THE GHOST

OF VALENTINE PAST

HAUNTING DANIELLE

HAUNTING DANIELLE - BOOK 7

THE GHOST
OF VALENTINE PAST

BOBBI HOLMES

The Ghost of Valentine Past
(Haunting Danielle, Book 7)
A Novel
By Bobbi Holmes
Cover Design: Elizabeth Mackey

ROBETH
PUBLISHING, LLC

ISBN 978-1-949977-06-6

Dedicated to those who I've loved and lost to death.
As we grow older, death visits more frequently.
I prefer to believe it's nothing more than a doorway into forever.

ONE

Meghan Carter doubted the building was haunted. There was normally a rational explanation for odd noises during the night, unexpected chilly drafts, flickering lightbulbs, and rearranged furniture. That didn't mean Meghan was a nonbeliever. In fact, she had been seeing ghosts for as long as she could remember. Of course, she didn't share that with her acquaintances. To them, she was simply a researcher of paranormal activities, and when she received calls like this one, they typically turned out to be non-ghost related.

Meghan parked in front of the boarded-up commercial building. From what she understood, this area of Sacramento, California, was considered prime commercial real estate. She thought it a shame the building was practically abandoned. Perhaps Tom was right, and the place was haunted. Why else would someone let the building sit idle for so long?

Just as she climbed out of her Jeep, Tom pulled up behind her. Meghan paused by the side of the Jeep and gave him a brief wave as he parked. A woman she didn't recognize was with him. Meghan assumed it was the building's owner.

"Hey, it's Ghost Busters!" Tom called out as he got out of his car and slammed its door shut.

"Funny, ha-ha," Meghan returned dryly. "You know, I can get

back in my car and go home. I should be there putting my Christmas decorations away, anyway."

"I'm sorry. I just couldn't resist," Tom said sheepishly. He gestured to his passenger, who had just gotten out of his car. The woman's eyes nervously darted from Megan to the boarded-up building.

"Meghan, this is Ann Reynolds, the owner. Ann, this is Meghan, who I've been telling you about," Tom introduced.

Megan smiled at Ann. "Hello."

"I'm not really sure how this is going to help," the woman said, wringing her hands. "But I'm at my wit's end and willing to try anything. Even an exorcism."

"I'm not sure what Tom's told you, but I don't do exorcisms." Meghan smiled kindly.

Ann's gaze darted from Meghan to Tom. "I don't understand."

"I told you, Meghan studies this sort of thing—paranormal activities. If your place is really being haunted, she'll be able to tell, and then she can help you figure out what you need to do next."

"I want it to stop!" Ann cried out. "I thought you said she could take care of it!"

Megan reached out and patted Ann's arm reassuringly. "Maybe I can. But first, why don't we go inside, and you can show me what's been happening."

"No." Ann shook her head. "I'm not going in there. Not until it's gone."

"Okay then," Meghan said patiently. "Why don't you tell me what's been happening, exactly."

Tom spoke up. "Ann and her husband used to run their business out of this building. Then, over a year ago, strange things started happening. About six months ago, Ann's husband passed away, and she found it impossible to keep running the business alone—not with all the strange occurrences going on."

"It didn't seem as frightening when my husband, Albert, was here. For one thing, Albert was getting forgetful, and I figured he was responsible for most of it. But he wasn't," Ann explained.

"What kind of strange things?" Meghan asked.

"Doors that were closed would suddenly be open. I'd clean up in the office and return to find drawers pulled out, the trash can tipped over. And lightbulbs—the lightbulbs kept popping. I even called an electrician. He said there was nothing wrong."

"That's when I thought of you. I remembered our conversation about lingering spirits screwing around with electricity."

"Well, that's one theory some have," Meghan said.

"I couldn't take it anymore. I closed the business. I started taking Social Security this last year anyway, and I had Albert's life insurance. But I need to sell the building, and I just don't feel right about selling it to some poor unsuspecting buyer, not if it's cursed. That doesn't seem right."

"Well, let me have a look. Did you bring a key?"

Ann nodded and dug into her pocket, pulling out a key chain. "I hope you don't mind if I stay here."

"I'll go in with you," Tom offered.

"No. It might be quicker if I do it alone." Meghan took the key from Ann. If she did encounter a spirit, she would feel awkward trying to communicate with it while Tom stood by and listened.

"I'm afraid the electricity is turned off, but the skylights let in plenty of sunshine," Ann told her.

A few moments later, Meghan unlocked the building's front door and gently pushed it open. She found it was fairly bright inside due to the sun streaming in through overhead skylights. Stepping into the building, she closed the door behind her and looked around. Dust coated the furniture and empty shelves.

Just as she reached the center of the room, the overhead light flickered on and off. Looking up to the light fixture, Meghan swallowed nervously and said under her breath, "Either Ann is wrong about the electricity being off or…"

Before she could finish her sentence, a ghostly apparition appeared just a few feet from her. A strikingly handsome, well-dressed young man, he seemed more confused and frightened than poor Ann outside. By his clothes, he was obviously of Tom's generation and not some ghost who had been lingering for decades.

"Hello," Meghan said.

Her greeting startled him. "You're willing to talk to me?"

"Willing?" Meghan asked.

"Everyone is so rude. All I want is directions. Why won't anyone help me?"

"I'll help you. Where do you want to go?"

He frowned thoughtfully for a moment and then said, "I'm not really sure. That's why I need someone to help me."

"Do you remember how you got here?"

3

He considered the question a moment before answering and then pointed to the doorway Meghan had just entered. "I came through that door, of course."

Meghan looked around the room. "Until I came in, there was no one here to help you. Why didn't you just leave?"

He frowned again. "There was. I'm sure there was. And then... then there wasn't."

"So why didn't you leave once you were alone?"

"Where would I go?"

"Can you tell me your name?"

"Lucas. Lucas Saunders."

"Hello, Lucas Saunders, my name is Meghan. Do you know where you were before you came in here?"

Lucas shook his head. "Things are a little confused for me."

"What was the last thing you remember before coming in here?" Meghan asked.

Lucas closed his eyes and tried to remember. "Everything is so jumbled up...but..." He opened his eyes again and stared at Meghan. "Danielle, Danielle is going to be worried about me."

"Danielle?"

"My wife, Danielle. She's expecting me. I just remembered. We have to go Christmas shopping. I promised I'd go with her. Christmas is in five days."

"No, Lucas. Christmas was almost two weeks ago."

"No. That's impossible. I couldn't have missed Christmas."

"Lucas, I have a feeling the Christmas you're talking about was more than two weeks ago."

"What do you mean?"

"What year is it?" she asked.

"You don't know?"

"Yes, I know. But do you? Remember, you've been wandering around this building for some time. You said there used to be people here. But I happen to know this building has been empty for almost six months now."

"That's impossible. I haven't been here for six months!"

"Then tell me what year it is."

"It's 2013, of course."

Meghan pulled her iPhone out of her purse and opened her calendar. She showed it to Lucas.

"That's impossible," he said dully, sitting down in a chair, staring ahead blankly. "I don't understand."

"I really hate to be the one to have to tell you this, Lucas. But I think you already know, you just haven't come to terms with it yet, which is why you keep rambling around this building. You know... deep down...you know, don't you?"

He shook his head in denial. "No. I can't be dead. No."

"I'm sorry, Lucas. Do you know how it happened?"

He looked up at Meghan and shook his head again. "No. I don't remember. Everything is confused...but something strange..."

"What?"

"It doesn't seem quite as jumbled as it was before you came."

"Sometimes a spirit just needs someone to help them acknowledge their death, which enables them to see things more clearly, and then they can move on," she explained.

"Move on? What do you mean move on?"

"When we die, we aren't supposed to hang around here. You have somewhere to go. Haunting this building is no way for you to spend your eternity."

"I've been haunting this building?"

"Yes. From what I understand, that's exactly what you've been doing."

"I can't go anywhere; I need to find Danielle first."

"Danielle? Your wife?"

"Yes. I remember now; I need to find her before I move on. It's important. But I don't know how to find her."

"Do you remember how you died?"

"No. That's still blurry."

"Well, maybe knowing how you died will help you remember the rest of it." Meghan opened a search window on her iPhone's browser and typed in Lucas's full name and Sacramento, California. Within less than a minute, she had the answer.

"Oh my," she said sadly.

"What did you find out?"

"I now understand why you're here. Apparently, you were killed in a car accident—across the street from this very building. You died on December 20, 2013." She pulled up a few more webpages connected to his name.

"Does it say where I can find Danielle?"

"Umm..." Meghan looked up from the phone. "I've a feeling your wife really does not want to see you—even if that was possible, which it isn't. I think you need to move on, follow the light, as they say."

He adamantly shook his head. "No, I need to find my wife."

"According to the second online article—you were killed with another woman. Someone named Kelsey Woods. Kelsey's spirit isn't around here, is she?"

"Kelsey…Kelsey is dead too…I remember now," he said dully.

"Do you also remember Kelsey was your lover? According to the article, you were killed with your lover, Kelsey Woods."

"Oh my god." Lucas started to pace the room. "That explains it. That's why I need to find Danielle."

"I'm sorry, Lucas, that's really impossible. You need to move on. There's nothing you can do about it now."

"I need to remember where I lived with Danielle…why can't I remember that? I need to get home."

"I'll see what I can find on her—but you have to promise me you'll leave here and not come back."

"I promise."

"You also have to promise not to haunt your poor wife."

"What do you mean?"

"I'd feel horrible if I helped you find your wife only to have you hang around her house, slam her doors, and make her lightbulbs explode."

"I need to find her. Please help me."

"Do you promise not to haunt her? Check on her, make sure she's okay, and then move on. Do you agree?"

He didn't answer immediately; finally, he nodded his agreement.

Meghan looked at her cellphone again and began searching for any information on Danielle Saunders. After a few minutes, she looked up and asked, "Was your wife's maiden name Boatman?"

"Yes! Yes, it is!"

"She's going by her maiden name now."

"Why would she do that?"

Meghan arched her brows. "Why do you think?"

"Oh…I wonder if she's still living in our house."

"No. She moved to Oregon."

"Oregon? Why would Danielle move to Oregon?"

"She's living in Frederickport, Oregon—on the coast. According to this article, she runs a bed and breakfast called Marlow House."

When Meghan looked up from her cellphone, Lucas was gone.

6

TWO

It was no longer raining. Normally, that would make Will Wayne smile, but now it was snowing—if one could call the slush covering his windshield snow. The wipers struggled to keep up, and he was grateful he was almost at his destination. Days like this made him long for Arizona and its reliable sunshine. He enjoyed summers in Portland, Oregon—winter, not so much.

Pulling into the parking lot, he turned off the engine and grabbed the umbrella off the passenger seat. He wasn't too proud to use an umbrella, especially on days like this. He had already traded his cowboy boots in for a pair of reliable rubber-soled water-resistant boots. It had only taken one tumble to realize slick-bottomed cowboy boots and wet asphalt didn't mix. He was too old to be breaking a hip. His cowboy hat remained, but he had no intention of getting it soaked in the rain and snow, hence the umbrella.

Five minutes later, he was being led into the office of Logan Mitcham, private detective. Wayne hadn't expected a thirtysomething, ruggedly stocky man of six feet, with a ruddy complexion and short buzzed strawberry-colored hair. Wayne thought marine when he saw Mitcham, not PI. To Wayne, a private detective should look like James Garner or Humphrey Bogart.

The two men shook hands, exchanged introductions, and Wayne took a seat facing Mitcham, who sat down behind his desk.

Mitcham opened a manila folder, glanced over its contents, and then looked up at Will and asked, "You want me to investigate your daughter's death?"

Wayne nodded. "Yes. A friend recommended you. She said you're familiar with Earthbound Spirits."

The private detective did not respond. Instead, he stared at Will.

"You are familiar with them, aren't you? She said you've investigated them before."

Mitcham closed the folder. "Earthbound Spirits? The cult? Yes, I'm familiar with them."

"And you know who Peter Morris is?" Wayne asked.

"Of course. He founded the group."

"I believe Peter Morris may have been responsible for my daughter's death."

Mitcham leaned back in his desk chair and studied Wayne for a moment. "I'm sorry about the loss of your daughter. But how exactly do you believe Morris was involved? How did your daughter die?"

"My daughter was Isabella Strickland. They say she died of a brain aneurism."

Mitcham leaned forward, resting his elbows on the desk. "Isabella Strickland, yes, I remember reading about that in the paper. She was your daughter?"

"Yes." Wayne nodded solemnly.

"I don't remember the paper mentioning she was married."

Will shook his head. "Married? No, Isabella wasn't married."

"I just assumed—since she didn't go by Wayne."

"Her mother and I divorced years ago. Unfortunately, I was never in Isabella's life."

"Why do you believe Morris had something to do with your daughter's death?"

"The oldest motive in the world, money, of course. She had made a will leaving everything to Earthbound Spirits."

Mitcham leaned back again. As he did, he picked up a pen from the desk and began absently tapping its end against the desktop. "I remember reading about her death—it was quite sensational, considering the uncle hid her body and tried to pass off another woman as her. From what I've read, your daughter left everything to that uncle."

"True. But there was an earlier will, where she left everything to Earthbound Spirits. They submitted that one to probate. But it was later thrown out when the evidence showed her uncle's will was the more current one."

"And you think they killed her over the inheritance?"

"I believe it may be possible."

"Have you gone to the police? I would assume this is a question for the coroner."

Will fiddled with the rim of his cowboy hat. It teetered on his right knee. Shaking his head, he said, "No. From what I've seen so far, no matter what crap Morris falls into, he manages to climb out smelling like he just rolled around in a rose garden."

"Roses have thorns," Mitcham reminded him.

"I'd like you to be that thorn. Can you help me?"

HE HAD JUST OPENED a menu when he heard a woman say, "Will Wayne?" Looking up, he broke into a smile—it was Danielle Boatman. By her drenched braid and wet jacket, it was obvious she hadn't brought an umbrella.

"Danielle! What are you doing in Portland on such a miserable day?" He then motioned to the empty seat across the table from him, silently inviting her to join him.

"I keep asking myself that same question," she said with a laugh as she hung her purse on the back of the chair and sat down.

"Are you alone?"

"Actually, I just dropped Lily and Ian off at the car dealer. Lily is finally getting a new car."

"Not the best day to go car shopping."

"She ordered it last week and was anxious to pick it up. There was no way she was going to be stopped by a little rain."

"You call this a little rain?"

"It is for Portland." She laughed.

"I'm surprised she's taken this long to get a car."

Danielle shrugged. "She really wasn't ready before, and I let her use mine, and she has Ian. But now, I think she wants to get back to her old normal again. So what brings you to Portland in this weather?"

Before Will had time to answer, the server came to their table and took their orders. When she finally left, Danielle repeated the question.

9

"I'll tell you if you promise not to say anything to anyone. I know you've become close to Chief MacDonald. I'd prefer he not know—at least not yet."

Danielle rested her elbows on the table and leaned forward. "You have my curiosity piqued; what's up?"

"I hired a private detective to investigate Isabella's death."

Danielle frowned. "I don't understand? We know what happened. And with Stoddard and Darlene both dead, I'm not sure how you could learn anything more about what happened that day."

"This has nothing to do with Stoddard and Darlene. It's about Peter Morris and Earthbound Spirits."

"But they weren't even around when she died. Stoddard found her. And according to the coroner, she died of natural causes."

"I know that's what they say. But I've reason to believe Peter Morris had Isabella killed. Stoddard just happen to be the one to find the body."

"You're thinking they intended to cash in on her old will?"

He nodded. "Yes."

"I'm not sure why you don't want to say anything to the chief. I know he's the last person to protect Morris. He'd love to nail the SOB. I'm sure if there was anything suspicious about Isabella's death, he'd be all over it."

"Coroner reports can be faked. We already know Morris had Isabella's attorney in his pocket. How difficult would it be for him to pay off someone in the coroner's office?"

"It would take more than just someone in the coroner's office. I would assume the coroner would have to be crooked to pull something like that off."

"We hear about politicians and government officials taking bribes every day," Will reminded her.

"Yeah, but something like that would make the coroner party to Isabella's death. Can't imagine someone would be willing to take that sort of risk unless a lot of money was involved, and a bribe like that would be something the chief could easily check out."

Will shook his head. "No, I don't want him blundering around and screwing this up. When I go to the authorities, I intend to take more than my suspicions."

The server returned with their beverages. They waited until she was gone before resuming their conversation.

"Why do you suddenly suspect foul play in Isabella's death?" Danielle asked.

Will let out a heavy sigh. "I've been getting phone calls."

"Phone calls?"

"I got the first call on New Year's Eve. It was a woman. She told me they had lied—that Isabella didn't die of a brain aneurism. That Peter Morris had her killed."

"Do you have any idea who she was?"

Will shook his head. "And then in the paper, a few days later, there was an article about Cleve Monchique's suicide note, and how he confessed to killing Clarence Renton, and how he tried to kill that other guy. After that, she called me again, said that proved they were capable of killing my daughter. She asked if I was just going to let Morris get away with murder."

"Morris was probably responsible for Cleve's death—but he didn't pull the trigger. There is no doubt Cleve killed himself."

"She told me she was a member of Earthbound Spirits, that she was frightened for her life, and she couldn't go to the police. She wanted to get away from the group, but she couldn't."

"Why was she calling you?"

"She hoped I could do something—prove what Morris had done to my daughter, to bring the organization down, weaken it, put Morris behind bars—so she could get out. According to her, she knew for a fact Morris ordered Cleve to kill my daughter, but that Cleve didn't want to; so Morris had someone else do it."

"According to the suicide note, Cleve admitted to killing Renton —and I know he tried to kill Richard Winston. I wonder why he would have balked at killing Isabella. You think because she was a woman? That is assuming Morris had her killed, which, honestly, I seriously doubt. Not because I don't believe he's capable, but I'm not quite willing to believe the coroner would do something like that."

"All I know is that this woman was adamant about Morris ordering Isabella's death. She wouldn't tell me who had done it; she just kept saying follow the money."

"Follow the money?"

"Danielle, we know Cleve was willing to kill for Earthbound Spirits. Is it so farfetched to imagine there are others in the group willing to do the same thing? From all accounts, Isabella was a young healthy woman, with a sizable estate. Isabella should have easily outlived Peter Morris—and what good would that do him? If he let things take their natural course, he probably would never have seen Isabella's money, even if she left everything to Earthbound Spirits."

"I don't think they're going to start killing off their younger, affluent members. Wouldn't people start noticing?"

"Yes, they would start noticing, Danielle. That's what this is all about."

"I never figured their motive for killing Renton was about money. It was to shut him up."

"Because he knew Earthbound Spirits was trying to cash in on an outdated will," he reminded her.

"But that doesn't mean Earthbound Spirits killed Isabella."

"What about that other man Monchique tried to kill?" Will asked.

"Richard?"

Will nodded.

Danielle silently considered all that he was telling her. Finally, she said, "Okay, you have a point. Cleve did try to kill Richard for his inheritance. So I suppose it's within the realm of possibility that they were willing to kill off members to cash out earlier."

"According to the woman on the phone, the ones they normally go after are those attempting to leave the group. Which would make sense. Isabella had backed away from Earthbound Spirits before her death. They obviously knew the will was fake, but Morris probably figured with what Stoddard had pulled with Lily, no one would believe his will was the authentic one, especially with Renton on their side."

"And Richard was pulling away from them after finding his sister," Danielle murmured.

"Exactly, which is why this woman—whoever she is—is so terrified to go public. She fears for her life."

"So what are you planning to do about it?"

"Like I said, I hired a private detective, Logan Mitcham."

THREE

Danielle's brown eyes fluttered open, greeted by sparkling sunshine. It took her a moment to comprehend her surroundings. She sat in a wooden hammock beach chair, her toes buried in the sand. Strangely, the sand was cold, a contradiction to the bright sunshine overhead. Walt sat next to her, in his own beach chair. If she wasn't mistaken, it was the Hawaiian shore, not Oregon's—or at least that was the effect Walt was going for, given the number of palm trees nearby and the blue and green Hawaiian shirt he wore. Glancing down, she noticed her muumuu was made from the same fabric as his shirt.

She could hear someone playing the ukulele in the distance. Yet there were no people in sight. The steady rhythm of the breakers pounding along the shore before retreating back into the sea added a haunting effect to the Hawaiian music.

Reaching up, she touched the ends of her long dark hair and noticed it was free flowing. She then remembered she had removed her braid before going to bed that night.

"Aloha," Walt greeted her with a smile as he leaned back in his chair and studied Danielle. He wore white slacks with his tropical shirt and a straw panama hat. Stretching out, he casually crossed his ankles. White sand covered his bare feet.

"Hawaii?" Danielle asked with a grin.

Walt shrugged. "I was going for a tropical feel. It could be Hawaii or any Polynesian island, I suppose."

"What's the occasion?" Danielle wiggled her toes in the sand and momentarily frowned. *Why is the sand so cold?*

"You've been complaining about the rain. I thought you might enjoy a little sunshine."

"It's been raining nonstop this month." Danielle let out a sigh and then added, "But you know, tropical islands get a lot of rain too."

Walt shook his head. "Not here. I won't allow it. Just sunshine."

"Thank you, I do appreciate the change of scenery." Danielle leaned back in her chair.

"I also miss talking to you without him around. It seems the only time we can be alone these days is if I dream hop."

"Him? I assume you mean Chris?"

"When did you say he's leaving?"

"As soon as escrow closes on his property. According to Adam, that should be by the first of next week."

Walt met Danielle's gaze with a frown. "I still don't understand why he had to buy something. I thought he was going to rent. He could've been out by now."

Danielle stretched out in the chair. "Oh, come on, Walt, admit it. You like Chris. You enjoy having another man around to talk to."

Walt let out a grunt. "I was doing just fine before he showed up."

Danielle smiled. "Well, I know Chris likes you."

"We know who Chris really likes."

"You didn't bring me to this lovely beach just to snipe at me, did you?"

"I suppose not. And if I'm being honest, I'd have to say if I had my choice between Chris or Heather leaving first, I'd vote for Heather."

Danielle chuckled. "You aren't fond of that particular guest, are you?"

"Admit it, she's getting on your nerves too."

"I know Lily will be relieved when Heather moves back to her own house. But she did save our lives. We could have burned up in Presley House if it wasn't for her."

"If her great-grandfather hadn't been a murderer and a thief, there would have been no reason for her to rescue you. Maybe when Chris moves out, he can take Heather with him."

Danielle laughed at the idea. "I don't see that happening."

"One can hope."

"So what do you think of our Valentine's Day guests? The love-birds, David and Arlene?"

Walt brushed his knuckles over the bottom of his chin as he stared out to sea. "I find it fascinating how open unmarried couples are about checking into an inn together."

"Ahh, you mean shacking up together." Danielle giggled.

"Shacking up?"

"According to my mother, that's what they called it in her day, when unmarried people lived together. I assumed the term was around when you were alive."

"I've heard the term, but back then, it didn't have anything to do with cohabitation without the benefit of marriage. Are you saying the behavior wasn't accepted when your parents were young adults? These loose morals are more a product of your generation?"

"Oh please, we've been over this before. Yours was the era of flappers, moonshine, and speakeasies. I suppose my generation is just less hypocritical. As for my mother's, it wasn't as scandalous as it was in your time; but I remember my mother telling me that her father was pretty old fashioned and would have had a fit had she and Dad lived together. Today, well, it's pretty common for people to live together without marriage. Although, there are still those who don't approve. I assume primarily for religious reasons."

"What about you, Danielle? Did you and Lucas live together before you were married?"

"I thought the topic was our new guests? You never told me what you thought about them, aside from the fact that they're unmarried."

"I haven't had much of an opportunity to observe them. They seem all right, nothing noteworthy, aside from how openly they flaunt their living situation."

"It's a different world today." Danielle wrapped her arms around herself and shivered.

Walt sat up in his chair and reached toward Danielle, touching her knee. "Are you all right?"

"It's just so darn cold here." Danielle looked up to the sun. "Why isn't it warmer? The sun is bright enough."

"You forget, the sun isn't real. I bet you've kicked your blankets off again."

"I need to do something about that heater. It gets so cold in the house, especially this time of year. I'm surprised the guests aren't complaining." Danielle shivered again.

"Try pulling the blankets up over you," Walt suggested.

Danielle glanced down at her chair and at the beach surrounding her. "And just how am I supposed to do that? I don't have a blanket."

"I'm not talking about a blanket here in the dream—back in your bedroom at Marlow House. Close your eyes and tell your hands to reach down and grab hold of your blankets and pull them up over you."

Danielle closed her eyes and tried what he suggested, but she was still cold. Opening her eyes again, she looked over at Walt. "It didn't work. I guess I'll have to wake myself up before I freeze to death."

"Don't be silly. It took you two hours to fall asleep, thanks to that extra cup of coffee you had with dinner. If you wake up now, you might be up all night."

"Maybe, but I'll also be warm!"

"Just hold on a moment, and I'll go cover you up."

"Really?" Danielle smiled. "I guess that would work."

"Certainly. I'll be right back. Enjoy the view, and you'll be warm again in no time," Walt promised.

WALT STOOD over Danielle's bed. Just as he suspected, her blankets had fallen to the floor. Curled up on the center of the mattress, she shivered in her sleep, her arms wrapped around her bent knees. Wearing plaid pajama bottoms and a red T-shirt, her feet were bare, and he suspected if he could actually touch them, they would be ice cold.

Moonlight flooded through the window, illuminating the bedroom. Walt reached down and grabbed the blankets from the floor. Just as he tossed them over Danielle's sleeping body, movement from the corner of the room caught his eye. At first, he expected to see Max. Yet it was not the cat, but a man silently watching him and Danielle.

Walt froze a moment, prepared to do battle with the intruder, when the stranger looked up into Walt's eyes and asked, "Who are you?"

"You can see me?" Walt found himself asking.

"What kind of question is that? Of course I can see you," the man snapped.

"Another one who can see me?" Walt muttered under his breath. He then glared at the stranger while standing guard over Danielle.

Instead of retreating from Walt, the man gazed down at the bed. "That's Danielle, isn't it?"

"How did you get in here?" Walt demanded.

The man looked up into Walt's eyes. "Who are you?"

"You're the intruder here. Answer my question." Walt wondered briefly if he should summon Chris. It wasn't that Walt wasn't fully capable of handling the intruder on his own, but Chris could call the police and get the man locked up. The last thing he wanted was for Danielle to suddenly wake up and find a stranger in her bedroom. He would prefer to handle the situation and then explain to her what had happened—after the intruder was apprehended and behind bars.

"I was looking for Danielle. What are you doing in her room? How did you get in here? I didn't see you come in," the stranger asked.

"This is my house," Walt explained. "And you are a trespasser. I'm calling the police."

Walt took a step toward the stranger, and when he did, the man disappeared.

"What the…" Walt looked over to Danielle, who continued to sleep peacefully; yet now she was contently snuggled beneath a pile of warm blankets.

After glancing around one last time, Walt stepped out of the bedroom and surveyed the hallway. All was quiet. Lily's bedroom door was closed, as was Heather's and the couple who had checked in that afternoon. A moment later, he heard the faint sound of the downstairs clock chiming three times. The couple who checked in yesterday, Walt corrected himself, when he realized it was no longer Thursday, but Friday morning. Friday the 13th. The day before Valentine's Day.

With haste, Walt moved through the rooms on the second floor of Marlow House. Yet all he found were sleeping guests, no spirits.

Before making his way to the attic, he checked on Danielle, just in case the intruding ghost had returned to her room. She slept soundly and alone.

In the attic, he found Max, who sat on the windowsill, looking outside, his black tail swishing back and forth.

"Max," Walt greeted him when he entered the room.

Max turned toward Walt and gazed at him through golden eyes.

"There's another spirit in the house; have you seen him?"

Max continued to stare at Walt, asking a silent question.

"I've no idea who it is," Walt replied.

Max leapt down from the windowsill.

"That's probably a good idea. You stay with Danielle while I check downstairs."

When the two reached the second floor, Walt let Max into Danielle's bedroom. She was still alone and sleeping. Max jumped onto the bed and curled up beside the sleeping woman.

Moving into the hallway, Walt left the door ajar, which would allow Max to escape the room if he needed to summon Walt.

Making his way down the stairs, Walt noticed movement coming from the direction of the parlor. Just as he stepped onto the first-floor landing, a gray-haired man rushed in his direction. The moment the man saw Walt, he froze.

"I have to get out of here!" the man shouted at Walt.

"Where did you come from?" Another one can see me? Surely he's not a spirit too…

Walt had his answer a moment later when the man vanished.

"What in the hell is going on here?" Walt muttered. Shaking his head, he made his way to Chris's room.

Standing over Chris's bed, Walt looked down at the sleeping man and shouted, "Wake up!"

With a startled bolt, Chris sat up in the bed and looked around frantically, his eyes wide. He found Walt standing over him.

Rubbing sleep from his eyes, Chris glared at Walt. "What is going on?"

"There's a ghost in the house," Walt explained.

"Yes, I know. And he can be annoying. Why did you wake me up?"

"I'm not talking about me. There's another ghost—actually two other ghosts—I just saw them. The first one was in Danielle's bedroom, and the second one I just saw downstairs."

"Two? Who are they?" Chris jumped out of bed. All he wore was a pair of boxers. Hastily he grabbed his robe from the end of the bed and slipped it on.

"I've no idea. I was hoping you could help me figure it out."

"Where's Danielle?"

"She's still sleeping. Max is with her."

"Don't you think you should wake her up?" Chris paused a moment and studied Walt. "Just what were you doing in her bedroom? Kind of creepy and stalkerish of you watching her sleep, don't you think?"

"I wasn't watching her sleep," Walt said indignantly. "I was covering her up. She was cold."

"And how did you know that?"

"She told me."

FOUR

F astening his robe's belt, Chris studied Walt. "I thought you said she was asleep."

Walt shrugged. "She was. Is."

Muttering something under his breath, Chris started for the bedroom door. He then asked, "Tell me about these ghosts."

"One was in her room."

"And you just left him there, with Danielle sleeping?" Chris threw open his bedroom door and stepped out into the hallway.

"He's not there now. That's why I came looking for you. I hoped we could figure this out together, without having to wake up Danielle."

Chris paused and turned to face Walt. "You have no idea who he was?"

"No. He was about your age, I suppose. The other one was much older."

"Where was he?"

"I saw the older one when I came downstairs. It looked as if he had just come from the parlor. He told me he had to get out of here —and then he just vanished."

"What did that one look like?" Chris asked.

Walt considered the question a moment. "There was something familiar about him, but I can't place it. Older gentleman, gray hair, in a hurry to leave."

"And you're sure they were ghosts? Maybe someone broke into the house?"

"Both men vanished before my eyes—and the fact they both could see and hear me—so my guess would be that they're other spirits. What concerns me is the first one knew Danielle's name, and he was watching her."

Chris tightened the belt on his robe and turned around. Instead of moving toward the staircase, he faced the parlor door.

"Maybe you should wake Danielle. You can get to her faster than I can," Chris suggested. "I'll check the parlor and see if anything's been disturbed. Random ghosts wandering through Marlow House can't be a good thing."

When Walt returned to Danielle's room a few seconds later, he found her still sleeping soundly, with Max curled up at her side.

"Any sign of a ghost?" Walt asked Max.

In response, Max closed his eyes and began to purr.

"I found another one downstairs."

Max stopped purring and opened his eyes.

"Yes, there were two of them. I have to wake Danielle."

DANIELLE STRETCHED out in the beach chair, enjoying the warmth of the sun—or possibly the blankets back at Marlow House. She assumed Walt had covered her up, but wondered what was taking him so long to return.

"You look comfortable," Walt said when he appeared a few seconds later. Instead of sitting in the empty beach chair, he stood by her side.

"I was beginning to wonder if you were coming back. Aren't you going to sit down?"

"I'm afraid there's a little situation back at Marlow House, and Chris thinks it might be a good idea if you wake up. I think he may be right." Walt sat down in the chair.

"Situation?"

"There appears to be two spirits wandering around the house."

"Spirits? You mean ghosts?"

Walt nodded.

"Did Chris see them?"

"No. I did. I thought it might be a good idea to wake Chris and elicit his help in discovering who they might be."

"Why do you think they're ghosts—oh no, maybe someone broke into the house!"

"No. It was two male spirits. They both could see me—and both vanished before my eyes."

"Any idea who they are?"

"No. Chris went to check the parlor while I came to get you."

"Parlor? Why the parlor?"

"I saw the second man rush out from there—I think that's where he was coming from. He seemed in a hurry. When he saw me, he said he had to get out of there, and then he just disappeared."

"What about the first man?"

"When I went to cover you up, I found him in your bedroom—watching you sleep."

"My bedroom?" Danielle squeaked.

"He seemed to know who you are. He said your name."

"What did he look like?"

"Tall—I suppose good looking. Dark hair, dark eyes. Serious looking."

"And the other man?"

"Older, maybe in his late sixties. Gray hair. I didn't recognize the younger man at all—but there was something familiar about the older one. I just can't place him."

"Well, crap." Danielle stood. "I suppose you should wake me up. Do you have any idea what time it is?"

"When I heard the downstairs clock chime, it was three. I don't imagine it's now much later than that."

"Then you better wake me up. The only way I can do it is to make myself scream—and I really don't think that would be a terrific idea with a houseful of guests."

"Waking up Heather like that might be particularly annoying. The last thing we need is for her to start burning her voodoo incense to cleanse the house of spirits."

"It's not incense; it's essential oils. And I doubt it works anyway."

"I should think not. I'm still here." In the next moment, he wasn't there.

Instead of contemplating the irony of Walt's declaration just a moment before he disappeared, Danielle felt someone repeatedly tugging her arm.

The beach faded away, and Danielle opened her eyes. A loud meow greeted her. Sitting up in her bed, she looked over to Walt, who stood nearby. Another meow caught her attention, and she looked down in time to see Max press his head against her arm as he wove around her body, loudly purring.

The light hadn't been turned on, yet it wasn't needed, thanks to the moonlight streaming through the window. In the next moment, a shrill scream pierced the silence. It came from downstairs.

Bolting from bed, Danielle raced to the bedroom door and threw it open. She found Lily and her new guests, David and Arlene, standing at their bedroom doors, looking nervously into the dimly lit hallway. They too had apparently heard the screaming. Heather's door was also open, but she was nowhere to be seen.

Lily glanced from Heather's open door to Danielle. "Was that Heather who screamed?"

David pushed Arlene back into the safety of their bedroom and stepped out into the hallway. He attempted to close the door, but Arlene refused to be shut up in the room alone.

"Maybe we should call the police?" Arlene suggested. She grabbed hold of David's arm and pulled him back into the room with her.

Danielle glanced at Walt and then looked back at Arlene and David. "It's probably nothing. I'll go downstairs and check. Chris is down there; I'm sure everything is fine."

"I'll go with you," Lily said, walking first to Heather's room and peeking inside. "She's not in there. That must have been her who screamed."

Hastily, Lily and Danielle raced down the stairs. "Please tell me Walt is with us," Lily said in a whisper.

"He was. I suspect he's already downstairs," Danielle explained under her breath.

Reluctantly, Arlene and David followed Lily and Danielle, yet not before Arlene retrieved her cellphone from their bedroom.

"IS THAT PETER MORRIS?" Walt asked as he looked down at the lifeless body sprawled on the floor in front of the small parlor sofa.

Instead of answering Walt's question, Chris looked up at Heather, who remained standing at the open doorway. No longer screaming and now mesmerized by the grisly scene, she clutched the edge of the parlor door. Someone had sliced Morris's throat, and considering the beige throw rug in front of the sofa was now red from blood, it was doubtful he was still alive.

In spite of the hopelessness of the scene, Chris had managed to check the man's vitals, only to verify what he already assumed—Peter Morris, founder of the infamous cult Earthbound Spirits, was dead. Still kneeling by the body, Chris was just about to stand up when Danielle and Lily came rushing into the room.

"I know now why he looked familiar," Walt told Danielle. Yet she wasn't listening to what he had to say. Instead, she stared horrified at the dead body on her parlor floor.

"Oh my god, is that Peter Morris?" Danielle gasped. "What happened?"

"Is he dead?" Lily knew it was a ridiculous question the moment she asked it.

"I'm calling the police!" Arlene shouted from where she stood in the hallway, peeking over Heather's shoulder.

"I know now why the man looked familiar," Walt repeated his assertion. In response, both Chris and Danielle looked in his direction. "The older man," Walt explained. "The second spirit I saw, it was Peter Morris. I didn't recognize him at the time because his hair was gray, practically white."

Danielle looked back down at the dead man on her floor—his hair was jet black, as it was the last time she had seen him.

Finding her voice, Heather stepped backwards, out of the parlor and into the hallway. She bumped into David and froze. Pointing at Chris, she shouted, "He killed him!" With shaking hands, she gestured from the dead man to Chris.

Now standing, Chris looked down at his hands. Both were covered with blood. "I found him like this," Chris explained. "I was just checking his vitals when Heather walked into the room."

"I need to call the police," Danielle said dully. Still staring down at the body, she asked—speaking more to herself than to anyone within hearing distance—"What was he doing here?"

"I already called the police! They're on their way!" Arlene called out.

"I have to wash my hands," Chris announced, pushing past Heather and Arlene, making his way to the bathroom.

"You're destroying evidence," David called out.

Chris paused a moment and looked back at David and the rest. They all watched him.

"I didn't kill Morris," Chris reiterated. Glancing down at his hands, he felt ill. "I got blood on me when I was checking to see if there was anything I could do for him. I'll tell the police I washed my hands—that I got his blood on me. But I'm not going to stand here like this." Without another word, he went to the bathroom.

"What in the world was Peter Morris doing in this house?" Lily asked.

Silently, Danielle glanced around the room. Her three guests— Heather, David, and Arlene—huddled by the doorway, looking in, while Lily stood next to her, and Walt stood just a few feet from the dead man.

"I never saw him arrive," Walt told Danielle. "But I did see him leave."

"You need to ask Chris," Heather said, looking nervously over her shoulder, expecting Chris to return in the next moment.

"I don't believe Chris had anything to do with this—he had no reason to kill Morris. And he explained, he found Morris here—he was checking his vitals. That's why he had blood on his hands," Danielle insisted.

"No, Morris came to see Chris. I saw them together," Heather told her.

"What are you talking about?" Danielle stepped from the parlor into the hallway, Lily trailing behind her.

"Tonight—around midnight—I was in the living room, watching TV, when I heard Chris go to the front door and let someone in. It was Morris. I got the impression Chris was expecting him. There was no knock at the door; the doorbell didn't ring. The two men went into the parlor. Chris is the reason Peter Morris was here—he obviously was the one who killed him."

As if on cue, Chris returned from the bathroom, his hands now clean. Nervous, Heather stepped back from Chris while David and Arlene followed suit, keeping a safe distance from the man who just moments before had been wearing Morris's blood.

"You're wrong, Heather," Chris said calmly.

"I saw you with him!" Heather spat.

"True, he came to see me—we were in the parlor together earlier—but I didn't kill him. You saw him after I did."

The next moment the front door opened—it was the police.

FIVE

G lancing down at his wristwatch, Brian Henderson cursed
himself for trading shifts with another officer. Frederickport
tended to be a quiet beach community—that was, of course, until
Danielle Boatman inherited Marlow House and turned it into a bed
and breakfast. Since that time, he seemed to be constantly tripping
over dead bodies.

Brian had assumed things had finally settled down, and the new
year meant Frederickport had returned to the sleepy beach community it had once been. Apparently, he was wrong. Any thoughts of
getting off work in a couple of hours and having Friday to himself
were killed—as dead as Peter Morris.

They had brought the residents of Marlow House to the police
station for questioning while processing the crime scene. They had
allowed each person to get dressed before bringing them to the
station, but not until the house was searched, in case the perp was
hiding in a dark corner. Then, each person was escorted to his or
her room to make sure no evidence was compromised while each
witness changed into street clothes.

Brian decided to talk first with the woman who had called the
police to the crime scene, Arlene Horton. He was already in the
interrogation room, sitting at the table, when Arlene was shown into
the room.

Before asking his first question, he studied her for a moment.

She was around Danielle's age—early thirties or perhaps a few years younger. He found her attractive, with almond-shaped hazel eyes and a pixie-like face. She wore her chestnut-colored hair in short curls, a look he felt only a woman with delicate features—as she had —could carry off.

While rounding up the group after he arrived at Marlow House, he had learned the man she was with was not her husband. Apparently, the two had come to Marlow House for a romantic Valentine's Day weekend. That bit of information seemed to contradict the woman's choice of nightwear, which she still had on when he had first arrived at the house: a prim, floor-length, flannel nightgown with long sleeves and a button-up collar. But considering the recent turn of events, he doubted there would be much romance in their weekend, even if she had a secret stash of Victoria Secret nightgowns up in their room.

"You're the one who called the police?" Brian asked.

Arlene nodded. "Yes, when that horrible scream woke us, I knew something awful had happened. I just never imagined it would be this."

"Why don't you start at the beginning and tell me what happened." Brian leaned back in the chair, his gaze focused on Arlene. "Start at when you first arrived at Marlow House."

"David and I checked in…" With her hands nervously fidgeting on her lap, she glanced briefly at the wall clock. It was almost 5 a.m. "I guess it was yesterday, late in the afternoon, before five p.m. We checked into our room, then went out to dinner; that was about six. When we returned, it was a little past eight. We were both exhausted, so we went right to our room. I was asleep when I heard it. Jolted me right out of bed."

"Heard what?" Brian asked.

"The scream. I know now it was Heather. But at the time, we had no idea what was going on. It woke up David too. When we opened our bedroom door, Danielle and Lily were standing at their doorways. They had heard it too."

"Then what happened?" Brian asked.

"Danielle insisted it was nothing. Reminded us Chris was downstairs." Under her breath, she muttered, "With blood all over him."

"Did you see Chris attack Peter Morris?"

Arlene shook her head. "No, but Heather said he did."

"Back up, and tell me what you saw, exactly."

"Danielle said she was going downstairs to see what was going on. Lily and David insisted on going too. I certainly didn't want to be left upstairs all alone, so I grabbed my cellphone and headed downstairs with them. I was already searching for your number when I reached the first floor and saw Heather standing by the parlor door. When I saw the man on the floor, I immediately called you."

"What was Heather doing?"

"She was standing by the parlor door, looking in, when we all got downstairs."

"What was Chris doing?"

"He was kneeling by the body. There was blood all over his hands."

"He didn't have any blood on him when we arrived," Brian reminded her.

"No. He washed his hands. David told him he shouldn't, that he was washing off evidence. But he did it anyway."

"Then what happened?"

"You arrived."

"Had you seen Peter Morris—the man who was killed—at Marlow House earlier?"

Arlene didn't answer immediately. Finally, she shook her head. "No."

"Is there anything you want to add?"

"Just that you should talk to Heather next."

"Why is that?" Brian asked.

"Because according to Heather, Chris killed that man."

———

"WHY DOES this feel like déjà vu?" Danielle asked Brian a few minutes later when she sat down across from him in the interrogation room. The two were alone.

"This isn't how I expected to spend my Friday," he told her.

"Friday…that's right, it's Friday the 13th," Danielle murmured.

"Tell me, what was Morris doing at Marlow House? I didn't think you two were that chummy."

"You know I couldn't stand the man," Danielle admitted.

"Not the best thing to confess, with him found in your house and his throat slit."

"You couldn't stand him either," Danielle reminded him.

"True, but he wasn't lying on my parlor floor, dead."

"I suspect you don't have a parlor," Danielle quipped.

"You're rather sassy considering your house is a crime scene —again."

"You know I do this when I'm nervous. I thought you'd know that by now."

"I was rather hoping I wouldn't be interviewing you about another homicide. At least, not so soon."

"Okay." Danielle took a deep breath. "I'll focus and try not to be a smart aleck. What do you want to know?"

"To begin with, why was Morris there?"

Danielle shook her head. "I have no idea. I didn't know he was in the house—not until I saw him on the parlor floor just minutes before you arrived."

"Start from the beginning." Brian studied Danielle. Instead of the pajama bottoms and T-shirt she had been wearing earlier that morning, she now wore blue sweatpants and an oversized sweatshirt. He was used to seeing her hair in a tidy fishtail braid, but this morning it was a bit of a tangled mess, pulled back into a haphazard bun, with stray tendrils framing her face. He had to admit she looked rather cute, and for a moment, he understood what Joe Morelli saw in the woman.

"I was asleep when I heard a scream—it woke me. When I got to the doorway, Lily, David, and Arlene were also up. I guess the scream woke them too. We all went downstairs to see what was going on, and we found Heather standing at the door to the parlor and Chris in the parlor, kneeling by Morris, checking his vitals."

"Wasn't that a little risky, just charging downstairs?"

With a frown Danielle asked, "Risky, why?"

"You hear a woman scream bloody murder—and in this case, there was an actual murder—and you just charge downstairs without considering your safety?"

Danielle shrugged. "I just assumed Heather went downstairs for some reason and something frightened her…maybe a mouse. She can be a little dramatic sometimes. Anyway, I knew Chris was downstairs."

"It's almost like you already knew the danger passed—or maybe you knew the only person in danger was Morris, and he was already dead."

Danielle let out a weary sigh. "Brian, please don't read more into this than there is. I really had absolutely no idea Morris was in my house. Trust me; no one was more surprised than I was to find him downstairs—dead."

"Do you have any idea why he was there?"

Folding her hands on her lap, Danielle closed her eyes briefly and let out another sigh. She opened her eyes again and looked directly at Brian. "I've an idea of why he was there. Please listen to what Chris has to say first. Don't jump to conclusions. You tend to do that, and they're often wrong."

"Chris? According to Ms. Horton, Heather seems to believe Chris killed Morris."

"That's only because he was found with the body. But I believe what he said—that he was just checking Morris's vitals and that's why he got blood on his hands, which I'm sure Arlene already mentioned."

"You said you have an idea of why Morris was there. Explain."

"According to Heather, she was watching television in the living room when she heard Chris answer the door. She saw him let Morris in, and the two went into the parlor together. But that was around midnight. And we found Morris in the parlor after three."

"When was the last time you saw Peter Morris?" Brian asked.

"Me?" Danielle frowned and considered the question. "Back in December, I think. When Richard Winston was taken to the hospital. I don't think I've seen him since then."

"Has he tried to contact you?"

"Morris? No. Why would he?"

"I seem to remember Morris was rather interested in recruiting you."

"Yeah, well, that was never going to happen. I would assume he finally realized that."

Brian's cellphone began to ring. Picking up his phone from the table, he looked at who was calling.

"I have to take this," he told her. On the other end of the phone was one of the officers still at Marlow House, processing the scene.

"I think we found the murder weapon," the officer told Brian on the phone. "I'm sending a picture now." In the next moment, an image popped up on Brian's phone. It was of a fishing knife resting on a bloody hand towel.

"Where did you find it?" Brian asked.

"It was shoved under the dresser in the entry hall bathroom, wrapped in that hand towel," the officer told him.

After Brian got off the phone, he showed Danielle the image. "Do you recognize the knife or the towel?"

"It looks like one of the hand towels from the downstairs bathroom," Danielle murmured, her attention on the knife in the photograph.

"What about the knife? Do you recognize it?" Brian asked.

Danielle swallowed nervously and said with a hoarse voice, "It looks like a fishing knife."

"It is, a very sharp knife. Have you seen it before?"

"Maybe…" Danielle squeaked.

"Maybe? Where have you seen it before?"

"I suppose…looks a little like the fishing knife I gave Chris…but I'm sure there are others like it in town. I bought it at the local sporting goods store."

"Do you know where Chris keeps his fishing knife?"

"I would assume in his tackle box. The last time I saw it—the tackle box—it was on the back porch. That was a couple days ago; I remember because I moved it out of the rain. But I didn't look inside."

"Do you have anything you want to add—something you believe is relevant to the case?"

"No. But…well…I was wondering, do you know when the chief is going to be in?"

"He normally comes in around eight. Why?"

"I…I just would like to talk to him."

"Danielle, I'm taking the lead on this case; if you know something, you need to tell me."

"I was just wondering when the chief was coming in, that's all." Danielle shrugged.

Narrowing his eyes, Brian studied Danielle for a moment. "I think I'll talk with Chris next. I suppose he should get used to being called by Chris Glandon from now on. With Morris's murder—especially considering who he was and the press this case is bound to catch—I doubt Glandon can continue using the name 'Johnson,' regardless of how much money he has. I seriously doubt your friendship with the chief will fix this one, Danielle."

SIX

Six Weeks Earlier—January 2, 2015

Officers Joe Morelli and Brian Henderson sat at a booth at Lucy's Diner, reading lunch menus. There was no reason for either of them to actually read the menus, they could easily recite them word for word—with their eyes closed. But habits were a hard thing to break, so they pored over the menus, though they would probably order what they normally did when visiting Lucy's for lunch.

They had just tossed their menus onto the table when Police Chief MacDonald entered the diner and walked in their direction.

"Hey, Chief, you want to join us for lunch?" Joe offered.

"Have you ordered yet?" MacDonald asked.

Joe slid over in the seat, making room for his boss. "No."

After MacDonald sat down, Brian handed him a menu.

"I don't need it." The chief waved it away. "I already know what I want."

Ten minutes later, after the server took their orders and brought their beverages, Joe asked the chief what he knew about Cleve Monchique's funeral services.

Before answering, the chief sipped his coffee and then set his mug on the table. "From what I understand, they aren't having one. Apparently, his estate goes to Earthbound Spirits, and he left Peter

Morris in charge of handling his arrangements. I heard this morning that Morris issued a statement that Cleve was being cremated and they weren't having any formal service—but he did ask for donations in lieu of flowers."

"Donations to Earthbound Spirits?" Brian asked with a snort.

"Of course." The chief shook his head in disgust.

"Didn't Cleve have any family?" Joe asked. "I would think they'd want to do something for him."

"From what I understand, he's been estranged from his family since he got involved with that group. I heard somewhere he had a sister—or maybe it was a brother." The chief shrugged. "Not sure his parents are still alive."

"There is no way Morris didn't know about Cleve's plot to kill Winston," Brian grumbled.

"I agree with you, but there's no way for us to prove it, especially after Cleve's handwritten confession he included with his suicide note." MacDonald picked up his coffee mug and looked across the table at Brian. "I know there are some who believe Morris blackmailed Darlene over your affair."

In response, Brian shrugged. Joe was about to comment when Adam Nichols walked into the diner with Chris Johnson. Adam waved at the officers, but led Chris to a table at the opposite end of the restaurant.

Brian watched as Adam and Chris sat down. "I wonder what those two are doing together."

"I imagine Adam is showing him property," MacDonald answered.

"What do you mean?" Joe frowned.

"According to Danielle, Johnson is planning to stay in Frederickport. Adam is helping him find a rental."

"Don't you mean Glandon?" Brian asked.

Before the chief could respond, the server returned to refill their mugs and inform them their lunch would be out in a few minutes. When she was gone, the chief pushed his mug aside and looked seriously from Joe to Brian.

"I think we need to talk about something," the chief began.

"Is there a problem?" Joe asked.

"No, not really. It seems Chris Johnson intends to make Frederickport his home for a while. And I expect you both to refer to him as Chris Johnson—not Chris Glandon."

"But his legal name is Glandon," Brian reminded him.

"That's true. But I understand why he chooses to use his mother's maiden name. As a new citizen of Frederickport, he deserves our protection, and I believe that if he uses that particular alias instead of his legal surname, our job will be much easier. I've already talked to the other people in the department who are aware of his real name."

"This doesn't have anything to do with the fact that he is some freaking bizzillionaire," Joe grumbled under his breath.

MacDonald looked over at Joe and smiled. "Actually, it does, but not in the way you imply. The fact is, if Johnson didn't have the money he has, his surname would not be an issue. I'm not courting any special donation for the department—but Mr. Johnson has not broken any laws, and I believe he has a right to his privacy. If his real name were to be made public, I imagine this place would be overrun by con men looking for some way to get a piece of Johnson's fortune. As it is, we already have Peter Morris and Earthbound Spirits to contend with; do we really want more like them?"

"Wouldn't it be easier if Johnson just moved on?" Joe asked. "And I bet if his real name was leaked, he would move on faster. That would make our lives easier."

MacDonald studied Joe for a moment. Finally, he asked, "Joe, this wouldn't have anything to do with Danielle Boatman, would it?"

"Of course not," Joe snapped. "But Danielle doesn't need someone like that guy hanging around."

"What, she doesn't need some good-looking rich guy?" Brian snickered.

"WHAT DO YOU THINK? Have you made a decision?" Adam asked Chris. The two men sat across from each other at a table in Lucy's Diner.

"I really liked that second house you showed me—the one right on the beach, three doors down from Ian's rental."

"The only problem with that one—like I told you earlier—the owners intend to list it, so they're only willing to rent month by month. As long as you don't mind moving again if it sells fast. The up side is the rent is reasonable, since they'll only go month by month."

Holding his water glass by its rim, Chris gently twirled the glass, watching the ice swirl around. He grinned and then looked up at Adam while setting the glass back down on the table. "How about if I bought it?"

"You want to buy it? Seriously?"

"Sure, why not? It's about time I settled somewhere for longer than a few months. I really like that house, its location."

"But you don't even know what they'll be asking."

"Do you know what they plan to ask?"

"I haven't gotten the comps together yet."

"You're the listing agent?" Chris asked.

Adam nodded. "I do mostly property management, but I also represent my owners when they decide to sell."

"Then talk to them. You can get both sides of the deal. Better for you. If they agree to sell, I'll talk to Danielle about renting the room until escrow closes; that way I only have to move once."

"While I hate losing a prime rental property, the commission on the sale will help ease the pain," Adam said with a laugh.

"Okay then!" Chris grinned. "Let's see if you can pull this together!"

A thought crossed Adam's mind and his smile quickly faded. "There's just one thing. Danielle assured me you wouldn't have a problem with the rent—but if you want to buy something, it's going to be a little tricky getting you financing. You aren't working right now, are you?"

Chris grinned again. "No, no, I'm not. But I'm not going to need financing. I'll be paying in cash."

February 13, 2015

WHEN CHRIS ENTERED the interrogation room, Officer Henderson was sitting down at the table, notebook in hand, reviewing his notes. Instead of standing up, he waved for Chris to take a seat and told him he would just be a minute.

After a few moments, Brian looked up from his notebook while one hand rested on the open page. "I was just telling Danielle it will be a bit more difficult for you to fly under the wire, what with Morris's murder and the investigation. I don't imagine it'll be possible to keep your true identity a secret. Especially if you had something to do with his death."

"I didn't kill Morris. I had no reason to kill him," Chris insisted.

"According to Danielle, you admitted he came to see you."

"Yes, but that was a few hours before I found him in the parlor —murdered."

"Let's start with why he came to Marlow House."

"I got a call from him last night—on my cellphone. It was right before midnight."

"What was the relationship between you and Morris?"

"We had no relationship. I only met the man a couple times—at Danielle's Christmas Eve party and again at the hospital when Richard was taken to the ER. Although, I don't recall talking to him at the hospital. I believe you were there."

"But he had your phone number?"

"Yes. I don't know how he got it, but he did."

"What did he say when he called you?"

"He told me he had to talk to me, that it was urgent. I thought it was pretty bizarre, him calling me, especially because it was almost midnight. And then…then he called me Chris Glandon."

"He knew your real name?"

"Apparently."

"So what happened then?"

"He told me that if I didn't want him sending out a tweet letting the world know where I'd landed, I'd meet with him for a few minutes. He promised the visit would be short. As it turned out, he was already parked in front of the house when he made the call."

"So you agreed to meet him?" Brian asked.

"Yes. I let him in the house and took him to the parlor. When I left him, he was still alive. I didn't see him again until I found him in the room some three hours later."

"What did he want to talk to you about?"

Chris let out a snort. "What do you think a man like Morris wanted? He wanted a donation. He actually believed I should join his cult and agree to giving sizeable—and frequent—donations. Or shall I say, blackmail payments."

"Blackmail? What did he have on you?"

"Nothing aside from knowing my real name. He actually

36

thought I'd be willing to pay him for that. To be honest, he sounded…panicked."

"Panicked?"

"Maybe frantic would be a better word," Chris suggested. "It was like he desperately needed money, and he needed it fast. That's just the impression I had. It was as if he wasn't thinking rationally, especially since he actually thought I'd pay him for something like that."

"What did you tell him?"

"I asked him how much he wanted."

"Why did you ask him that? You just said you'd never pay him."

"He didn't know that. I saw it as an opportunity to catch Morris. I know Danielle believes he was the one behind Cleve's actions—and death. I was planning to talk to Chief MacDonald this morning, see if we could arrange some sort of sting to catch Morris in his blackmail scheme."

"But wouldn't something like that potentially expose your true identity after trapping Morris? You would have to go to court as a witness. Something like that would get media attention."

"Murdering Morris a few feet from the room I was staying in would also risk exposing my true identity to the world. If it was you, which one would you choose?"

"Fair enough. What happened after you told Morris you were willing to give him a donation?"

"I told him I'd have to arrange a transfer with my bank, that the checking account I use for my day-to-day living expenses doesn't have that much money in it."

"He agreed to that?"

"Not at first. He suggested I make the transfer online or with my cellphone. He also told me to turn over all the cash I had on me." Chris laughed.

"Why is that funny?"

"I had less than twenty bucks on me. I asked him if he seriously expected me to hand over my pocket change. For some reason he assumed I carried a large sum of money on me."

"Then what happened?"

"I told him I never kept much money on me. And that I wasn't able to transfer money like that. I explained I'd expressly set up the account with my bank that any transfers of large funds had to be made in person—for security purposes."

"So he was okay with that?"

"What else could he do? We agreed to meet late Friday afternoon. I told him I'd call him as soon as I made the transfer. And I started to walk him out—"

"What time was this?"

"I didn't check the time, but I don't think we talked for more than thirty or forty minutes."

"So he left?"

"I thought he did."

"What do you mean you thought he left? Did you lock the door after you walked him outside?"

"I didn't walk him to the door."

"I thought you said you walked him out?"

"No, I started to. When we got into the entry hall, Heather stepped out of the living room and told me Danielle was looking for me and that she'd gone to the kitchen. She offered to walk Morris out, so I left her with him and went into the kitchen to see what Danielle wanted."

"That was pretty late by then, wasn't it? Almost one in the morning?"

Chris shrugged in response.

"When you went into the kitchen to see Danielle, you didn't tell her about Morris's visit?"

"She wasn't in the kitchen. I thought maybe she'd gone into the library, but she wasn't there either. I walked upstairs, but all the doors were closed and the lights were out, so I just went back downstairs. I didn't want to wake up the guests. Figured whatever she needed me for must not have been that important."

"Did you say anything to Heather about Danielle not being in the kitchen?"

Chris shook his head. "No. When I came back downstairs, all the lights were off. Figured she had locked up and gone to bed while I was off in the kitchen and library, looking for Danielle."

"What did you do then?"

"I went back to the kitchen and got a piece of cake and then went to bed."

"Did you eat the cake in the kitchen?"

"Yes."

"And you didn't hear anything downstairs?" Brian asked.

"No."

"What time was this?"

"Like I said, I never checked the time. But I suspect it was around one a.m."

"When you went to your bedroom, did you go right to sleep?"

"Yes."

"But Heather found you in the parlor two hours later, which you don't deny. Why were you there?"

"Something woke me up."

"Something?"

"I don't know what exactly. But I woke up...thought I heard something. When I went out into the hall, I noticed a light coming from under the parlor door, and I went to check it out. That's when I found Morris."

"A light coming from under the parlor door? When you went back downstairs, after looking for Danielle, did you notice a light coming from the parlor then?"

A frown crossed Chris's face, and he cocked his head slightly, considering the question. He began to shake his head. "No, no, I didn't. I remember it was pitch black when I came back downstairs, which is why I assumed Heather had locked up the house, and I didn't bother checking the front door. No, the parlor light was off then. All the downstairs lights were off."

"If it was pitch black, you really couldn't see if Heather was still downstairs or not? Or Morris, for that matter."

"When I said pitch black, I just meant the interior lights were off. There was enough moonlight coming in the window to get around without turning on a light—and I'm certain the parlor light was off."

"I have one last question for now."

"What's that?"

"Danielle tells me she gave you a fishing knife?"

"Fishing knife? Yes...why?"

"Can you tell me where the knife is?"

"Why? Why do you need my fishing knife?"

"Just tell me where we can find it," Brian told him.

"I don't know where it is."

"Did you conveniently misplace the knife Danielle bought you?" Brian asked.

"I didn't conveniently misplace anything," Chris snapped. "I put it in my tackle box, and the last time I looked, it wasn't there."

"Are you saying someone stole your knife?"

"Or borrowed."

"And where do you keep this tackle box?"

"On the back porch."

"On the back porch where anyone can get into it?" Brian asked.

"The yard is fenced."

"Did you tell anyone the knife was missing?"

"No."

"Why not?"

"I didn't want to embarrass whoever borrowed it. Figured they would put it back when they were done with it."

"I think they're done with it," Brian said. "But I don't think they're going to be returning it to your tackle box."

SEVEN

"I'm surprised you didn't talk to me first," Heather said when she walked into the interrogation room. Taking a seat across from Brian, she crossed her legs and stared at him while waiting for his first question.

"I understand you believe Chris murdered Peter Morris."

"I don't want to believe that. I actually like Chris. But I did see him covered in blood, and I know Peter Morris was at the house to talk to him. Who else could it be?"

"Tell me what you remember from last night."

Repositioning herself in the chair, Heather uncrossed and recrossed her legs. "I'd been watching television and had just turned off the set when I heard what sounded like someone coming in the front door. I looked into the hallway and saw Chris leading Peter Morris into the parlor."

"Did you recognize Mr. Morris immediately?"

Heather shrugged. "Rather hard not to, with that ridiculous black hair of his, for a man his age." She paused a moment and blushed. "I suppose that's rather harsh, considering he's dead."

Brian reserved comment. Heather's own hair was unnaturally black for her complexion. "Then what did you do?"

"I...I didn't do anything. I went up to bed."

"Chris tells me you were still downstairs thirty or forty minutes after Morris first arrived."

"I guess that's about right. I wanted to straighten up the living room a bit before I went upstairs. I try to do my part around the house."

"According to Chris, you showed Peter Morris out."

"No, I didn't."

"Are you saying Chris is lying?"

"No." Heather uncrossed and recrossed her legs again. "I'm just saying I didn't see the man out."

"According to Chris, when he came out of the parlor with Mr. Morris, you told him Danielle wanted to speak to him, and you offered to show Mr. Morris out."

"I suppose that's true."

"You suppose?"

"Well, I did offer to show him out, but he didn't leave; he had something else to tell Chris. I just assumed Chris showed him out."

"Why don't we back up a little bit; explain exactly what happened when Chris and Peter Morris came out of the parlor."

"I was just getting ready to go upstairs for bed. Chris had to go to the kitchen, so I offered to show Mr. Morris out. But when we got to the door, he told me he'd forgotten to tell Chris something, so he said he would just wait there for Chris to return. Then I went upstairs."

"Did you see Chris with Mr. Morris again?"

"You mean, aside from in the parlor after Mr. Morris was murdered?"

"Yes."

"No. But it was late. I figured he'd be going to bed as soon as he returned from the kitchen. There was no way he'd miss seeing Mr. Morris standing there, not far from his bedroom door."

"Why did Chris go to the kitchen?"

"I guess Danielle wanted to talk to him about something."

"Did she tell you that?"

Heather frowned. "No."

"According to Chris, you told him Danielle wanted to see him in the kitchen."

"That's not exactly what happened."

"Are you saying Chris lied?"

"No. I thought I heard Danielle calling for Chris. It sounded like it was coming from the kitchen. I…I just assumed it was Danielle."

"If I understand correctly, you saw Chris let Peter Morris into the house a little after midnight. They went into the parlor. Then thirty or forty minutes later, you thought you heard Danielle calling for Chris from the kitchen; he came out of the parlor with Mr. Morris; you told him Danielle needed to talk to him; you offered to show Mr. Morris out. He told you he needed to tell Chris something, and you left the man at the front door and then went upstairs to bed. Is that correct?"

"Yes, pretty much."

"So did you turn the downstairs lights off?"

"The downstairs lights? Why would I do that and leave Mr. Morris standing in the dark?"

"So the lights were on?"

"I suppose so."

"Why did you come downstairs again? How did you happen to be standing at the door to the parlor while Chris was inside the room, kneeling by Mr. Morris?"

"I woke up. I was thirsty. So I came downstairs. I heard something coming from the direction of the parlor, so I went to investigate."

"What was the first thing you saw?"

"I noticed the door to the parlor was open and the light was on. I went to see who was up. When I got to the door, I saw Chris kneeling by the body, blood covering his hands."

"And your first thought was that he'd killed Mr. Morris?"

"I think it was a rational assumption."

"AM I SPECIAL? You want to see me again? What about Lily or David?" Danielle asked Brian when she returned to the interrogation room.

"What time did you go to bed last night?"

"It was about ten when I went upstairs." Danielle sat down. "I took a shower, read for a while. I remember checking my phone before I turned off the lights. It was not quite 11:30 p.m."

"So you were probably sleeping when Morris arrived around midnight?"

"I doubt that. Took me a couple hours to finally fall asleep. I drank a couple cups of coffee at dinner last night—something I shouldn't do. Had me wired."

"Did you go downstairs?"

"Not until later, after we heard Heather scream."

"According to Heather, she thought she heard you calling for Chris from the direction of the kitchen. It would have been after midnight."

Danielle shook her head. "No. I don't know what she thought she heard, but it wasn't me. For one thing, I'm not in a habit of shouting for people—especially in the middle of the night."

"Could it have been Lily?"

"I seriously doubt it. I checked in on Lily after I finished my shower, and her bedroom door was already locked; there wasn't a light on in her room. I'm sure she was asleep, but you can ask her."

"I've a question about Heather."

"Yes?"

"Why is she staying at Marlow House?"

Five Weeks Earlier—January 9, 2015

"SO YOU'RE REALLY CHRIS GLANDON?" Adam Nichols asked for the third time. He sat with Danielle and Chris in Pier Café.

"If you keep saying that, someone is going to hear," Danielle whispered.

"I just thought you needed to know the truth, since you're my real estate agent," Chris told him.

"I'm glad you told me now before I wrote up the purchase contract," Adam said.

"You do understand Chris prefers to remain anonymous. Do you think that'll be possible?"

"It shouldn't be a problem. The sellers live out of state. I doubt they'll give the buyer's name much thought." Adam picked up his coffee and took a sip.

"If I can maintain my anonymity through this purchase, it could be very profitable for you," Chris told him.

Adam set his mug back onto the table. "What do you mean?"

"I've been considering purchasing property in Oregon for several projects I've been working on. I need a local real estate agent. I know you specialize in property management and these—"

"Are you suggesting you might use me?" Adam interrupted.

"Yes. If I'm able to continue flying under the wire."

Adam reached across the table to shake Chris's hand. "I'd be more than happy to help you find the perfect properties, Mr. Johnson."

With a laugh, Chris accepted the handshake.

A few minutes later, the server brought their order. Just as she left their table, Heather Donovan entered the restaurant. Instead of stopping by to say hello, Danielle's neighbor took a table on the other side of the room.

Danielle watched Heather, who stared blankly at her menu. "Heather doesn't seem particularly friendly today."

Both Chris and Adam glanced briefly to Danielle's neighbor.

"From what Bill tells me, she has a mess on her hands," Adam said just before he picked up his burger and took a bite.

"Mess? What do you mean?" Danielle glanced from Adam to Heather.

"She called Bill about a water leak. I guess it's been leaking for some time. There's some major mold going on in the walls between the kitchen and living room."

Danielle cringed. "Mold?"

"Yep. And she needs to move out while they make repairs. She called me the other day about somewhere to stay, but she has that cat. I don't have anything available right now that'll allow pets."

"There has to be some place she can stay," Chris said.

"I have owners willing to take small dogs, but not cats. It's allergies. There are a lot of people who are allergic to cats and won't rent from us if a cat's stayed in the house."

Danielle let out a sigh. "Yeah, we have that problem with Max, which is why I disclose the fact we have a cat before I accept someone's reservation."

"You can afford to turn away guests; I can't." Adam took another bite of his burger.

"She really looks unhappy, doesn't she?" Danielle said.

Chris eyed Danielle. "What are you thinking?"

"Well, I rent rooms. I think we could handle another cat."

"Oh really?" Chris laughed. "I wonder if Max would agree.

Danielle sighed. "You have a point. Max loathes other cats. But...we could explain it to him..."

Adam paused mid-bite and looked across the table to Danielle. "Explain it to him?"

"She did save my life," Danielle murmured, still looking at Heather.

"If she takes a room, you might as well change the name of Marlow House Bed and Breakfast to Marlow House Boarding-house," Chris teased.

Danielle laughed. "You have a point. I have you and Lily…" Danielle stood.

Adam looked up. "Where are you going?"

"Do you really need to ask?" Chris said after Danielle flashed them both a smile and walked to Heather's table.

"HI, NEIGHBOR," Danielle greeted her when she reached Heather's side.

Closing her menu, Heather looked up at Danielle. "Umm…hi. I saw you when I came in, but I didn't want to interrupt."

"Do you mind if I sit down a moment?"

"Umm…sure…I mean…no, I don't mind."

"I heard you have a mold issue." Danielle took a seat.

Heather groaned. "If that was my only problem. What do they say, when it rains, it pours?"

"Yeah, I understand you've been having a hard time finding someplace to stay because of Bella."

"Right…that too." Heather tossed the menu to the table.

"You mean you have more problems than mold and finding a place to stay?"

"I've lost Presley House, Danielle."

"Yeah, I know. I was there when it burned down."

"No, I mean the property. I've lost it."

"I don't understand."

"I told you Mother had power of attorney for my grandfather after he was committed. I didn't realize what a mess everything was. The property manager wasn't getting paid; the electric meter was pulled. But what's worse, the property tax wasn't being paid."

"You've lost the land for back taxes?"

Heather nodded. "I had no idea. They sent the notices to the wrong address. I spoke to someone in the assessor's office, and she told me she was looking into it…that something looked odd."

"Odd?"

"Yeah. Just between you and me, she said there was something odd about the file. I may have to get an attorney. Not that I can afford one now."

"Have they sold the property yet?"

"Yes. Deep inside I know this entire thing isn't kosher. Something crooked went on."

"Seriously?"

"Yes. But I can't think about it right now. I'm trying to figure out where I'm going to stay tonight. As it is, I have to get rid of most of my upholstered furniture—even my bed. The mold got into everything."

"It's that bad?"

"Worse. I don't know what I'm going to do. I suppose I should just find a home for Bella, but I don't want to do that."

"Stay with me. Bella's welcome."

"Stay with you? I can't do that. I can't afford to stay at an inn."

"We'll work something out. Heather, if it wasn't for you, I could've died in that fire. And you didn't have to give me the emerald. I can give it back to you. You can use it to pay for an attorney, help get your property back."

Heather shook her head. "No. I can't do that. That emerald belongs to you. The sins of my great-grandfather demand that it be returned to the rightful owner."

"You had nothing to do with what he did."

"I feel cursed enough these days. I don't want to test fate."

"You're serious, aren't you?"

"Very."

"At least accept my invitation to stay while your house is fixed."

"Danielle, they say it's going to take a month or more."

"That's okay. I'm letting Chris rent a room while he waits for his house to close escrow."

"Chris is buying a house?"

"Yes, on our street. He'll be our new neighbor."

"Sweet. When does he move in?"

"I don't know. The sellers have just decided on an asking price; they haven't even written up a purchase contract yet. But I don't imagine it'll take more than a month."

"It'll probably take longer than that. Getting loan approval can be a bitch, and Chris isn't working yet, is he?"

"Umm…I believe he has a little inheritance he's using to help him buy the house."

"Nice."

"So you want to stay at Marlow House?"

"I'd like to…but I honestly can't afford to pay what you normally charge."

"I told you we can work something out."

February 13, 2015

"DANIELLE? DANIELLE?" Brian repeated.

"Oh…I'm sorry." Danielle gave her head a quick shake. She looked over at Brian and smiled.

"Where did you zone out to?"

"I'm sorry, I was just thinking of something. Now, what was it you wanted to know?"

"I was wondering why Heather is staying at Marlow House."

"Oh…that…her house has mold."

EIGHT

W alt had changed from the beach apparel he had been sporting in Danielle's dream back to his normal attire—a three-piece suit, circa 1925—and his feet were no longer bare. He stood in the middle of the entry hall and watched as the responders processed the crime scene. They were preparing to move the body.

Earlier, they had discovered what they believed was the murder weapon, a fishing knife. Upstairs, officers combed through every room, but so far, they hadn't found anything else related to the crime. Walt had already completed his own search. He had been looking for the second body, but so far, he hadn't found it. Perhaps it was outside.

He suspected the younger man, who had been watching Danielle sleep, was somehow connected to Morris's death. Had the killer murdered them both? Or perhaps the younger man was the killer, but had met some fatal accident when fleeing the crime scene, which would explain his appearance earlier.

Peter Morris's spirit had fled the premises, but Walt knew there was no guarantee the ghost wouldn't return. Spirits often felt connected to the site of their death, especially when it was a violent one. Walt himself had stuck around Marlow House after his murder, and Darlene seemed connected to Pilgrim's Point, where she had been killed. Walt found the thought of sharing Marlow House with a spirit of Morris's ilk highly repugnant.

He preferred to believe Morris had moved on, and if he hadn't, then Chris or Danielle would simply need to convince him to leave permanently. However, at the moment, Walt was more concerned about the spirit of the younger man. Who was he? And where was his body?

Upstairs, Max was in the attic with Bella. While Max wasn't thrilled about having the younger female cat trail after him, he was getting used to it. Walt had given him a firm lecture, preaching the necessity of exerting patience with the smaller feline, who was practically a kitten in comparison. He reminded Max it was only a temporary situation. As soon as Heather was able to return to her own house down the street, the unwanted cat would go with her. Bella no longer hissed at Max. Instead, she found it far more amusing to pounce on his tail when he wasn't looking.

Walt was about to go upstairs and check on Max and Bella when he heard an officer call out from the parlor doorway, "You can't come in here."

Walt turned to the front door. It was open, with crime tape blocking the entry.

Ian stood on the front porch, looking in. "What in the hell is going on? Where's Lily? Danielle?"

Ian sounded frantic. Sadie was nowhere in sight. Walt assumed Ian had left the golden retriever at home across the street and had rushed over when he'd woken up and seen the police cars parked out front. Walt smiled. *He really does love Lily.*

"Oh, Mr. Bartley, it's you. I'm sorry, I didn't recognize you," the officer said. "But I'm afraid you can't come in; this is a crime scene."

"My god, Lily? Danielle?" Ian looked prepared to leap over the tape.

"Ms. Miller and Ms. Boatman are fine. They went down to the station with Mr. Johnson and the others to give their statements."

"What happened?"

"I'm sorry; I really can't discuss it at this time. Like I said, this is an active crime scene, so you need to leave."

Ian didn't argue with the officer. Instead, he turned and rushed away from Marlow House. Walt walked to the open doorway and watched Ian's hasty departure. He suspected Ian was going home to get his car so he could drive to the police station to find Lily.

Walt was about to turn from the doorway when he saw him:

Peter Morris. Unlike the body in the parlor, Morris's ghostly form looked a good ten years older, with gray-white hair. Yet Walt did not doubt for a moment that it was indeed Morris's ghost outside.

Walt was tempted to call out to Morris to find out who had murdered him and ask about the identity of the younger man. Yet he was reluctant to invite the spirit back into the house, for fear that he would not leave.

Voices from behind Walt caught his attention. He turned around. They were bringing Morris's body out. Moving to one side, out of their way, he watched as they carried the corpse from Marlow House to a waiting van parked outside.

Peter Morris trailed behind his body and climbed into the van. A few minutes later, the vehicle drove away, carrying both the body and spirit of Peter Morris.

Walt turned from the open doorway and made his way down the entry hall and up the stairs. By the time he reached the last stair leading to the second-floor landing, the officers were coming downstairs, moving right through him. Startled by their hasty departure, he paused a moment and looked down at his body as one officer after another rushed through him as if he were an open doorway. Disgusted with the invasion of his space, he was tempted to give one of them a shove, but resisted. He didn't think Danielle would appreciate some officer falling to his death on her staircase. Plus, the last thing he needed was another spirit haunting Marlow House.

The officers were all downstairs now. He wondered when they would finally leave and when Danielle and the rest would be allowed to return. It was then that he heard a new voice downstairs, one he recognized: Chief MacDonald. He suspected the police chief had stopped by on his way to work to check out the crime scene.

Walt continued on his way to the attic. But first, he decided to look through the rooms on the second floor to see what damage—if any—had been done during the police search of the property.

The first room he stepped into was Danielle's. It was no surprise that the bed remained unmade. A few of the drawers were partially opened and the closet door was ajar, yet other than that, he didn't see any damage.

He was about to move back into the hallway when a male voice asked, "Why were the police here? Where did Danielle go?"

Turning to the voice, Walt looked into the dark eyes of the man he had seen earlier, watching Danielle sleep. "You've returned."

"I didn't really go anywhere. Just outside. I'm surprised you can see me," the man said.

"Why is that?" Walt asked.

"Since I've arrived, no one has been able to see or hear me except for you," the man said, "and Peter Morris."

"Who are you?" Walt asked. "What do you have to do with Peter Morris?"

"Why does it matter? He's dead. Are you dead too?"

"Did you kill Peter Morris?" Walt asked.

"Is it possible for a ghost to kill a living person? I hadn't considered that possibility," the man muttered, more to himself than Walt.

"I'm talking about when you were alive, of course," Walt said impatiently. "Where is your body?"

"I suppose I could ask the same of you. Where is your body? Did you kill Peter Morris?"

Walt sighed impatiently. "This is my house. You're the one who needs to answer the questions."

"If you're dead, how can you own this house? How is that even possible? I understood Danielle owns this house."

"You just stay away from Danielle and answer my questions."

The man laughed. "Now, that is definitely something I will not do."

Before Walt could respond, the man vanished.

NINE

When Ian arrived at the police station on Friday morning, they wouldn't take him in to see Lily. The residents of Marlow House were still being interviewed. No one would tell Ian what had happened. He just knew Lily was unharmed.

He had been waiting for about thirty minutes in the front lobby when Chief MacDonald arrived. MacDonald was preoccupied and wouldn't answer any of Ian's questions, but he asked Ian to wait, telling him someone would be out in a few moments to get him. Twenty minutes later, Joe Morelli stepped out from the inner offices.

Ian stood up. "Can I see Lily now?"

"In a minute. But first, would you come with me?" Joe asked.

After leading Ian into his office, Joe closed the door, gestured for Ian to sit down, and said, "I thought we could do this in here since all the rooms are full."

"Do what?" Ian asked as he sat down.

Joe took a seat behind his desk and grabbed a pen and pad of paper. "I need to ask you a few questions." Joe couldn't help but remember how well he and Ian had hit it off when Joe had briefly dated Danielle some eight months earlier. The two men were about the same age, and the four of them—Ian and Lily, and Danielle and Joe—had enjoyed each other's company. There had been laughter and a promise of a bright future, a romance with Danielle, and a friendship with Ian and Lily—until everything changed. While Joe still considered Ian a friend, any bromance had cooled sufficiently.

"What's going on, Joe? I get up this morning, see cops parked all over the street, crime tape in front of Marlow House, and they tell me everyone has been brought down here. What happened?"

"Ian, where did you sleep last night?"

"My house. Why?"

"You didn't stay at Marlow House?"

"No."

"What time did you get up this morning?" Joe asked.

"It was almost eight. Why?"

"What time did you go to bed last night?"

Ian let out a deep sigh and leaned back in the chair before answering. "It was after midnight. What's going on?"

"Did you go outside at all last night? Did you ever look out the window? Look across the street to Marlow House?"

Ian shook his head. "No. I was pretty exhausted. I'd been working all day. Hit the bed and that was pretty much it. I would probably have slept longer, but Sadie woke me up. She had to go out. That's when I looked across the street and saw all the cop cars."

Joe tossed the pen onto his desk and leaned back in the chair. His gaze met Ian's. "Peter Morris was murdered last night."

"Damn, are you serious? That's going to change everything."

"Change what?" Joe frowned.

"I've been working on an exposé on Morris and Earthbound Spirits. This will change the direction of my piece. What happened? Any idea who did it?"

"I guess you'll have to ask Lily and Danielle about that."

Ian frowned. "What are you talking about?"

"That's the reason for the crime tape. Early this morning, Peter Morris was found murdered at Marlow House."

"What do you mean found at Marlow House?"

"In the parlor, to be exact. With his throat slashed."

"Holy crap." Ian stood up and briefly lifted his Cubs baseball cap from his head before putting it back on. He paced in front of the desk for a moment and then paused and looked at Joe. "Have you arrested anyone?"

"Not yet."

"Do you know who did it?" Ian asked.

"It's an ongoing investigation. Like I said, we haven't arrested anyone yet."

"I can't believe this. He was murdered at Marlow House? What happened?" Ian sat back down.

"As far as we know, his body was found in the parlor of Marlow House between three and four this morning. His throat had been slashed. Initially, Heather found Chris standing over the body with blood on his hands. Chris claimed he'd just found Morris and was checking his vitals. We do know Morris had come to Marlow House at midnight to see Chris. He threatened to reveal Chris's real name if he didn't make a large donation. That's pretty much all that we have right now. Oh…and we found the murder weapon."

"No way Chris killed him," Ian insisted.

"Why do you say that?" Joe asked.

"Why would he?" Ian scoffed. "And even if he wanted to, Chris has enough money to make Morris disappear without anyone suspecting him. Not to mention, he has absolutely no motive."

"He was being blackmailed; that's a motive."

"Blackmailed, for what?"

"I told you, he threatened to reveal Chris's real last name."

"Come on, Joe, you aren't serious. If Chris was so desperate to keep his identity a secret—which I don't believe he is—then he certainly isn't going to commit a sensational crime just a few steps from the room he's staying in. That makes absolutely no sense."

"I'm not saying it was premeditated. But a crime of passion—maybe. He seems intent on staying close to Danielle. Found a way to keep renting a room from her even though she doesn't operate a boardinghouse. Maybe he panicked when Morris made his demand. He grabbed the first thing he could find—his own knife—and in a fit of rage, slit Morris's throat. He waited for everyone to go to bed before moving the body. But Heather surprised him, and when she screamed, it got the entire house up."

Ian stared at Joe. "Are you saying the murder weapon belonged to Chris?"

Joe nodded. "It was his fishing knife."

"You're serious, aren't you?" Ian said dully. "You actually believe Chris murdered Morris?"

"Yes, I do," Joe said solemnly.

Ian stood up abruptly, and just as he did, the office door opened. Standing at the doorway was Chief MacDonald.

"They told me you were in here with Joe," MacDonald greeted them. He then looked at Joe and asked, "Are you done with him? Lily is ready to leave, and I told her Ian was here for her."

"Yes," Joe said with a nod.

Without another word, Ian rushed from the room.

"Is Danielle still here?" Joe asked.

"Yes. I haven't had a chance to talk to her yet. I asked her to wait, but I have to run to my office and make a phone call first."

"Would you mind if I talk to her?"

"That's fine. When you're done, send her to my office. Give me at least ten minutes."

JOE WAS SITTING at his desk when Danielle came into his office.

"They said you wanted to talk to me for a minute?" Danielle asked wearily.

"You look exhausted." Joe stood up and motioned to the empty chair. "Would you like me to get you a cup of coffee?"

Danielle shook her head and flopped down in the empty chair. "No, thanks. I think I've already downed about three, maybe four cups. Which I'm going to regret. But if you happen to have any bacon and eggs lying around, I'll take it. I'm starved."

Joe smiled. "Sorry, I don't. But I'll be happy to take you out to breakfast after you finish talking to the chief."

Danielle flashed him a kind smile. "Thanks, Joe. I appreciate the offer. But Chris is waiting for me. We drove over in my car." Danielle watched as Joe sat back down behind his desk. He'd had a recent haircut, she thought. The style he normally wore reminded her a bit of an old-fashioned boy's haircut, one that allowed his soft dark curls to remain. While this new cut was longer than a buzz cut, it was far shorter than Danielle had ever seen him wear his hair, and the curls were gone.

"Are you okay, Danielle?"

"Well, aside from the fact I got about an hour of sleep last night —if that—and someone was murdered in my house, I guess I'm terrific."

"It really does seem Marlow House wasn't meant to be an inn."

Danielle frowned. "Why do you say that?"

"Looking back, most of the bad things that have happened to

you since you arrived never would have happened if you hadn't pursued the bed and breakfast. Opening your house to strangers just invites danger."

"Now you're making up rhymes?" Danielle smirked.

"This is serious, Danielle. You know what I mean."

She let out a weary sigh. "Unfortunately, yes, I do. But don't start that again. Please, not right now. I'm too flipping exhausted to argue with you."

"I don't want to argue with you," Joe insisted.

"Sure sounded that way. And it's always the same argument."

"I just worry about you, Danielle. I won't apologize for that. You have no idea how I felt when I heard Morris had been brutally murdered under your roof. What would've happened had you walked into the parlor at the wrong time? It might have been you lying in the morgue right now."

"I appreciate your concern, Joe. And trust me, that thought has crossed my mind too."

"How about I take you away from all this ugliness—at least for a couple hours. Let me take you out to dinner tonight. You need a break."

"Thanks, Joe. But honestly, all I want to do is go home and crawl back into bed and sleep. Which will not be so easy, considering all that dang caffeine I consumed this morning."

"Then let me take you out tomorrow night."

Danielle studied Joe for a moment before responding. "Tomorrow is Valentine's Day."

"Do you have a date already?"

"Umm…no…but…well, restaurants are always swamped on Valentine's Day."

"I'm sure I can get us in somewhere."

"Thanks for the invitation, Joe. But I just don't think it would be such a terrific idea."

"Ah, come on, Danielle. We're still friends, aren't we?"

"Sure we are."

"Then what will dinner with a friend hurt?"

"On Valentine's Day?" Danielle shook her head. "I don't think so. I don't want to give you the wrong impression. We are friends, Joe. But just friends. Nothing else."

Joe leaned back in his chair and studied Danielle. "It's Chris, isn't it?"

"Chris has nothing to do with this."

"I think he's dangerous, Danielle. I believe he murdered Morris."

"Don't be ridiculous. There is no way Chris would've killed him. He had no motive."

Joe then proceeded to share his theory with Danielle—the same theory he had given Ian. When he was done, Danielle silently stood up.

"Where are you going?" Joe asked.

"I imagine the chief is off the phone by now." Danielle turned toward the door, but then paused and turned briefly back to Joe. "You're wrong about Chris. Please don't do this again." Without waiting for a response, Danielle left the office.

TEN

"I swear, Joe drives me insane," Danielle told MacDonald when she entered his office a few minutes later. She shut the door behind her. Without waiting for an invitation, she sat down across from him. They were alone.

"Let me guess, Joe told you his theory of who murdered Peter Morris," MacDonald asked.

"You mean how Chris killed Morris in a fit of rage and then left him in the parlor for a couple hours, waiting for everyone to fall asleep so he could sneak back later and dispose of the body?"

"It's not a bad theory, since Morris did come to see Chris."

Danielle slumped down in the chair. "I suppose from Joe's limited perspective, it is a reasonable theory."

"Of course…" MacDonald absently tapped his fingertips on the desktop. "I'd have to ask myself, wouldn't Chris worry about Peter Morris's ghost sticking around and telling you or Walt what he'd done?"

"Well, actually, Morris's ghost did stick around."

The chief leaned forward. "You saw Morris's ghost?"

Danielle shook her head. "No, Walt did."

"Did he say who killed him?"

"No. But it's always possible he's talked to Walt since we've been here. Although, the thought of Morris's spirit lingering around Marlow House rather freaks me out."

"I can't say I blame you. You already went through that with Stoddard."

Danielle leaned toward the desk. "I've a question for you. One I couldn't ask Brian."

"What's that?"

"Was there a second body? Did your people find another man's body?"

He frowned. "A second body? Why would you ask that?"

"Because last night—technically early this morning—Walt saw two spirits. One was Peter Morris, and the other was a younger man Walt didn't recognize. I have to wonder, if two ghosts suddenly appear, and we find the body of one—shouldn't there be another body out there?"

"If there's a second body, we haven't found it. Tell me what you know—what you couldn't tell Brian."

"I was having this lovely dream hop in Hawaii," she said with a sigh. "At least I think it was Hawaii."

MacDonald frowned. "Dream hop?"

"Some spirits have the ability to visit people in their dreams—even people unlike me, who can't normally see spirits."

MacDonald smiled. "I sometimes dream about my grandmother. Those dreams always feel a bit...different."

"I assume it's the grandmother I met at the cemetery?" she asked.

"Yes."

"Wouldn't surprise me if it wasn't a regular dream. I call it a dream hop. Walt does it with Lily sometimes. It gives them a chance to have a real visit where she can see and hear him. And sometimes, well, sometimes he does it with me."

"Why would Walt have to dream hop with you?"

Danielle smiled softly. "Because in a dream, you make your own reality. We can set sail on the sea, kick back on a sandy beach, or go skydiving."

"Seriously?"

Danielle grinned. "Yep. Last night I was lounging on a tropical beach when I started to get cold. Unfortunately, in a dream our body is still vulnerable to the real world. My blankets had fallen to the floor, and I was freezing. Instead of waking up, Walt offered to leave the dream world and return to my room and cover me up. When he got there, he saw the two spirits."

"They were together?"

"No. He saw the first one in my bedroom. It was the younger man. Walt asked him a couple questions, but he just disappeared. So Walt headed downstairs, looking for him, and that's when he saw Peter Morris's spirit running down the hall. Morris said something about having to get out of there and then vanished."

"So what did Walt do? Did he find the body?"

Danielle shook her head. "No. He decided to wake up Chris. I guess he thought Chris could help him figure it out without waking me up. Chris was asleep when Walt went into his bedroom. That's how I know Chris was telling the truth about finding Morris later, after he thought Morris had left."

"Was Walt with Chris when he found the body?"

"No. Chris went to investigate the parlor because that's the direction Walt had seen Morris coming from. Walt went to wake me up. I had just woken up when I heard Heather scream. And you know the rest."

"In all fairness to Joe, what you told me really doesn't discredit Joe's theory. If Walt was with you in a dream, it was possible Chris killed Morris in a fit of rage—not thinking out the possible consequences of his actions."

"And then just left his body in the parlor and went to bed? I don't know about you, but if I'd just killed someone in a fit of rage, I couldn't go to bed and fall asleep. And according to Walt, Chris was sound asleep when he woke him up."

"I'm not saying I agree with the theory, just that it's not without merit." The chief reached over and snatched a manila folder from the corner of his desk.

Danielle watched MacDonald open the folder. "Maybe Walt has found out something since we left him."

"I wanted to ask you a few questions about one of your guests."

"Which one?"

"David Hilton."

"David? What about him?"

"We did a brief background check on the couple staying for the weekend, to see if anything came up."

"You mean a connection to Earthbound Spirits or Morris?" she asked.

"I remember reading an article a while back about how Earthbound Spirits' headquarters was bequeathed to the organization by

Helen Hilton—along with her entire estate, which was a considerable fortune. It caused quite a stir at the time, family sued, lost."

"Hilton? As in the hotel chain?"

"No relationship to the hotel chain. But there is a connection to David Hilton. He's Helen Hilton's youngest grandson."

"No kidding? Does this mean he was involved with a lawsuit against Earthbound Spirits?"

"He and his siblings."

"He didn't mention anything last night about his connection to Morris," Danielle murmured.

"No, no, he didn't." From the folder, MacDonald removed a printout of an online news article regarding the lawsuit. He handed it to Danielle.

After she read the article, she tossed it back on his desk. "While David had a reason to hate the man, I can't imagine he was involved in his murder. How would he have known Morris was going to be at the house? Why would he have killed Morris under the same roof he was staying? That's even more implausible than Joe's theory."

"Maybe it wasn't premeditated. Maybe David came downstairs to get a drink of water—like Heather did later that evening. He saw Morris waiting in the entry after Heather had gone up to bed and Chris was in the kitchen looking for you. For whatever reason, he confronted Morris, wanted to tell him what he thought of him. The two men went into the parlor and things escalated, got out of control, and David killed him."

"And how did David conveniently get ahold of Chris's fishing knife? Chris's tackle box was on the back porch. I assume whoever used it to kill Morris—assuming it is the same knife—stole it earlier and intended to use it to frame Chris," Danielle said.

"I suppose that is possible, Danielle," MacDonald conceded. "But according to Chris, his knife had been missing for a few days. Perhaps it wasn't stolen. Maybe he misplaced it—set it in the parlor and forgot it. Or maybe whoever borrowed it earlier did the same thing. And when David was confronted with Morris in the parlor, he was just so angry and happened to find the knife…"

"And managed to slit Morris's throat? Just tell me, Chief, where's the blood evidence? Your people have gone through the house; did you find any bloody clothes that might've belonged to David? Now that I think about it, that would go for Chris too. I can't imagine it's possible to cut someone's throat without getting blood on them.

While Chris had some on his hands when we found him with Morris, I'm pretty sure he didn't have any on him when Walt woke him up. I can't imagine going to bed in bloody clothes. And if he did, that blood would be transferred to the sheets."

"It doesn't mean Hilton wasn't able to dispose of his clothes before the body was found several hours later. He could have buried them on the beach—they could have gone out with the tide. There's a number of possibilities."

"I suppose we'll have to wait, then, to see if any clothes wash up on shore."

"So who do you think did it?" he asked.

"I honestly have no idea." Danielle shook her head. "But if you would just let me go home, maybe we'll get the answers we need. When can I go home, by the way?"

"When I left your house, they had a couple more hours, maybe more. I'll call you as soon as you can go back."

The chief's phone began to ring. He picked it up and looked to see who was calling. He raised his hand briefly to Danielle, signaling he was about to take the call. A few minutes later, when the call ended, he smiled up to Danielle.

"If Walt doesn't have any new information for us, maybe we won't have to wait for any bloody clothes to wash up," he told her.

"What do you mean?"

"Apparently, they found a bloody fingerprint on the wrought iron fencing along the front of Marlow House, down by the street."

"Do they know who it belongs to?" Danielle asked.

"My guess, the killer."

ELEVEN

D avid and Arlene turned down Lily and Ian's invitation to join them for breakfast. None of them were allowed to return to Marlow House. According to Police Chief MacDonald, they wouldn't be able to do that until after three that afternoon. By the time David and Arlene left the police station, Lily and Ian were already gone, but Danielle and Chris were still inside, talking to officers.

———

ARLENE SILENTLY STARED out the side window of the Honda Accord as David steered the vehicle down the road, looking for somewhere to stop for breakfast.

With both hands firmly on the steering wheel, David glanced briefly at Arlene and asked, "I thought you'd look happier."

Still gazing out the side window, she said, "Maybe we should go home now."

"Just because Morris is dead, it doesn't mean this is over for us. Maybe this isn't what we planned, but I don't see the point of leaving now."

A few minutes later, David pulled into a restaurant parking lot. After he turned off the engine, they both got out of the vehicle, neither of them saying a word. They were just about to step onto the walkway leading to the front door of the restaurant when they heard someone call out, "Arlene!"

They both paused and looked in the direction of the voice. Arlene reached out and touched David's wrist. "Go on in, and get us a table."

"Who's that?" David watched the man walk toward them.

"Just someone I know." Arlene gave David a gentle nudge, urging him to continue to the restaurant. Without another word, David turned and hurried up the walkway and entered the building.

"I wondered if that was you!" the man greeted her when he reached Arlene, giving her a quick hug.

"Adam, Adam Nichols, it's been a long time," Arlene said when the hug ended. They stood together on the sidewalk, their gazes locked, and his hands lightly holding her fingertips.

"You look amazing. Of course, you always did," Adam told her. He gave her fingers a quick squeeze and then released his hold.

She took a step back, her eyes still on his. "You look pretty good yourself. I'm really sorry about Isabella."

"You heard?" Adam asked.

"You knew I would, considering everything. Anyway, it was in all the papers."

"You probably also heard Isabella and I hadn't been together for a long time. Almost a year when she died."

Arlene readjusted the strap of her handbag, which hung over her right shoulder. "Well, you know what I always said: Earthbound Spirits has a way of destroying relationships."

"I don't know, I always thought they were responsible for..." Adam didn't finish the sentence.

"For us?" Arlene asked in a whisper.

Adam shrugged in reply.

"You could have called me after...well...after you and Isabella broke it off." Slipping her handbag strap off her shoulder, she clutched it in her hands, nervously fidgeting with the leather loop.

"I considered it. But then, I didn't think you would've been thrilled to hear from me."

Glancing down at her purse, Arlene sighed. Looking back up into Adam's face, she said, "Yeah, you're probably right. Things were always a little complicated for us."

"So..." Adam nodded toward the restaurant door. "Your boyfriend...husband?"

"Not married," Arlene explained. "He's a...friend...we're spending the weekend in Frederickport."

Adam shoved his hands into his coat pockets and glanced from Arlene to the restaurant door and then back to Arlene. "Ahh, a romantic Valentine's weekend."

Arlene shrugged. "So what about you? Any woman finally get you to settle down?"

"No. Still single. I'm not the settle-down type."

Arlene looked over to the restaurant. "I guess I should go. I imagine David's got us a table by now."

"Yeah, and he's probably wondering what's keeping you so long."

Arlene flashed Adam a weak smile. "It really was good seeing you again."

"You too. Have a nice weekend." Adam leaned over and brushed a kiss over her cheek.

Flashing him a final smile, she said, "Take care of yourself."

When Arlene turned from Adam and started toward the restaurant, he called out, "Arlene, wait!"

She paused a moment and looked at him.

"I was sorry to hear about your brother," he called out.

"I'd understand if you really weren't," she told him.

Adam watched as Arlene turned from him and made her way into the restaurant. When the door closed, Adam mumbled to himself, "Now where are you having breakfast? Not here."

Shaking his head, Adam turned back toward the parking lot.

———

WHEN ADAM PARKED in front of Pier Café ten minutes later, he spied Danielle and Chris walking toward the restaurant. Hastily getting from his car, he slammed the door shut and sprinted to catch up with them while calling out, "Chris! Danielle!"

They both came to a stop and turned to face Adam.

Slightly out of breath when he reached them, he said, "I tried calling you about an hour ago. I wanted to let you know I spoke to escrow this morning."

"Is everything okay?" Chris asked.

"Looks like escrow is closing early. By this afternoon you'll be a Frederickport home owner."

Before Chris could respond, Adam turned his attention to Danielle, looking her up and down with a curious expression. "When did you take up jogging?"

"Jogging?" Danielle frowned.

"I just figured..." Adam looked her up and down again, taking in her disheveled appearance. "Have you looked in a mirror this morning?"

Wrinkling her nose, Danielle backhanded Adam's arm. He only laughed at her tepid assault. He then looked back to Chris, noting that he didn't look much better.

"Ahh, now I get it," Adam said with a dry chuckle. "Active morning in bed for you two? Grabbing some food before round two?"

Danielle rolled her eyes and turned toward the restaurant. As she started for its door, she said, "Adam Nichols, you have a dirty mind."

"Actually, I rather like how he thinks," Chris said with a laugh as he and Adam trailed behind her.

"So you really didn't spend the morning in bed together? That's rather disappointing," Adam said as he and Chris followed Danielle inside the restaurant.

"Tell me about it," Chris said dryly.

"So why do you two look like something the cat dragged in?"

"We spent the morning at the police station," Chris explained.

Without asking for an invitation, Adam followed the pair to a booth and sat down with them.

"We don't have to eat with him, do we?" Danielle said with mock seriousness.

Chris picked up the menus at the end of the table, handing one to Danielle and then one to Adam. "He's my Realtor, Danielle. And I want to hear about my new house."

"What do you mean you spent the morning at the police station?" Adam asked.

Peeking over her menu, Danielle looked at Adam. "Peter Morris was murdered last night."

"You're kidding me? Who killed him?"

"That's the question of the hour," Chris replied. "And technically, he was murdered early this morning, not last night."

The next moment the server came to their table, filled their coffee cups, and took their orders. When she left them, Adam asked, "Where did it happen?"

"In the parlor at Marlow House," Danielle told him.

"Holy crap, seriously? Not really surprised someone finally killed the hustler. But in Marlow House?"

"I always figured it would be in the library with the candlestick, not in the parlor with the fishing knife," Chris quipped.

Danielle couldn't help but laugh. "Are we awful? The man is dead. And it was horribly gruesome." She shook her head and took a sip of coffee.

"That's pretty cold. Even for me," Adam said. "What happened? I take it neither of you killed him, or you'd be in jail right now. Although with Chris's money, you'd probably be out." He looked at Chris and arched his brows. "You didn't kill him, did you? After all, I'm counting on making a lot of money from you on real estate commissions in the future, and I'd rather not have to do it from your prison cell."

"God no." Chris snorted.

Danielle went on to tell Adam about how they had found the body in the parlor and spent the morning at the police station, answering questions.

"Any idea who did it?" Adam asked when she finished recounting the morning's events.

Chris picked up his coffee cup and looked across the table at Adam. "Officer Morelli seems to think it was me."

"I suppose if Joe has to pin this murder on someone, you'd be the best candidate," Adam said.

"Why me?" Chris asked incredulously.

"Maybe the blood on your hands when Heather walked in?" Danielle suggested.

Looking at Chris, Adam nodded toward Danielle. "I was thinking more along the lines of getting rid of the competition."

"I'd hate to think Joe would do something like that," Danielle said with a sigh. "It's one thing if he sincerely thought Chris did it. Hell, he once believed I'd kill my cousin. But I can't imagine him trying to pin a murder on someone for a personal reason. And anyway, Joe knows there will never be anything between us, and Chris and I are just friends."

Adam glanced over to Chris, noting his unreadable expression.

"So what was your motive? Hell, I'd have more of a motive to kill him than you."

"Don't say that too loud," Danielle scolded. "From what I recall, jail didn't agree with you."

"You have a point." Adam cringed.

"What would your motive be?" Chris asked.

"I suppose you could say I lost a girlfriend to Earthbound Spirits. Isabella and I broke up after she got hooked up with them," Adam explained.

Danielle was just about to take a sip of water when she paused and looked across the table at Adam. Lifting her brows, she said, "According to Will Wayne, you might have even more of a reason to kill Morris." She sipped the water and then set the glass back on the table.

"Will Wayne? Isabella's father?" Adam asked.

"I ran into Will a few weeks back. He told me someone called him up and claimed Morris was responsible for Isabella's death," Danielle explained.

"Who called him?" Adam asked.

Danielle shook her head. "I've no idea; neither did he. Some anonymous caller."

"It was probably a prank call. A crappy one," Adam said.

"That's what I told Danielle when she told me," Chris said.

Danielle shrugged. "Will seems to think it might be possible."

"What did the chief say? Something like that would have to involve the coroner," Adam said.

"That's pretty much what I told Will. But I haven't said anything to MacDonald about it."

"Not even this morning when you were being questioned?" Adam asked.

Danielle frowned. "Why would I say anything?"

"I'd imagine they're looking at all possible motives," Adam explained.

"Will didn't have anything to do with Morris's death," Danielle insisted.

"I'm not saying he did." Adam set his mug on the table and looked over at Danielle. "I don't believe anyone murdered Isabella. She had an aneurism, according to the coroner. Anyway, if Earthbound Spirits had something to do with her death, they wouldn't have been so careless with the body. Kind of hard to cash in on her will without a body."

"They didn't know Stoddard was going to hide it." Danielle grew silent for a moment and then looked up. "Maybe you guys are right; it probably was a prank call."

"Why do you say that?" Chris asked.

"Isabella had already changed her will when she died. And I'm sure Earthbound Spirits knew the will they had was outdated."

"But they did put it into probate," Adam reminded her.

"When Will and I discussed a motive for killing Isabella, we agreed that Earthbound Spirits probably felt confident claiming Stoddard forged the current will, because of what he'd done with Lily. Not to mention, Stoddard was dead and not there to defend his claim on Isabella's estate."

"I see where you're going," Adam said. "At the time Isabella died, Morris had no idea Stoddard would hide the body or end up getting murdered."

"If Earthbound Spirits was responsible for Isabella's death, the motive certainly wasn't to get their hands on her estate. If Stoddard had called the police the moment he found Isabella's body, the chances of the courts favoring Earthbound Spirits' claims over Stoddard's would have been a long shot."

"So I wonder who the caller was, and why pick on poor Will?" Chris said.

"Obviously it wasn't anyone who knew anything about Earthbound Spirits," Adam said.

"Why do you say that?" Danielle asked.

"Well, you said they accused Morris of killing her. Morris never did the dirty work. It would have been Cleve."

"Actually, the woman mentioned Cleve," Danielle said. "According to the caller, Cleve refused to kill Isabella, so Morris got someone else to do it."

Frowning, Adam looked from Danielle to Chris. "I find that hard to believe."

"Why is that?" Chris asked.

"Cleve would never refuse Morris anything."

"According to the caller, he did," Danielle insisted.

"Caller...did you say it was a woman?" Adam asked.

"Yeah, why?"

Adam shook his head. "Nothing...just thinking."

TWELVE

After leaving the diner, Chris and Danielle headed for Ian's. It was still too early to get into Marlow House. When they arrived, Lily was asleep in Ian's bedroom while he worked in the dining room on his newest project. Chris and Danielle lounged on the sofa, watching an old movie, with Sadie napping by their feet.

They had been watching the movie for about thirty minutes when Danielle glanced over to Chris, silently studying his profile. *He really could be a model,* she thought. His sandy-colored hair was slightly longer than it had been when he had first arrived at Marlow House before Christmas. While it could benefit from a comb—as could hers at this point—she had to admit there was something sexy about the tumbled and casual look. The dark circles below his blue eyes reminded Danielle of their stressful morning.

"You've been awful quiet. Are you okay?" Danielle asked.

His eyes still on the television, he asked, "Do you think we'll see Morris?"

"Walt saw him before he woke you up, so it's possible. But I really hope he's moved on."

They were quiet for a few minutes, watching the old black-and-white movie, when Chris asked, "Danielle, you know back at the diner when you told Adam we were friends?"

She smiled. "Yeah. We are friends."

"Actually, you said just friends."

"Well...you know what I mean." Danielle scooted down on the sofa, propping her feet up on the coffee table.

"Before all this happened...I was going to ask you today if you wanted to go out with me tomorrow night...for Valentine's Day dinner."

With her arms folded over her chest as she remained slumped down on the sofa, her feet on the table, Danielle looked over at Chris. "You always ask women out at the last minute? And Valentine's Day? Sheesh. I always heard Valentine's Day dates were made at least a week in advance."

"You're the one who said we were just friends." Chris smiled.

Danielle shrugged. "True. But it is Valentine's Day. Maybe I already have a date."

"With who, Walt?"

Danielle arched her brows and smiled. "Maybe. After all, he did take me to Hawaii last night. Although our trip was cut short due to Morris's untimely demise."

Chris looked from the television to Danielle. "I know about the dream hop—or at least I figured it was something like that. Walt said you told him you were cold, but you were asleep."

"If it had been a little warmer, it would have felt just like a beach in Hawaii."

"It wasn't real, Danielle."

"It felt real."

"You know what I mean."

"There's no harm in a dream hop," Danielle said defensively.

"It is if it becomes a substitute for..." Chris let out a sigh and leaned back on the sofa.

"Substitute for what?" Danielle asked.

He studied her for a moment before answering. "Substitute for a real relationship."

"I'm not ready for that kind of relationship, anyway," Danielle said in a whisper.

"Why, because of Joe? And how he didn't turn out to be what you thought?"

Danielle shook her head. "I know now I wasn't ready to get into a relationship when I first went out with Joe. So much was going on back then. I'd lost my husband just six months earlier, had just moved to Oregon, was trying to get a new business off the ground. And then everything spun out of control with Cheryl being

72

murdered. Even if all that hadn't happened, I wasn't ready for anything but casual friendship. It was probably for the best that things didn't work out between Joe and me."

"Just as long as you don't allow the—unique relationship you have with Walt to interfere with your—your real life."

"What Walt and I have is real."

"You know what I mean."

"I'm just not in a hurry to get into a serious relationship. There is so much I need to do first."

"Then agree to go out with me tomorrow. You know I'm anything but serious."

Danielle laughed. "You have a point there. Most of the time I think of you as that unemployed guy who prefers to live on some friend's boat and enjoy life rather than a secretive philanthropist."

"Not sure if I should be insulted or flattered."

"I suppose a little of both. About tomorrow night, why don't we see how things are going by then? Who knows if the cops will descend on us again or what might come up. And it probably will be difficult to get a table at a restaurant anyway."

"Fair enough."

Sadie leapt up, knocking Danielle's feet from the coffee table. The golden retriever started to bark and then ran to the front door.

Leaning toward the coffee table, Danielle picked up the remote and turned off the television. "It sounds like someone's at the door."

They both started to stand up when Ian entered the room with Adam Nichols. "I found this guy on my front porch." Ian flashed Adam a smile and then returned to the dining room to work, leaving the new arrival with Chris and Danielle.

"Are you stalking us?" Danielle teased.

"Be nice," Chris scolded.

"Sometimes I wonder why my grandmother thinks you're sweet," Adam told Danielle.

"What's up, Adam?" Chris asked.

"Figured you two would still be here. I've got sort of a good news, bad news thing going on. Couldn't really deliver the good news by phone, so I thought I'd bring it in person."

"What good news?" Danielle asked.

Adam held up a set of keys. "Thought I'd bring you the keys to your new house. Technically speaking, you really shouldn't go in until it records, which should be by four this afternoon." He tossed the key chain to Chris.

"So what's the bad news?" Chris asked. He and Danielle sat back down on the sofa.

Adam took a seat in the recliner. "I just got a call from my grandmother. She was telling me all about the nice young man I'd just sold a house to—and how his last name is really Glandon, and he's loaded."

"How did she find out?" Danielle asked.

"She already knew I'd sold Chris a house and that it was closing any day now. As for the rest—she heard it on the radio. I guess the story of Peter Morris's murder—and how Chris Glandon found the body—is out there. I believed they referred to you as the elusive philanthropist who'd been holed up in the quaint bed and breakfast —site of today's grizzly murder. They didn't mention anything about Chris Johnson, but Grandma figured it out."

"I'm surprised she still referred to me as a nice young man considering I was found with a dead body—one that had been brutally murdered."

"Well, Grandmother loathed Morris, and if she thought you were the one who killed him—which I don't believe she does—she would probably want to give you a medal."

Chris looked at the set of keys in his hand, giving them a brief toss. Clutching them, he looked from Danielle to Adam. "I guess this changes everything. I suppose I was being overly optimistic thinking I could live here as Chris Johnson."

"What are you going to do now?" Danielle asked.

"Considering Chris put the house under one of his companies, I don't think it'll be all that easy for people to just come into town and find where he lives. At least not by looking in the property records. Hell, half of the houses in my property management program are held by some company set up by the owners for tax purposes," Adam said.

"I'm not really surprised this came out," Chris said with a sigh.

"If you decide not to stay in Frederickport, I could list it for you or put it in my property management program," Adam suggested.

"While I'm not thrilled, I have no intention of leaving. I'd hoped I could fly under the wire for a bit longer, but I always knew this was a possibility. And it's not like I've droves of paparazzi chasing me. I can handle the letters and inquiries from people asking for a donation; I just hate when they show up at my door."

"What if you purchased another property in the area, under your real name, while you live in the house you just purchased?" Adam suggested.

"Chris could afford that, but wouldn't it be pretty obvious no one was living at the house?" Danielle asked.

"I was thinking more of a house he could use as his headquarters. He did tell me he was looking for something."

"Headquarters?" Danielle looked from Adam to Chris.

"Since my parents' death, I've been doing most of my charity work through my attorneys. And while I trust them, I know I need to get more hands-on—there's too much money involved, too much temptation and possibility for fraud."

"I told Chris I'd be more than willing to take over the responsibility for him. I already have an office." Adam grinned.

"Oh my…" Danielle closed her eyes briefly and fought the urge to laugh. "That thought is rather frightening."

"You have no trust in me, Danielle," Adam scoffed.

"Do you blame me?"

He shrugged. "Not really…but I do have an ideal property for Chris, one that will solve all his problems."

"Hmm…and a nice commission for you?" Danielle asked.

Adam smiled, reminding Danielle a bit of Alice in Wonderland's Cheshire Cat. "Oh, yeah."

"So what is this great—and undoubtedly expensive—property?" Chris asked.

"The Gusarov Estate," Adam told him.

"That monstrosity?" Danielle gasped.

"That monstrosity, as you call it, is on prime ocean-front real estate and would make an excellent headquarters, with plenty of rooms to use as offices, a state-of-the-art security system, and is the kind of home people would expect someone like Chris Glandon to live in."

"I prefer a sailboat cabin," Chris reminded him.

"No. Chris Johnson likes living on a borrowed sailboat—or in a room at a bed and breakfast—but Chris Glandon has more expensive tastes," Adam told him.

"You know, he has a point. While I personally wouldn't want to live at the Gusarov Estate, I could so see it as the Glandon Head-quarters."

"Now we're calling it the Glandon Headquarters?" Chris asked.

Ignoring Chris, Danielle asked Adam, "Is the property for sale?"

"Yes. It has been for a while."

Danielle looked at Chris. "It does have a good security system."

"Isn't that the house you broke into?" Chris asked her.

"One of them," Adam answered with a laugh.

THIRTEEN

L ily had just woken up when Danielle received the phone call
that they could return to Marlow House. Curious to see the
condition of the property after the police search—and Morris's
murder—Ian followed them across the street. Sadie tagged along.

"Have you talked to Heather, or David and Arlene?" Lily asked
as they made their way up the walk to Marlow House's front door.

"I sent Heather a text message. As for David and Arlene, I tried
calling them on their cellphones, but they didn't pick up. I have no
idea where they went. But I left a message and told them they could
come back."

"You think they'll check out early?" Ian asked.

Danielle unlocked the front door. "I wouldn't be surprised."

Danielle and Chris found Walt anxiously waiting for them in the
entry hall. While Lily couldn't see Walt, she knew he was there,
especially considering the way Sadie greeted him. As for Ian, he was
unaware of Walt's existence, yet once again wondered why his dog
always acted so peculiar in Marlow House.

"I didn't think the police would ever leave!" Walt told Danielle
as he followed her and the rest of the group into the parlor.

"So this is where it happened..." Ian murmured. He walked to
the sofa and looked down at where the throw rug had been. Blood
stained the wood floor.

"Oh my," Lily gasped, her eyes riveted on the red stain. "Just seeing that blood brings it all back."

Ian took Lily's hand in his and squeezed. He looked over at Danielle and Chris, who silently stared at the red stain. "Do you think it's safe for you all to stay here?"

"I don't believe anyone from Marlow House is responsible for Morris's death," Danielle said. "From now on, I'm going to make sure the doors stay locked. We know the door was unlocked when Morris was waiting for Chris in the entry—anyone could have come in."

"How do you know that?" Ian asked.

"When I answered the door for Morris around midnight, I don't remember relocking it. I might have, but I don't remember," Chris told him.

"Even if you had locked it then, we know both you and Heather went to bed without checking the front door. You assumed Morris had left. The lights were all turned off. The only thing that makes sense, someone came into the house after Heather left Morris alone in the entry. Either Morris let him in—if Chris locked the door—or whoever the killer was let himself in," Danielle said.

Lily shuddered. "I wonder if it was someone out to get Morris or had a grudge against Earthbound Spirits?"

"Either way, not a short list, from what I've discovered," Ian said. "I prefer to think Morris was the intended target. I'd hate to consider the possibility that some homicidal maniac is running around knifing people in our neighborhood."

Danielle knelt down by the bloodstain. Reaching out with one hand, she lightly touched the spot. "I wonder if I'll ever be able to get this out of the wood." She stood up.

"The police must have taken the rug," Lily noted.

"I feel a little guilty worrying about a bloodstain—considering a man was murdered in this spot just hours ago," Danielle confessed.

"It's hard for me to muster a great deal of sympathy for the man," Ian said. "Especially considering everything Kelly told me about him."

"Kelly?" Danielle asked.

"Kelly's working with Ian on the Earthbound Spirits exposé," Lily said. "She was here yesterday, working with him on the project, but went home last night."

"Your sister was here?" Danielle asked.

78

"She wanted to come over and say hi, but we had so much work to do, and by the time we wrapped it up, it was awful late."

"What time did she leave?" Chris asked.

"It was after midnight," Ian told him.

"I'm surprised the police don't want to interview her. You did tell them she was here, didn't you? That was about the time Morris was murdered," Danielle said.

Ian shuffled his feet, glancing down at the bloodstain. "Well, actually, I sort of forgot to tell Joe that bit of information when he questioned me this morning."

"Why wouldn't you tell him?" Danielle asked.

"To begin with, he never asked me if I was with anyone. I simply answered his questions. Had he asked me if someone was at my house last night, I would've told him."

"Come on, Ian," Chris chided. "Why didn't you really tell him?"

Ian looked up at Chris. "I wanted to talk to my sister first. We are working on an exposé about Earthbound Spirits—and Morris's murder totally changes the direction of the piece. I thought if Kelly saw something last night, it might give us something to use. I didn't really want to just hand it over to the cops without first checking it out."

"It could also help the police find the killer!" Danielle reminded him, sounding somewhat annoyed.

"Well, she didn't see anything. I talked to her after Lily and I came back to my house."

"Where was I?" Lily asked.

"You were already sound asleep on my bed."

"Brian may still want to talk to her," Danielle said.

"I know. I already told Kelly she needs to call Henderson and let him know she was here last night."

"You mentioned Kelly knew some stuff about Morris—something she found when researching him?" Danielle asked.

Ian shook his head. "Not exactly. It's about her college roommate. But hey, you can read about it when I finish the article." Ian flashed Danielle a grin.

CHRIS KNELT by the fireplace in the library, arranging the logs and strategically positioning the kindling. Lily and Ian had just gone out to get something to eat, and the other guests had not yet returned to Marlow House. Danielle sat on the sofa, Sadie by her feet, watching Chris prepare the fire, while Walt paced the room.

"So Morris said nothing?" Danielle asked Walt.

"He was outside when I saw him again. I was leery to call him inside. I doubt he would have listened to me anyway. He seemed pretty intent on following his body."

"I suppose I could go down to the morgue—see if he's still hanging around his body. Maybe he'll tell me who murdered him," Danielle suggested.

"That doesn't seem like a good idea," Chris said, still kneeling in front of the fireplace. The flame began to flicker and expand. He closed the screen and stood up, wiping his palms off on the sides of his pants.

"For once, I agree with Chris. Stay away from the morgue," Walt told her.

"It's not that I want to go down there. But knowing he was murdered under this roof is a little more than disturbing," Danielle said.

"I'll make sure no one sneaks into the house—and I'll keep an eye on your guests," Walt promised.

"I suppose that means no more dream hopping," Chris said as he sat down next to Danielle on the sofa. Walt flashed him a cool look.

"Perhaps I should consider installing an alarm system," Danielle suggested. "I really don't expect Walt to stand guard at night."

"Oh no, we wouldn't want to interrupt your little trips to Hawaii."

Danielle frowned at Chris. "That was rather snarky."

"Maybe Chris is jealous," Walt smirked. "Perhaps I should do a little hop with him, maybe a little skydiving over a live volcano?"

"You just stay out of my dreams," Chris snapped.

"Or a snake pit?" Walt suggested.

"Oh please." Danielle shuddered. "Don't mention snake pits, even in jest. That was the worst."

Chris glared at Walt. "Don't tell me you took Danielle to a snake pit during a dream hop?"

"Of course not." Walt sounded insulted.

"Please. I don't want to talk about it. But no, it wasn't Walt." Danielle cringed.

After a few moments of silence, Walt said, "Something we do need to talk about—the second ghost."

"You mentioned you saw him again," Danielle said.

"Yes. I'm certain he has something to do with Morris's death. Maybe he's the one who killed Morris and something happened when he tried to get away," Walt suggested.

"Like after Chuck Christiansen murdered Bart Haston?" Danielle asked.

Walt nodded. "Exactly."

Chris turned to Danielle. "That's the one who drove off the cliff?"

"Yes. At the same place Darlene Gusarov was murdered," Danielle explained.

Chris frowned. "You know, there sure have been a lot of people killed here since you moved to town."

"Yeah, so Brian Henderson keeps telling me," Danielle said with a sigh.

"Now, is this Darlene Gusarov the same one from the house I'm buying? The Gusarov Estate?" Chris asked.

"You're buying the Gusarov Estate?" Walt asked. "Why would you do that? I thought you just bought a house."

Danielle told Walt about Adam's idea and why it was necessary for Chris to buy a second piece of property.

"Wouldn't it be easier for you to just move?" Walt suggested. "Like you mentioned, the mortality rate is high around here. You'd probably be happier somewhere else."

"Admit it, Walt, you'd be sad to see me go." Chris smiled.

"I'd get over it," Walt mumbled.

"I want to hear more about this second ghost," Danielle said.

"Since he showed up around the same time as Morris, I have to assume they are in some way connected. I asked him if he killed Morris," Walt explained.

"What did he say?" Danielle asked.

"He just gave me some double-talk. But what concerned me, he seemed overly interested in you."

"In Danielle? Why?" Chris turned to Danielle again. "Is it possible you know this spirit—or knew him when he was alive?"

"I can't think of any man I've ever met with a close connection to Morris, except for Cleve, and he's dead—and Walt knows what he looks like. Plus, I've already encountered his spirit, and I'm certain he's moved on."

"What did he say about Danielle?" Chris asked.

"When I asked him some questions, trying to figure out how he was involved in all this—if he knew anything about Morris's death —he kept asking me about Danielle. And then I...well...I told him to stay away from her."

"What did he say to that?" Chris asked.

"He...made it clear he didn't intend to leave her alone."

The three sat in silence for a few moments, considering Walt's words. Finally, Danielle asked, "Walt, can you describe what this spirit looks like?"

Walt considered the question a moment before answering. "He appeared to be about Chris's age. He's tall, a few inches taller than Chris, but slender."

"Skinny?" Chris asked.

Walt shook his head. "No, just slender. He looked fit—well, that is, had he actually been alive instead of a reflection of his former self. Dark hair, dark eyes. His manner of dress—not casual like yours—more like Adam—yet a better cut of clothes. Tailored. Yes, I'd say his clothing was tailored."

Danielle frowned. "Well dressed? Dark hair and eyes?"

"Yes." Walt nodded.

"It's possible whoever it is, assuming he is connected—was connected—to Earthbound Spirits, simply knows who I am and doesn't know me personally. After all, Morris was intent on recruiting me into the organization. Maybe this was some guy Morris recruited to get close to me, like with Richard."

"That was before he decided to blackmail me," Chris added.

"I don't know." Danielle shook her head.

"Hello, Danielle," a male voice said from the far corner of the library. They all heard it. Their heads turned to the direction of the voice. Shadows concealed the person or spirit attached to it.

Slowly, Danielle stood, staring into the shadowy corner.

He stepped out, revealing himself. Danielle let out a startled gasp. "Lucas!"

FOURTEEN

The moment Danielle uttered "Lucas," the apparition vanished. She remained standing, staring into the now empty corner.

"That was him!" Walt said. "That's the other spirit who was in the house today!"

Chris looked at Danielle. "What did you call him?"

Frowning, Walt looked from the now empty corner to Danielle. "You said Lucas. Why did you call him Lucas?"

"That's who it was," Danielle whispered.

"Are you saying the second spirit is the ghost of your dead husband?" Chris asked incredulously.

Danielle nodded.

"That's impossible. Danielle's husband has been dead over a year now. She never saw him after he died. Why would he show up here now?" Walt asked.

Danielle glanced from Chris to Walt. "He looked...he sounded...just like Lucas."

"It doesn't work that way, Danielle. Once a spirit moves on, he can't just come back," Walt told her.

Turning from the corner, Danielle looked at Walt. "What about my Christmas dream? Was that nothing more than something you orchestrated? My parents...Cheryl...it was just an ordinary dream?"

"It wasn't an ordinary dream." Walt's voice softened, his eyes focused on Danielle's face. "But visiting a dream after a spirit moves on…is not the same thing as staying on this plane, as I am…as those other spirits are doing…the ones you and Chris see."

"What makes you so certain about that?" Chris asked.

Walt looked from Danielle to Chris. "What do you mean?"

"How do you know a spirit can't come back after it's moved on?"

"It's just something I feel," Walt told him.

"But you don't know for certain," Danielle said.

"As certain as I can be," Walt insisted.

"Okay, let's say you're right. Maybe a spirit can't come back after it's moved on. But how do you know Danielle's husband moved on? Maybe he never did. And now he's here." Chris looked around. "But where did he go?"

"That doesn't make sense. Danielle didn't see him at his funeral; he never showed up at the house they shared. It sounds to me like he moved on. I think this spirit just looks like her husband."

"It was Lucas." Danielle sat back down on the sofa. "But where did he go?"

Walt paced the room. "I want to know what he has to do with Peter Morris's death."

"Maybe he has nothing to do with Morris," Chris suggested. "It could all be a coincidence."

"This is so strange," Danielle muttered. Holding her hands on her lap, she looked down and closed her eyes for a moment before opening them again and looking up. "Why would he show himself now? And where did he go?"

"Maybe he wants to talk to you alone," Chris suggested.

"Absolutely not!" Walt said.

Chris frowned at Walt. "Why not? And since when have you started monitoring Danielle's paranormal associations?"

"If it is Danielle's husband, he needs to beat it! But I'm not convinced it's him."

Danielle stood up. "Maybe Walt's right—it isn't Lucas. I mean, why would he be here now, after all this time? If he had something to say to me, why didn't he come before?"

"He died in a car accident, didn't he?" Chris asked.

Danielle walked to the corner and looked at where the apparition had been standing. "Yes. Right before Christmas."

"Did you ever go to the site of the accident?" Chris asked.

Danielle reached out to where Lucas had been standing just moments ago. There was nothing there. She turned back to Chris. "Yes. Well, I drove down the street once. But I couldn't get myself to stop the car and get out."

"It's always possible his spirit lingered there," Chris suggested.

"But wouldn't I have seen him when I drove down the street?" Danielle asked.

"Not necessarily. I remember this one spirit. He haunted a movie theater at the beach. People would tell stories of their popcorn flying out of their hands in the middle of the show, or how someone would knock a soda out of their hands, yet no one would be there. I decided to check it out, and sure enough, the theater was being haunted."

"What does this have to do with Danielle's husband?" Walt asked.

"It turned out the guy had been murdered in the alley behind the theater. After his death, he ran into the building and never left. He wasn't murdered in the theater, but that's the place he haunted."

"What happened to him?" Danielle asked.

"I helped him understand what had happened, and once he realized he was dead and came to grips with his murder, he moved on," Chris explained.

"You're a regular do-gooder," Walt muttered.

Ignoring Walt, Danielle said, "Sometimes that's all it takes for them to move on...to realize they're no longer alive."

Chris looked over at Walt. "Unfortunately, it doesn't always work that way. Sometimes they hang on and on, like an uninvited houseguest."

"If it was Lucas, where did he go? Why is he here?" Danielle asked.

"He might have left when he saw us here. I'd think after not seeing you for more than a year, he doesn't want an audience," Chris suggested.

"I'm going to my room." Danielle started for the door. Sadie lifted her head and looked around. She had slept through Lucas's brief appearance and had no idea another spirit other than Walt had just been in the room.

"You shouldn't be alone," Walt said. He started to follow her.

Danielle turned to him. "No. You stay here. I want to know why

Lucas is here. And Chris is probably right. I doubt he'll come if either of you are with me."

"Danielle, you don't want to do this," Walt insisted.

"Walt, let her go," Chris told him.

A few moments later, after Danielle had left the room, Walt directed his attention to Chris. "Why would you encourage this?"

"Don't you think Danielle deserves closure? This could give it to her."

"Closure? Her husband's been dead for over a year now. She's just fine. Let dead husbands lie," Walt said.

"Danielle's not just fine. Don't you think it's been eating at her, not having a chance to confront her husband? She probably feels guilty for being angry with him."

"She has no reason to feel guilty."

"I know that. But he left her in limbo. And then when she starts dating again, it's with Joe Morelli and—"

"Morelli was all wrong for Danielle."

"I don't disagree. Both men basically betrayed her. Her husband by having an affair and Morelli by not believing in her when she needed his support."

"What's your point?"

"Unless she works this out, she's never going to feel confident enough to trust a man again."

"Danielle trusts me," Walt snapped.

"I'm speaking about a living, breathing man."

Walt lifted his brows. "You?"

"I understand Danielle in a way Morelli never could."

"I understand her too," Walt insisted.

"I hate to be the one to point this out, but you're a ghost, Walt."

"I loathe that term." Walt turned from Chris and walked to the window. He stared out at the side yard.

"Don't you want Danielle to fall in love someday, with a man she can marry—have children with?"

Walt gazed out the window, his back to Chris. "Danielle's always telling me things have changed since I was alive, that a woman doesn't need marriage and children to be fulfilled."

"You don't have to necessarily need something to want it."

"You think she wants that?" Walt asked.

"She might if she found a man she could trust."

"Do you think you're that man? Are you saying you want to marry Danielle?"

"I haven't known Danielle that long, but I'd like to get to know her better. I've never really considered getting married before." Chris sat on the sofa. Sadie stood up and rested her chin on his knee while Chris absently stroked her ears.

"You say you want to get to know her better, but you never considered getting married. Are you saying your intentions are to enter into some casual relationship with her—no different from the current Valentine's Day guests? Use her and then what?"

"Settle down, Walt. I know we have this generation thing going on, but really, get off your soapbox."

"Generation thing? I happen to be younger than you!"

"Just because I happen to be older than you were when you died does not mean I'm older than you now. Anyway, I was referring to the era you lived in. And when I said I never considered marriage before, what I actually meant—I never imagined I could date a woman and feel confident she wasn't with me for my money. I don't worry about that with Danielle."

"You want to marry Danielle because she has money and isn't particularly interested in yours?"

"That's not what I meant. I'm interested in Danielle—because of who she is. But when I say I'm interested in her, I mean I want to get to know her better—go out with her. And someday, if things did progress with us, I could see her as someone I could consider marrying. I wouldn't be afraid she wanted me for my money. And you have to admit, we've a lot in common."

"What, that you both see ghosts?"

"I thought you loathed that term."

"Only when someone applies it to me."

"I think it gives us something unique in common—something we can't share with anyone else."

"Danielle discusses her abilities with Lily—and with Chief MacDonald."

"Yes, but not in the same way she can with me. Lily or MacDonald will never really truly understand all that Danielle's had to deal with because of this thing we share."

"I wonder…if you were unable to see spirits…how would you react to Danielle? In the same way Joe Morelli did?"

"I suppose I could say the same about Danielle. But the fact is, for both of us, our ability to see and communicate with spirits has shaped us into who we are, what we've become."

"What happens if you and Danielle get closer and then you decide she's not the one—maybe you fall in love with someone else."

"Walt, there're no guarantees in life. Have you really been dead for so long that you don't remember what it was like to want to get to know a woman better?"

"Those types of feelings don't necessarily die with your body," Walt said, his voice almost a whisper.

"I want to get to know Danielle better—I understand there's no guarantee either of us will want more than friendship after we do. Yet there is one thing I am fairly certain about, as long as she carries around the baggage of her marriage, I don't see anyone getting too close to her. And as long as you..."

When Chris failed to finish his sentence, Walt asked, "As long as I what?"

"I know Joe Morelli is still interested in Danielle. Considering they've a brief history, I imagine some might see him as my competition, but I don't. But the same can't be said about you."

"Are you saying you see me as competition?"

"I see how you look at her, Walt."

"Chris, I'm not a fool. I know there's no future for Danielle and me. I won't interfere if something develops between you two. I didn't interfere when she went out with Morelli. But don't expect me to simply move on. I'm staying here." Walt vanished.

Sadie jumped up and let out a bark. She looked around and then raced from the library. Chris could hear the golden retriever running up the stairs. He guessed the dog was headed for the attic, where she would probably find Walt.

"WHERE IS BELLA?" Walt asked Max when he got to the attic.

Max let out a high-pitched meow.

"Sleeping where?"

Max yawned.

"As long as you didn't do something to her."

Max rolled over on his side.

"Yes, the police are finally gone. I just wish I was downstairs last night when Morris was here."

Max meowed.

"Morris is the man who was killed. The body the police took out of here."

Just as Sadie raced into the attic, Walt asked Max, "What do you mean you saw Arlene go downstairs around the time Morris was killed?"

FIFTEEN

Tree limbs swayed in the afternoon breeze, scraping against the exterior of Marlow House in a steady and repetitive rhythm. Danielle sat silently on the edge of her mattress, her back straight and hands folded in her lap. She listened to the tree limbs hitting the house as she waited. Twenty minutes had passed since she had come upstairs, and still he had not shown himself again.

Danielle stood up and walked to the window. She wondered briefly if it was going to rain again. Looking outside, she spied David Hilton's car pull up in front of the house. Turning from the window, she headed for her bedroom door.

When Danielle reached the first floor, she greeted David and Arlene, who had just let themselves into the house. Guests of Marlow House were given both a key to their room and to the front door. The locksmith made periodic visits to Marlow House to rekey the door. With Morris's murder, Danielle was anxious to call the locksmith, although she suspected the killer had entered through an unlocked door.

Arlene stood outside the parlor, peeking in. "I don't know how you can ever go into that room again."

"I'll feel much better when the police catch the killer." Danielle closed the parlor door. She stood with Arlene and David in the entry hall.

Turning away from the now closed door, Arlene faced Danielle. "Do they have any leads?"

"I believe they found something that might help them."

"What was that?" David asked.

"They didn't tell me exactly," Danielle lied.

"I can't imagine what that could be," Arlene said. "We were all in the house when the police arrived, and I sure didn't see anything —aside from Chris standing over the body."

"Chris had no reason to kill Peter Morris," Danielle insisted.

"Well, I certainly hope you're right, since he's staying here."

"Actually, I'm moving out tonight."

Arlene startled from Chris's sudden appearance. He walked toward them from the direction of the library.

"Tonight? Why?" Danielle asked.

"The house will be officially mine by the end of the day. I have the key. It's fully furnished, so all I need to do is toss a set of sheets in the washing machine, and I'll be set."

"Chris, none of us got any sleep last night. Why don't you plan on moving in the morning after you've had some rest?" Danielle suggested.

"Don't rush out on our account," David told him. "Arlene really didn't mean anything. We know you didn't have anything to do with that man's death. If the police thought you were involved someway, I don't believe they would've let you go already."

"Thanks, David. I appreciate that." Chris flashed him a smile and glanced over to Arlene, who looked sheepishly to the floor.

"I want you to know," Danielle began, "I realize this is not the Valentine's Day weekend you two planned. Not by a long shot. If you want to leave early I'll refund your money—even for last night."

"I appreciate the offer," David told her. "But Arlene and I already discussed this, and we decided to stay."

Their conversation was interrupted when the doorbell rang. Danielle answered the door. It was Adam Nichols.

"I hope you don't mind, I dropped by without calling. I wanted to see Chris." Adam peeked over her shoulder and saw Chris standing in the hallway. He noticed another couple standing near him, but couldn't see their faces.

"Sure, come in." Danielle stepped aside and opened the door wider.

The moment Adam stepped through the doorway, Arlene turned and looked in his direction. He paused a moment, his dark eyes wide in surprise as he glanced from Arlene to the man by her side. "Arlene?"

So this is her boyfriend? Adam thought. He'd caught a brief glimpse of the man at the restaurant, but not a clear view of his face. He was rather ordinary looking and slightly overweight. He was obviously older than Arlene, but Adam didn't think by more than a few years. Adam surmised the man's thinning hair and extra weight added several years to his appearance.

"Adam…" Arlene stammered. She immediately reached out to David and took his hand.

"You know each other?" Danielle asked as she closed the door.

"We had some mutual acquaintances," Adam explained. "It's nice seeing you again, Arlene."

"You too." Arlene squeezed David's hand.

"Are you staying here?" Adam asked.

"Yes…yes, we are. Adam, this is David…my…my boyfriend. David, this is Adam Nichols."

With a frown, Adam looked from Danielle to Arlene. "Were you here last night when Peter Morris was murdered?"

"You know about that?" Arlene asked.

"Yes. Strange you didn't mention it," Adam said.

"Mention it?" Danielle asked.

"Arlene and I bumped into each other this morning before breakfast."

"I just figured we weren't supposed to discuss the case," Arlene explained, flashing Adam a pleading expression.

"Well…it's nice seeing you again. Nice to meet you, David."

"If you'll excuse us, we're going to head up to our room," David explained. "We didn't get much sleep last night, and I'm exhausted."

AFTER DANIELLE LED Adam and Chris into the library a few minutes later, she closed the door behind her and turned to Adam.

"Okay, what is the deal with you and Arlene?" Danielle asked.

"What do you mean?" Adam asked.

"Come on, Adam, the looks you two were giving each other. There has to be some story there."

"Danielle, you're sounding an awful lot like Lily right now," Chris chided.

"Why, because Lily tends to ask what everyone is thinking?"

"It really is nothing," Adam insisted. "I was just surprised to see her staying here, that's all. I knew her back when I was going out with Isabella."

Danielle paused a moment, considering Adam's statement. Cocking her head to one side, she asked, "Was she a member of Earthbound Spirits?"

"Why would you think that?" Adam asked.

"You said it was when you were dating Isabella."

"No, she was not a member. Arlene would be the last person in the world to hook up with an organization like Earthbound Spirits."

"Why do you say that?" Chris asked.

"She just wouldn't do it, that's all. So what do you know about the guy she's with? What's he like?"

"Aha! So there is something between you!" Danielle teased.

"Don't mind her," Chris said with a laugh. "She's sleep deprived and doesn't realize how she sounds."

Danielle scowled. "How do I sound?"

"Nosy," Adam and Chris said at the same time.

Danielle waved her hand dismissively, went to the sofa, and sat down. "In all fairness, Adam was the one asking questions about the boyfriend."

Adam walked over to the sofa and sat down in a chair facing Danielle. "And? You haven't told me anything about him yet."

Danielle started to say something and then paused, looking quizzically at Adam. "Why are you here anyway?"

"To see Chris, remember?"

"I suppose I should leave and let you talk to him before you two start accusing me of being nosy again." Danielle started to stand up.

"Oh, sit down," Adam scoffed.

Danielle sat back down and smiled. "I found out something interesting about her boyfriend from Chief MacDonald." She looked at Chris. "I haven't even told you yet."

"What's that?" Chris said.

"You know his last name is Hilton. I guess his grandmother was Helen Hilton."

"Helen Hilton?" Adam said in surprise.

Danielle looked at Adam. "You know her?"

"If it's the same Helen Hilton who left her estate to Earthbound Spirits, then, yeah, I know who she is. The lawsuit was big news back then. Family lost. Morris won."

"Apparently David is the youngest grandson."

"Doesn't that make him a prime suspect?" Chris asked.

"That lawsuit was a number of years ago," Danielle explained. "You were here last night. David was in his room when you found the body. Whoever killed Morris had to have gotten some blood on them, considering the number they did on Morris. As far as I know, the cops didn't find any bloody clothes. If they had, I don't believe they would've let David leave. I think it's just a bizarre coincidence. If he had the patience to wait that long to kill the man, I'd assume he wouldn't plan to murder him under the same roof where he was staying."

"This morning he never mentioned the connection to Morris," Chris noted.

"No. And apparently, he didn't offer the information to the cops when they interviewed him. The chief told me he ran background checks on the guests, and that's what they came up with."

"How did he explain that to the cops?" Chris asked.

"I have no idea."

"What did they find out about Arlene?" Adam asked.

"Arlene?" Danielle shrugged. "The chief didn't mention anything aside from the fact she's David's girlfriend."

"Not sure how I feel about him staying here now," Chris said.

"Why? You think David's dangerous?" Danielle asked.

"He's the only one staying at Marlow House with a real motive to kill Morris."

"If he came here to kill Morris, I'd assume he would've taken my offer to leave early. After all, no one would have thought anything suspicious about them leaving, under the circumstances. Why stay longer if he came here to kill Morris?"

"You certainly seem calm about all this," Chris noted.

Danielle shrugged. "I just don't feel him being here has anything to do with Morris's death."

The three were silent for a few moments; then Chris let out a sigh and looked at Adam. "So what did you need to talk to me about? Everything okay with the house?"

Adam picked up the manila folder from his lap and opened it. "I called the title company right before I came over here, and the house is officially yours. But that's not why I'm here. I brought over a purchase contract for the Gusarov Estate for you to look over if you decide to make an offer. I assume you'd want to look at the property first."

"I've driven by it, and I think it would work." Chris put his hand out to Adam.

Standing up briefly, Adam handed Chris the contract.

"But don't you want to look at it?" Adam asked.

"Not particularly. It's not as if I intend to live in it. And from what Danielle tells me about the property, I believe it'll be perfect for what I need."

Chris walked over to the desk and sat down with the purchase contract, reading it over.

Adam smiled over at Danielle. "You know, if you ever decide to close up the bed and breakfast, I think we'd make a great real estate team."

ADAM WAS JUST ABOUT to climb into his car when he heard a woman call out, "Adam, wait!" He looked up to see Arlene running toward him from the direction of Marlow House's front entry.

"Arlene…" Adam stood on the sidewalk next to his car.

"I wanted to talk to you before you left…alone."

"Yeah, I imagine you do."

"What did you tell them?"

"You mean Danielle and Chris?"

Arlene nodded.

"I didn't tell them anything aside from the fact we used to know each other."

Arlene sighed in relief.

"But they do know who your boyfriend is. Is he really your boyfriend?"

"What do you mean?"

"Oh, come on, Arlene, Helen Hilton's grandson? Really? What are the chances of you two getting together?"

"Maybe we just have a lot in common."

"Yeah, I bet you do. But you need to know the cops have done a background check on both of you. They know David is Helen Hilton's grandson. And if they figure out your connection to Earthbound Spirits, I've a feeling you'll be pushed up to the top of the suspect list."

"I didn't kill Peter Morris."

"Frankly, I don't care who killed that SOB. They did the world a service. But I'd hate to see you go to jail over that dirtbag."

"I didn't kill him, I promise."

"Please be careful, Arlene."

"Are you going to tell anyone?"

Adam looked into Arlene's pleading eyes. He studied her a moment and then finally shook his head. "No."

SIXTEEN

Leaning back in his desk chair, cellphone in hand, Police Chief MacDonald read Danielle's text message. "No news."

With a disgruntled sigh, he tossed the phone onto his desk. He had hoped when Danielle returned to Marlow House, Walt would tell her the identity of the killer—or perhaps she would run into the ghost of Peter Morris. But so far, having someone on his side who could communicate with spirits wasn't giving him an edge in this investigation.

A knock came at his office door. Looking up, he watched as one of his officers peeked in.

"Carla, the waitress from Pier Café, insists on seeing you. Says it has something to do with Morris's murder," he told MacDonald.

"Show her in."

A few minutes later, Carla sat in a chair facing the chief. They were alone in his office, the door closed.

"Was Peter Morris really murdered at Marlow House?" she asked.

"Yes. Now, what did you want to tell me?"

"I heard on the radio that he'd been murdered—after midnight at Marlow House. I just knew I had to come talk to you! I think I saw the killer running away from the house last night."

"You were by Marlow House last night?"

Carla nodded. "I drive right by there every day for work. When

I was coming home last night, I saw someone running away from Marlow House. I almost hit her!"

"Her?"

Carla nodded again. "Yes, I'm sure it was a woman. She looked right into my headlights. But she was wearing one of those hoodies, you know, like those gang kids wear."

"Hoodies? Are you talking about a hoodie sweatshirt?"

"Well, I guess it was actually a coat. But it had a hood, and she had it pulled up over her head. Real suspicious like. Of course, at the time I had no idea she had just killed someone."

"You say she looked into your headlights?"

"Yes, when I almost hit her. I had to slam on the brakes. I'm so afraid!"

"Why are you afraid?"

"Now I know she killed someone, and she saw my car. She might track me down and kill me too! After all, I'm a witness!"

"If she looked into the headlights, you must've seen her face."

Carla shook her head. "It happened so fast. I just know it was a woman. Or I suppose it might have been a man, a very slender man. Maybe a boy?"

The chief pressed the heel of his hand against his forehead. He could feel a headache coming on. "Let's slow down a bit, Carla. Do you know what time this was?"

"Sometime between midnight and one. I can't be sure exactly."

"Don't you know what time you left work? It's only a few minutes from Pier Café to Marlow House. What time did you get off work?"

"Last night I got off work at 11:30, but I didn't go right home. I ran into someone in the parking lot, and we started talking...time just sort of got away from us."

"You were having a conversation in the dark parking lot in the middle of the night, with the weather we've been having?"

Carla scooted down in her chair. "I wasn't exactly standing in the parking lot. I was sitting in his car."

"Whose car?"

"He said his name was Martin Smith, but I don't think it was."

"You don't know the name of the man whose car you were sitting in during the middle of the night?"

"He said he was staying at the Seahorse Motel, but when I went over there this morning, they had no Martin Smith registered."

"Why were you talking in his car?"

"Oh, come on, Chief, I came here to help you. You know Martin and I weren't actually talking. He's a cute guy. We were having fun. And when it got a little out of hand, I told him I had to go. But I didn't check the time."

The chief lifted his brows. "But you went to the motel to find him this morning?"

Carla shrugged. "Like I said, he was real cute."

Shaking his head and putting aside images of Carla and a strange man rolling around in the backseat of a car like two teenagers, he asked, "So tell me about this person you almost ran over."

"I was driving down the street and this dark shadow seemed to jump out in front of me from the direction of Marlow House. This person just appeared in my headlights, and I slammed on my brakes. It was like she didn't realize a car was coming. She looked up at me and then kept running."

"Did this woman get into a car?"

"Like I said, I'm pretty sure it was a woman, but I suppose it could have been a man or maybe a teenage boy."

"Did this person get into a car? Did you see where she—or he—went?"

"That's the funny thing…" Carla leaned forward, lowering her voice. "I was so shook up; I watched to see where she went. Ran right over to the house across the street and climbed into a car parked in the driveway and drove off."

"House across the street?"

"Yes. The one Ian Bartley rents. But I know it wasn't Ian. I would've recognized him. Although, now that I think about it, it looked a little like Ian."

"It was Ian?"

Carla shook her head. "No, it definitely was not Ian, but it looked a little like him."

After the chief finished with Carla, he phoned Ian. According to Ian, he and Lily were just heading back to Marlow House, but he agreed to stop at the station first.

"WHAT'S THIS ABOUT, CHIEF?" Ian asked when he was led into

the interrogation room, and Lily was asked to wait in the front lobby.

The chief motioned to one of the empty chairs at the table before closing the door. The two men sat down.

"Joe talked to you this morning when you came to pick up Lily?"

"Yes." Ian watched the chief pick up a file from the table and open it.

Glancing over the contents of the file folder, the chief looked up at Ian and asked, "You told Joe you went to bed around midnight last night?"

"That sounds about right."

"Can you tell me what cars were parked in your driveway from...let's say...about thirty minutes before you went to bed until this morning when you woke up?"

"What cars?" Ian frowned.

"From what I remember about your driveway, you have enough room to park maybe—two cars there?"

"Yes."

"So tell me. What car—or cars—were parked in your driveway last night?"

Ian let out a sigh. "My car...and Kelly's."

"Kelly? Your sister?"

"Yes."

"You didn't say anything to Joe about Kelly being in Frederickport."

"She's not. She went home last night."

"Last night? When?"

Ian shrugged. "It was around midnight."

"Why didn't you tell Joe?"

"I answered Joe's questions; he didn't ask me if there was anyone at my house."

The chief slammed the folder shut, his hand hitting the tabletop with a loud slap. "What are you hiding, Ian?"

"I'm not hiding anything."

"Don't give me that. Don't try playing stupid, it doesn't suit you. Why did you withhold information regarding your sister being in Frederickport? Joe asked if you'd seen anything last night; I don't believe for an instant you wouldn't realize Joe would want to question your sister about what she saw when leaving your house."

Ian leaned forward, resting his elbows on the table. "Kelly's been working with me on my current project. It's an exposé on Earthbound Spirits—and Peter Morris. Obviously, Morris's death changes the direction of our article. I confess; I wanted to talk to Kelly before you did—I wanted to see if she saw anything."

"I assume you've spoken to her?"

"Yes. I called when Lily and I got back to my house. Kelly told me she didn't see anything unusual last night."

"And you didn't realize we'd still want to interview her?" MacDonald snapped.

"Yes, of course. I told Kelly to call Henderson. I understood he was taking the lead on this case."

"She hasn't called."

Ian shrugged. "I assumed she would've called right away. But I guess she figured since she didn't see anything, there was no rush."

"Did Kelly go back to Portland?"

"No. She went to Astoria to stay with some friends."

"Ian, something has come up, and I need to talk to her as soon as possible. Can you get her to come back to Frederickport?"

"You mean today?"

"Yes. I'd rather not have to send someone to Astoria to pick her up and bring her back here."

"You're serious, aren't you?"

"Very."

MACDONALD WAS ALONE in his office an hour later when his cellphone began to ring. It was Danielle.

"What's this about you ordering Kelly back to Frederickport?" Danielle asked McDonald the moment he answered her call.

"Why didn't you tell me she was in town last night?" he asked.

"I didn't know. Ian mentioned it after we left the police station, but he told me Kelly would be calling you."

"He told me he didn't tell Joe about Kelly being here because he wanted to talk to her first—in case she saw something he might use in his article," the chief explained.

"Yeah, that's pretty much what he told me. I really don't think it's any big deal. I know you're probably irritated, which I assume is why you told him to have her come back to town, but I think you could've probably just talked to her on the phone. She told Ian she didn't see anything."

"I know Ian's a good friend of yours, Danielle—"

"He's your friend too, Chief," she reminded him.

"I know, but this is a murder investigation. I can't let personal feelings hinder the investigation."

"Will Brian be interviewing Kelly?"

"I sent him home to get some sleep."

"Is Joe still there?" Danielle asked.

"I think so, why? You want to talk to him?"

Danielle sighed. "No. I was just curious. He's the one who initially questioned Ian; just wondered what he thought about Kelly being here."

"I spoke to him. Actually, he blamed himself. Said Ian did answer his questions—Joe just didn't ask the right ones."

"It's really pretty typical of Ian. He's always closemouthed about whatever he happens to be working on."

"I hope that's all it is," MacDonald muttered.

"What did you say?"

"Oh, nothing," he lied. "But I was wondering, have you figured out who that second spirit might be?"

"I think so—saw him once—he hasn't shown himself again. But I don't think it has anything to do with Morris's murder. It's just a coincidence, a second spirit showing up at this time."

"How can you be so sure?" he asked.

"Because it's Lucas."

"Lucas?" he asked.

"My late husband."

He didn't respond immediately. Finally, he said, "I didn't think you'd ever seen his spirit before."

"I haven't. I need to figure out why he's here. It would be nice to solve at least one of today's mysteries. Have you learned who that bloody fingerprint belongs to?"

"I really shouldn't have mentioned that to you," MacDonald grumbled.

"Do you know who it belongs to?"

"Yes."

"Well, who? Is it someone I know?"

"I'm sorry, I can't tell you that. Not at this time."

Danielle groaned. "I can't believe you aren't telling me."

SEVENTEEN

Steam escaped the teakettle just before it began to hiss and whistle. Alone in the kitchen, Danielle lifted the kettle from the stove and filled her teacup. Just as she walked to the table with her cup of hot green tea, Walt appeared.

"I wanted to talk to you, but someone always seems to be around. Where did Lily take off to again?" he asked.

Instead of taking a sip of tea, Danielle set the cup back on its saucer. "She and Ian went back to his house. When they were out, they stopped by the police station."

"Why?"

"The chief found out Kelly was at Ian's last night. He wants to interview Kelly since she left around the time the murder may have occurred. The chief was annoyed Ian failed to share that bit of information with Joe."

"Did she see anything?" Walt sat down.

Picking up the cup again, Danielle gently blew on the tea. "According to Ian, she didn't. But I guess sometimes we see things we aren't even aware of." She sipped the tea.

"Have you seen Lucas again?"

"No. I waited in my room for a while, but nothing. Then I came back downstairs. Adam stopped over with a purchase contract for Chris. I guess he's putting in an offer for the Gusarov Estate."

Danielle lifted the tea bag from the cup, gently jiggling off any liquid before setting it on the saucer.

Walt noticed Danielle had changed her clothes and fixed her hair. Instead of her normal fishtail braid, she had pulled her dark hair back into a high ponytail. No longer wearing sweatpants, she had slipped into a pair of blue jeans. While she looked vastly improved from this morning, Walt couldn't accuse her of dressing up for a potential meeting with her deceased husband.

"What are you staring at?" Danielle asked with a frown.

"Oh, nothing, I was just thinking how you look rather… young…with your hair like that."

"I'll take that as a compliment." Danielle sipped her tea.

"I think you need to have the chief take a closer look at Arlene."

"Arlene, why?"

"According to Max, she came downstairs last night after Heather went up to bed. Which would have been about the time Morris was still here and Chris was in the kitchen looking for you."

"Hmm…she didn't say anything. And Chris didn't mention seeing her downstairs."

"From what he told me, it was dark when he came back down the hall after looking for you. Arlene could have easily been downstairs—even in the parlor with Morris."

"With the lights off?" Danielle asked.

"If Morris was already dead, she might not have felt she needed a light."

"There's still that issue of blood evidence. I don't see how someone could've cut his throat like that and not have gotten blood all over them. And do you honestly believe a woman Arlene's size could've slit his throat like that? Maybe he wasn't a young man, but he wasn't small or frail."

"The coroner had an interesting theory," Walt told her.

"Coroner?"

"I'm not sure it was the coroner, exactly, but one of the people in that group this morning."

"You were listening in."

"Of course I was."

"That's probably why the chief told me about that fingerprint," Danielle muttered.

"You mean the one they found outside?"

Danielle nodded. "He probably figured you would hear what

was going on and tell me, so keeping that bit of information from me served no purpose. Of course, if he tells me these things, then it appears we're working together, and I'll share what I find with him."

"Are you saying you aren't working together?"

"No, but I spoke to him on the phone not long ago, and he knows who the fingerprint belongs to, but he's not willing to tell me at this time."

"I suppose I can understand. This is an ongoing investigation."

"Why do you suddenly sound like Brian and Joe?"

"Probably because I spent the morning with their co-workers," Walt suggested.

Danielle let out a grunt then asked, "So tell me, what's the coroner's theory?"

"Morris was sitting down at the time of the attack. There didn't appear to be a struggle in the room. It's as if someone came up from behind him, surprised him, and slit his throat before he knew what happened."

Danielle cringed. "That's gruesome."

"The sight this morning was gruesome."

"True." Danielle set her cup back on its saucer and pondered the possibilities. "That would mean whoever killed Morris was probably someone he knew. Someone he was talking with in the parlor. If the killer took the fishing knife out of Chris's tackle box on the back porch, then that would have to indicate this was premeditated. According to Chris, that knife had been missing a few days, before Arlene and David even arrived."

"I still think you need to tell the chief," Walt told her.

"I suppose you're right." Danielle glanced up to the ceiling. "I certainly hope our current guests had nothing to do with Morris's murder."

Walt stood up. "If you will excuse me, I think I'll do a little eavesdropping."

"I assume you mean on David and Arlene."

"Yes."

"While I generally don't condone listening in to our guests' private conversations, I suppose this is one of those times I have to make an exception."

"That's what I thought." Walt disappeared.

Now alone in the kitchen, Danielle put her feet up on the empty chair across from her at the table. About to finish the rest of her tea, she noticed the space behind the chair she currently used as a footstool darken, as if someone had turned off the kitchen light illuminating just that space. Hastily removing her feet from the chair, she sat up straight, pushed the teacup aside, and stared at the darkening spot. Her eyes widened as it darkened a few shades more before it brightened again, as if someone were fiddling with a dimmer switch. In the next moment an apparition appeared. It was Lucas. He stood just five feet from her.

"Oh my god," Danielle murmured. Stumbling to her feet, she stood up, her gaze locked with his.

"It's really you, isn't it?" Lucas asked in awe.

"I believe that's my line. What are you doing here?" Danielle stood behind the chair she had moments earlier been sitting on, gripping its back.

"I never truly believed you. You can really see people like me, can't you?"

"People like you? You really aren't a person anymore, Lucas. I asked you, what are you doing here?"

"I don't remember you being cruel, Danielle. I know I have a lot to explain, but I thought at least a part of you would be happy to see me."

"You've been gone for almost fourteen months now, Lucas. I would have expected to see you months ago, not now. Where have you been?"

"So that's it?" Lucas smiled. "You're upset I didn't come sooner."

"No, that's not it. It's just that if you were to show yourself to me, I expected it to happen months ago—maybe at your funeral."

Lucas shook his head. "I missed my funeral. Were many people there?"

"Yes," Danielle said without emotion.

"My mother, how is she? This must have devastated her."

"Yes, it did."

"She adored you," Lucas told her. "I hope you've kept in contact; I know that would mean so much to her."

"Honestly, I haven't seen or talked to your mother in months. We really have nothing to talk about."

"I need to explain things," Lucas said.

"Explain where you've been. This is confusing to me."

"I thought you told me you've been seeing spirits all your life."

106

"I have. But not after they've moved on. I assumed you had moved on."

"Moved on? Ahh…yes…Meghan explained that to me."

"Who's Meghan?"

"She's like you, I suppose. She found me. I had been wandering around in a building since it happened—since the accident."

"What building?" Danielle frowned.

"Just a commercial building not far from where I had the accident. I went in there, looking for someone to help me. But no one could see or hear me. No one until Meghan found me. Helped me."

"I don't understand how you found me."

"Meghan helped me track you down. She used the Internet. Told me you were using your maiden name. That hurt, Danielle. To think you didn't keep my name."

"You hurt me, Lucas."

"I'm sorry about that. But I can explain."

In the next moment, Chris barged into the kitchen. "Danielle, I was wondering…" He froze when he spied Lucas standing by the table with Danielle.

Lucas turned toward Chris and looked at him. In the next moment, he vanished.

"I APPRECIATE YOU COMING IN, JOANNE," Joe Morelli told Joanne Johnson as he brought her into his office.

"Danielle called me this morning, told me not to come in for work—explained what had happened. I still can't believe it." Joanne shook her head.

"It does seem Marlow House is cursed."

"I'll admit, it has had more than its share of trouble."

"I wanted to ask you a few questions."

"Certainly, Joe."

"Have you ever seen Peter Morris at Marlow House?"

Joanne considered the question a moment and then said, "The only time I can recall was at Danielle's Christmas Eve party. She wasn't thrilled he showed up, but I believe one of her guests—Richard Winston—invited him. Of course, we all know how that turned out."

"What do you mean? How that turned out?"

"Mr. Morris's right-hand man tried to murder Mr. Winston just days later. Danielle believes Mr. Morris was behind the assassination attempt, but of course, nothing could be proved, not with Cleve Monchique's handwritten confession."

"What do you think of Chris Johnson?"

"Chris? He's a likable young man. But I haven't spent that much time with him."

"Danielle told me Chris keeps his tackle box on the back porch. Have you seen it?"

"Of course. My duties include cleaning the back porch. I wasn't particularly happy when he put it out there. Each time I sweep, I have to move it. But Danielle set it on a bench under the overhang because of all the rain. Why are you asking about the tackle box?"

"It's my understanding Danielle gave Chris a fishing knife that he used to keep in his tackle box."

Joanne smiled. "That's normally where one keeps fishing knives."

"Are you familiar with the knife Danielle gave him?"

She shook her head. "I had no idea Danielle had given him a fishing knife."

"According to Chris, he kept the knife in the tackle box on the back porch, but the last time he looked in the box, the knife was missing. Have you ever seen anyone other than Chris get into that tackle box?"

"No...but..." Joanne frowned.

"Is there something you remember?" Joe asked.

"Are you trying to figure out where the fishing knife is?"

"Actually, we have the knife. We're just trying to determine who removed it from the tackle box."

Joanne smiled weakly. "Well...I guess that would be me."

EIGHTEEN

Kelly Bartley sat alone in the Frederickport Police Department's interrogation room. She had been waiting for over fifteen minutes to be interviewed. Glancing to the mirror on the far wall, she remembered what Danielle had once told her. It was a two-way mirror. She wondered if someone was watching her. Shifting nervously in the chair, she regretted not stopping first at Ian's house and picking up her brother. Instead, she had driven directly from Astoria to the police station.

She was considering standing up and pacing the room to burn off nervous energy when the door opened, and Joe Morelli walked in.

"Hi, Joe. I was wondering if you'd forgotten about me." She smiled.

"Kelly, we appreciate you coming in." Joe sat down across from her.

"Ian called me earlier today and told me what happened to Mr. Morris. He asked me to call the station and talk to Brian Henderson to let him know I'd left Ian's house around the time you think Mr. Morris was murdered. I did try calling, but they told me Officer Henderson had left for the day."

"Did you leave a message? Ask to talk to someone else?"

Kelly shrugged. "No. I just figured that since I really didn't see anything, it wasn't urgent. I was going to try calling again in the morning."

Resting his right hand atop the closed manila folder, Joe looked across the table at Kelly. "Why don't you tell me about last night. From when you left your brother's house and got into your car to leave."

"There really isn't much to say. I'd been helping him do some Internet research on his current project."

"The piece on Earthbound Spirits and Peter Morris?"

She nodded. "Yes. After Cleve Monchique's attempt on Mr. Winston's life, and then when nothing happened to Earthbound Spirits after Monchique's suicide, my brother decided to research the group and write an exposé."

"So what time did you leave your brother's house?"

"I honestly don't know. I remember looking at the clock around 11:30 and saying we needed to wrap it up. I was planning to stay with a friend for the weekend in Astoria. So we finished up; I tossed my stuff in a suitcase and left."

"Do you have any idea what time that was?"

"I didn't really pay any attention to the clock after that. But it was probably thirty minutes or maybe an hour or more later by the time I left."

"That's rather a big difference—thirty minutes opposed to over an hour."

She shrugged again. "I sometimes lose track of time. Ask my brother. I get doing stuff, tell him I'll be ten minutes, and then when I finally show up, it's maybe an hour later. I'm sorry. If I'd known the exact time would be important, I would've paid more attention to the clock."

"When you left, did your brother walk you to your car?"

"No. He was in the shower when I left. I'd already said goodbye to him."

"So when you went outside, did you go directly to your car?"

Kelly frowned. "What do you mean?"

"Maybe you took Sadie out? Walked around the yard, looked over to Marlow House? Maybe you saw some cars on the street?"

"I honestly didn't pay that much attention. I just got into my car and left. I didn't notice any strange cars parked on the street."

"Kelly, did you bring a coat with you?"

"Coat? Well, sure, it's been cold."

"Does your coat have a…hood?"

Instead of answering immediately, Kelly stared at Joe. Finally, she said, "Sure. It's a raincoat."

"And did you have that coat on last night when you left your brother's house to go home?"

Kelly shifted nervously in the chair. "What's this about, Joe?"

"I think you need to tell me what really happened between the time you stepped out of your brother's house and got into your car last night. Although technically, it was early this morning."

Looking down at the table, she closed her eyes. "That person, the one who almost hit me…"

"Kelly Bartley, did you kill Peter Morris?"

Kelly's eyes flew open, and her head snapped up. She looked into Joe's dark eyes. "Is that what you're thinking? Good lord, Joe! Of course I didn't kill him!"

"Then I think you need to tell me what exactly happened last night."

Kelly let out a deep sigh before proceeding. "Last night, while I was putting my suitcase and things into my car, I looked across the street and noticed a light on in the parlor of Marlow House. I had intended to stop and say hi to Danielle while I was here, but I never got around to it. So I decided to run over real quick, see if she was the one in the parlor so I could surprise her and say hi. I knew it was late…but it sounded…well, like a good idea at the time."

"What happened?"

"By the time I got over there, someone had turned off one of the lights in the parlor."

"What do you mean one of the lights?"

"When I first looked over, the parlor window was lit up—like the overhead light was on. But when I got across the street, it looked pretty dark downstairs, but there was still some light coming from the parlor. I looked in the window. There was a nightlight on."

"Was anyone in the room?"

"I saw what looked like a silhouette of a man. I figured it was probably one of Danielle's guests, and I started feeling like a peeping tom, so I ran back across the street. When I did, I almost got hit by a car. I was so frazzled and embarrassed from peeking into Marlow House's window, I didn't see the car coming. It stopped; I ran to my car, got in, and left."

"Did you see any other cars parked on the street?"

"No. I'm sorry. I really was not paying attention."

"Have you ever met Peter Morris?"

"No. I've never met him."

"Are you sure? Not even at Danielle's Christmas Eve party? You were both there, I remember."

Kelly shook her head "No. I didn't want to meet him."

"Why was that?" Joe asked.

"Because…" Kelly took a deep breath. "Peter Morris arrived at the party around the same time I was walking across the street from Ian's. I was on my way over to the party when I saw him drive up. I recognized him. I didn't want him to spoil Christmas Eve, so I waited until he went into the house, and then I went over and avoided him, making sure I stayed away from the man."

"That's quite a reaction for a person you've never met."

"I didn't have to meet the man personally to know what a piece of garbage he was. I suppose I should say I'm sorry he's dead, but I'm not. I hope he went straight to hell, where he belongs."

Joe studied Kelly, surprised by her outburst.

"Kelly, I think you need to tell me why you had such a strong dislike for Peter Morris."

Tears filled Kelly's eyes. Biting her lower lip in an attempt to stem the flow of tears, she shook her head. "It will all be in my brother's article. You can read about it there."

Setting his elbows on the table, he leaned forward, his voice low. "No, Kelly, I need you to tell me now. Why did you have such a personal dislike of Peter Morris, so much so that you didn't want to run into him at Danielle's party?"

Wiping away her unshed tears, Kelly took a deep breath, attempting to calm herself. "Peter Morris killed my best friend."

"Excuse me?"

"Well, he didn't pull the trigger exactly. But he might as well have."

"Why don't you start at the beginning," Joe suggested.

"Candice and I went to high school together. During college, we were roommates. She was a sweet girl, but she had some emotional issues. After a particularly painful breakup with a boyfriend, she started looking for answers."

"Looking for answers?"

"A lot of people do it. Life starts to throw nothing but hardballs, and you figure religion will give some meaning to it all. She started searching for answers—like why did her boyfriend leave her? Why was her mother such a looney tune? Why did her grandmother have to die? Unfortunately, she went to Earthbound Spirits for the answers."

"How did your friend die?"

"She overdosed. It was intentional. She left a farewell note. An odd handwritten suicide note."

"What do you mean odd?" Joe asked.

"Odd. It said something like Don't cry for me. It was my idea to do this, no one else's. Goodbye."

"What was Peter Morris's part in this?"

"I knew she had gotten involved with some church. That's what she called it. I assumed it was a Christian church. I had no idea at the time it was Earthbound Spirits. I wasn't really concerned when she first got involved with them, because she seemed content—at peace. Which was saying something for Candice."

"What happened?"

"A day before she killed herself, we got a little drunk. I had no idea at the time it was her going away party to herself. We were both pretty wasted when she started giggling and told me she was going to miss me, but that we'd see each other someday. I asked her what she was talking about. She told me her spiritual advisor had told her it was time for her to move on—time to leave this world. I asked her what she meant, but she just started giggling again. I figured she was just wasted."

"Did she say who her spiritual advisor was?"

"No. But the next day I slept in. And when I woke up, I went to check on Candice. She was dead. I found the note."

"When did you find out she'd been involved with Earthbound Spirits?"

"I just found out before Christmas. It'd been years since her death. I thought she just had some sort of mental breakdown. Like I said, she always had some issues. But in November, I ran into her sister, Baily. I hadn't seen her since Candice's funeral. We went out to lunch, started talking about Candice…and it all came out."

Joe quietly listened to what Kelly had to say.

"Candice came from a very wealthy family. I always thought her mom was sort of nuts, and her father was too busy making money to notice what was going on around him. Mrs. Bradford—Candice's mother—was one of those people who obsessed over what the world thought of her—of her family. After Candice died, the money she had inherited from her grandmother was left to Earthbound Spirits."

"So Candice had her own money?"

"Yeah. Candice was always close to her grandmother. When the woman died, she left a couple million to each of her granddaughters, Candice and Baily."

"Did her parents contest the will?"

"I suppose they could have, even though Candice was of legal age to leave her money to whomever she wanted to. But a couple million was not that big a deal to the Bradfords. What was a big deal was letting the world know their daughter had gotten tied up with that crazy group. It was bad enough their daughter committed suicide. They did all they could to keep the entire thing a secret, even signing an agreement with Earthbound Spirits not to contest the will, providing the group didn't publicize the fact that Candice had left them her estate. I'd no idea Candice was that involved with Earthbound Spirits, not until Baily told me in November."

"Why would her sister tell you now?"

"For one thing, Baily never knew—not until her mother died and she came across the written agreement between Earthbound Spirits and her parents. Their father died a few years after Candice. But their mother, she passed away just a few weeks before I ran into Baily in November. Baily had just found out the truth, needed to talk to someone, happen to run into me, and she knew I loved Candice."

"What did she tell you about Peter Morris?"

"Nothing specific. Of course, I already knew about the group. I didn't tell Ian immediately. I, well, at the time I didn't really think there was anything I could do, and in some ways, I was dealing with Candice's death all over again. But when Ian decided to do an exposé on Earthbound Spirits, I told him what I knew. And when we started digging into it, I found some people who knew Candice back then—who were in the group. And they told me Peter Morris was Candice's spiritual advisor."

"Why didn't you or Ian come to us with what you knew? Especially after Cleve's suicide?"

"We would have eventually."

NINETEEN

"Can I go now?" Kelly asked. "I've really told you all I know, which isn't much."

Joe's hand toyed with the upper right-hand corner of the manila folder, preparing to open it. "Why did you lie about going over to Marlow House before you left your brother's?"

Slumping back in her chair, Kelly let out a sigh. "I didn't lie exactly. I just sorta left out that part."

"A significant part."

She sat up straighter and looked at Joe. "Why? I didn't see anything, honest. It was dark when I got over there, and I'm not even positive if it was a man or woman I saw in the parlor."

"I still don't understand why you didn't tell me…unless…"

"I didn't want to get involved, okay?" Kelly snapped.

"What do you mean you didn't want to get involved?"

"Since I've been helping Ian research Earthbound Spirits, the more I learn about the group, well, they sort of scare me. They kill people. I just figure whoever murdered Peter is probably someone from the inside. A lot of money is at stake. Now with Cleve gone, Morris was vulnerable."

"I thought you believed Morris was behind Cleve's death?"

"Yes. I think he got Cleve to kill himself, just like he did with Candice. But with Cleve—I suspect Peter began to realize he acted rashly, because with Cleve gone, there was no one who had his back.

Although, I'm not sure he could've done anything differently—I mean, from Peter's perspective. From what we've learned in our research, the group seems to be unraveling."

"What does any of that have to do with you not telling me the truth about going over to Marlow House last night?"

"Don't you see, maybe the killer was in the room when I looked in. Maybe he had just killed Peter right before I peeked in. If he thinks someone saw him—if it gets out that I looked in the window last night—I may be the next person on the killer's list. If I'd seen something, something that would really help you, I would've already told you. But I didn't. But the killer doesn't know that."

"You knew someone saw you—the car that almost hit you."

"Yes. But it was just a car driving down the street, and I assumed it was unrelated to the murder. When Ian called me, told me about the murder, he asked me what I'd seen. I didn't even tell him about me going over there. What was the point? And I figured if I told Ian, he would probably tell Lily. I like Lily, but I really wouldn't trust her with my secrets. So I hoped the driver of the car never realized they'd driven by a crime scene, and then no one would have to know I'd looked in that damn window."

Joe didn't respond. Instead, he silently studied Kelly, his fingers still fiddling with the folder's edge.

After a few moments of silence, Kelly looked up into Joe's eyes and asked again, "Can I go now?"

"Not quite yet." Joe opened the folder and pulled out a photograph. He set it before Kelly. "Do you know this man?"

Kelly's eyes visibly widened when her gaze set on the photograph. Nervously chewing her bottom lip, she looked from the picture to Joe. "Yes. Why are you showing me this?"

"Who is he?" Joe asked.

Kelly shrugged. "It's Mitch."

"What's your relationship with him?"

Kelly shook her head. "I don't have a relationship with him. He…he lives in a condo below mine."

"Are you friends?" he asked.

"Not exactly. He's just a neighbor. I'm not even sure I ever knew his last name."

Joe smiled and removed a second photograph from the envelope. "Oh, you do." He placed the second photograph on top of the first one.

Kelly let out a gasp and snatched up the picture Joe had just placed before her. Holding it in her hand, she looked from the picture to Joe. "Where did you get this?" The photograph was of her and Mitch.

"That doesn't matter right now. But you look like more than casual neighbors in that picture."

Kelly shook her head and tossed the picture onto the table. "I don't understand what Mitch has to do with this. Why are you showing me these pictures?"

"This morning, during our processing of the crime scene, we found a fingerprint—a bloody fingerprint—on Marlow House's front gate. The fingerprint belongs to your friend Mitch, and we are fairly certain the blood belongs to Peter Morris. We should know that sometime tomorrow."

"Mitch?" Kelly pressed her right hand against her brow. She began to rub her now throbbing head and closed her eyes. "No, this can't be happening. It doesn't make any sense."

"Now maybe you might want to tell me again, what's your relationship with Mitch?"

Kelly stopped rubbing her forehead and opened her eyes. She stared at Joe, her expression unreadable. "I told you. He is just a neighbor. We have a very casual relationship. I don't even know his last name."

"You don't look very casual in that photograph, practically cheek to cheek."

"It was a stupid selfie Mitch took. I ran into him at the Starbucks down the street from my condo. This was about a month ago, right after he moved in. He started up a conversation, and I recognized him as my new neighbor. As we're talking, all of a sudden he grabs his phone, tells me he wants to take my picture, and before I know it, he practically knocks my head with his while he takes the picture. That's about the extent of our friendship."

"You never went out again?"

"Technically speaking, we didn't go out that day. We simply ran into each other at the coffee shop."

"So is that a yes or no?"

"No. We never went out—ever."

"Did you ever run into him again—like you did that day? Maybe at Starbucks or some other place?"

"I saw him a few times at Starbucks, but I never sat with him again. We said hello; that was it. The baristas there know me; you can ask them. They can tell you we didn't hang out there together."

"Did you ever go to his apartment? Did he ever go to yours?"

"No…" Kelly paused a moment, rethinking his question. "Well, actually, he did come into my place a couple times. But it wasn't like we were hanging out together or anything. A few times he helped me bring up my groceries."

"That was neighborly of him."

"It's not like he always helped me with my groceries. But our parking spots are next to each other, and a couple times, he pulled in at the same time I got back from the grocery store, so he'd offer to help me bring my groceries up. I have those stairs…but he never stayed. We never went out or anything."

"Do you know what he does for a living?" Joe asked.

Kelly shook her head. "I don't know. We never talked about it. Like I said, the only time we really talked was at the Starbucks that one time when he took that selfie. And then the conversation was just silly. We didn't really share any personal information other than first names."

"Silly, how?"

"Oh, I don't know—we talked about the high price of coffee, speculated on why Starbucks doesn't use small, medium, and large. That sort of stuff."

"Do you know of any connection between him and Earthbound Spirits?"

"No. And I find it hard to believe there is one. He didn't seem like someone who would get involved with a group like that." Cocking her head slightly, she looked at Joe. "Are you sure it was Mitch's fingerprint on that gate?"

"Did you know he was in Frederickport yesterday?" Joe asked.

"No. What does he say about all this?"

"I don't know. Your neighbor seems to be missing. He wasn't at his home this afternoon. And he wasn't at his office."

"His office? I don't know where he works. Where's that?"

"Downtown Portland."

"None of this makes any sense." Kelly picked up the photograph of her and Mitch and stared at it.

The door to the office opened and another officer walked in. He silently handed Joe a piece of paper and then left the room. Kelly looked up and watched the officer leave, wondering what Joe had been handed. In the next moment, she had her answer.

"Kelly, I've a warrant here—to search your car."

IAN ANXIOUSLY PACED the living room of Marlow House while Lily, Danielle, and Chris silently watched from where they sat: Lily on the recliner, and Chris and Danielle on the sofa. Walt observed from his place by the fireplace. Earlier, Chris had built a fire; the flames flickered and snapped from the hearth. David and Arlene had gone out for dinner, and Heather had finally returned. She was upstairs in her room.

Ian looked at his watch again. "What's taking Kelly so long?"

"I'd call the chief again, but I'm sure he's gone home by now," Danielle told him.

"Want me to call down there again?" Lily offered.

"No." Ian sat down on the arm of Lily's recliner. "The last time I called, they said she was still in the interview room with Joe."

"That can't be good," Walt said from his place by the fire. Both Danielle and Chris glanced over at him.

"Well, it can't," Walt reiterated. "We all know Joe has an overactive imagination and a penchant for trying to pin crimes on attractive young women."

Danielle flashed Walt a frown.

"It's true—she is an attractive young woman." Walt then turned his attention to Chris. "You know, Chris, I've said all along Kelly was perfect for you. And tomorrow is Valentine's Day. Since Kelly will probably be here for Valentine's Day—can't imagine she'll head out tonight—you should really think about asking her out for tomorrow. Might help Ian and Lily too. From what I understand, Ian was planning some romantic dinner at his house, and with his sister now back in town, it might spoil his Valentine's Day plans. A win-win for both of you." Walt smiled.

The doorbell rang. Ian jumped up from the sofa. "Maybe that's her!" He dashed from the room to answer the front door.

When Ian returned to the living room, a weary Kelly by his side, Danielle thought Ian's sister looked as if she hadn't slept in days.

"They searched my car." Kelly burst out in tears.

"You let them search your car? Why?" Chris asked.

"They had a search warrant." Kelly used the back of her hand to wipe away the tears. Ian led her to a chair. She sat down and then proceeded to tell them everything that had happened.

"Well, they didn't find anything, and they let you go. So that's good, isn't it?" Lily said.

No longer crying, Kelly sniffled. "But they kept my coat. And it's the one I got for Christmas."

"I'm sure you'll get it back," Ian said.

"I just hope they don't ruin it while checking to see if there's some trace evidence of blood! As if I would actually cut a man's throat!"

"I just wish you would've been up front with me when I asked you what you saw last night. Then we could've avoided all this," Ian said.

"In fairness to Kelly," Danielle reminded him. "You're the one who withheld information from the police first—not your sister."

"I still can't believe it was Mitch's fingerprint!" Kelly shook her head. "And you know what, his name isn't even Mitch."

"He lied to you about his name?" Lily asked.

"Not exactly. His real name is Logan Mitcham. But he goes by Mitch."

"Logan Mitcham?" Danielle asked. "Why does that name sound familiar?"

TWENTY

"Logan Mitcham, that's the name of the private detective Will Wayne hired to look into Isabella's death," Danielle said when she finally made the connection. "Is this neighbor of yours a PI?"

Kelly shrugged. "I have no idea. Joe didn't say what Mitch does for a living. And I was so frazzled, I didn't even think to ask. Although, now that I think about it, he asked me what Mitch does for a living. But since he said something about checking Mitch's office, I figured he already knew; he was just trying to see what I'd say."

"You think it's the same Mitcham?" Chris asked.

Kelly frowned. "Wait a minute, why would Will Wayne hire a detective to look into his daughter's death? She died of a brain aneurism. Ian and I haven't come across anything that would indicate foul play. The medical records were pretty clear. Can someone induce an aneurism, like a heart attack?"

"This all stems from some phone call Will received. He asked me not to say anything to the police until he found out more, but considering what's going on, I think I should talk to the chief." Danielle stood up. "Do you think your Logan Mitcham could be a PI?"

"He is hardly my Logan Mitcham. Heck, I didn't even know him by that name. And frankly, I would prefer to distance myself from him, especially if he killed Peter Morris." Kelly then looked at her brother in a panic. "They haven't found him yet. I can't go home until they do. What if he thinks I saw something? That I'm a witness?"

"You can stay with me, Kelly," Ian told her.

"WE COULD GO IN THE PARLOR," Danielle told the chief as she led him into the library thirty minutes later. "But I really don't feel comfortable going back in there."

"I can't say I blame you," the chief said as he took a seat. He watched Danielle shut the library door.

"You look tired," she noted.

"You too." He smiled wearily. "It's been a long day."

"I wanted to talk to you about Logan Mitcham." Danielle sat down.

"Ahh, I see Kelly has talked to you already."

"She stopped here after she left the police station."

"Is she still here? I didn't look in the living room when I came in. Can't imagine she'd be in the parlor."

"No. She went across the street with Lily and Ian. By her appearance, Joe was pretty rough on her."

"Joe was doing his job, and she was being less than forthcoming."

"I want to know—is Logan Mitcham a private investigator?"

The chief smiled. "So Kelly was lying about that too."

"Lying about what?" Danielle frowned.

"When Joe asked her what he did for a living, she said she didn't know. We figured if nothing else, she and Ian had hired Mitcham in the past."

"No, Kelly didn't know what he does for a living. And Ian had never heard of him before. He'd never even noticed the guy when he stopped by his sister's."

"Then how do you know he's a PI?"

"Because Will Wayne told me he hired a PI to investigate Isabella's death. And the detective he hired was some guy by the name Logan Mitcham. I wanted to know if it was the same man."

"Why would Will hire a PI? Isabella died of natural causes."

Danielle told MacDonald about running into Will Wayne when

visiting Portland in January, how Wayne had told her about the phone calls, and the suspicion surrounding his daughter's death.

"I really wish Will had come to me. That call was a hoax. Not sure why someone would do that, but I've no doubt the only thing criminal surrounding Isabella's death were her uncle's actions after she was already dead. But this does add new names to my suspect list."

"Certainly you don't think Will had anything to do with the murder. He hired Mitcham to investigate Morris, not kill him."

"I'll need to talk to Will, see what he knows."

"What does Mitcham say? According to Kelly, he wasn't at his condo or office. Have you located him?"

"Not yet. Brian drove to Portland this afternoon. When he got there, Mitcham wasn't at his condo or office. No one had seen him since yesterday morning. But we have someone watching the place and his office."

"When I talked to you earlier, you told me Brian had gone home —to sleep. That he'd had a long day."

MacDonald shrugged. "He did have a long day. I just figured it was easier to tell you he went home instead of trying to explain why he took off to Portland in the middle of an investigation. You have to understand, there will always be some things I simply cannot tell you. Nothing personal, Danielle."

"Hmm…well, I'll remember that when I know something."

MacDonald laughed. "You mean like knowing Will hired a detective to investigate Morris and believes Isabella was murdered? Which, if true, could mean there was corruption in the coroner's office?"

Danielle sighed. "Okay. You got me there. But I didn't really think the PI would find anything, and I certainly never imagined the PI's fingerprint would show up at a crime scene—on my property!"

"I just hope we find him soon and that he has some answers for us."

"Me too. Kelly's afraid to go home. She's paranoid about living next to a possible murderer, especially considering she was over here last night, peeking in the windows."

"So she told you everything?"

Danielle nodded. "Yep. She was pretty freaked."

"Any chance that you, Chris, or Walt might have run into

Morris's spirit since the last time we talked? It would make it a lot easier on me if he'd simply name his killer."

"Sorry. The last time Walt saw Morris's spirit was when they were taking his body away. He went with it. So I suspect if he hasn't moved on, he might be hanging around the morgue."

"Any chance you might be willing to go to the morgue with me?"

"No. Nada. Ain't happening. Nope."

"Well"—MacDonald stood up—"if you change your mind…oh, how about that second spirit? You still say it's your late husband?"

"It is. But I haven't really talked to him either. He just sort of shows up and then vanishes."

"Considering that, I suppose I understand your reluctance about going down to the morgue with me. You have your hands full."

Danielle stood up. "Oh…I just remembered. But considering you have the fingerprint, this isn't that big a deal."

"You remembered what?"

"According to Max—"

MacDonald arched his brows. "Max your cat?"

"Yes, sweet black furry little guy, white-tipped ears, likes to chew on your fingers."

"Yes, I'm familiar with the little demon."

"Ahh, that's not nice. Plus, he has information for you."

"I'm not quite sure if I'll ever get used to the idea of getting tips from ghosts—but a cat? That one always makes me stop and wonder if I'm losing my mind."

"Well, you're not. And if it makes you feel any better, it's not like Max talked to you—or even me, for that matter. It's just that thing between spirits and animals."

"Okay, what information does—Max—have?"

"Last night, after Heather came upstairs to go to bed, Max saw Arlene slip out of her bedroom. This was after Heather went into her bedroom and closed her door. Arlene went downstairs."

"Where was Chris?"

"I'm pretty sure he was in the kitchen about that time, looking for me, because a few minutes later Chris came upstairs. According to Max, he walked to my bedroom door, but then looked as if he had second thoughts, so he went back downstairs."

"Wouldn't Chris have seen Arlene downstairs?"

"I didn't ask Chris or Arlene about it. But I don't think he saw her, or else he would've said something."

"When did Arlene come back upstairs?" the chief asked.

"I don't know. Max went up to the attic after Chris headed back downstairs."

"I wonder why Arlene didn't say anything about going downstairs?" the chief murmured.

"I wondered that myself. But this was late—after midnight. It's always possible Arlene was half asleep when she got up, was thirsty, and maybe doesn't even remember going downstairs."

"And avoided running into Chris?"

"It's possible. But I guess you can ask her about it. But like I said, now that you have that fingerprint, I don't really think it's anything significant. And plus, how do you ask her? I mean, you really can't say according to the cat…"

WHEN LILY RETURNED from Ian's house later that evening, Marlow House was locked up and the only illumination came from nightlights plugged into random sockets throughout the house. Tiptoeing past the parlor, she noticed the door was shut. Just looking at it gave her chills. Chris's door was also shut. She knew he had decided to spend one final night at Marlow House and start moving into his new place in the morning.

Upstairs, all the doors were closed and there was no light coming from under any of the doors—except for Danielle's. Danielle was still up. Instead of knocking on Danielle's door and risking waking up Heather and the others, Lily used her cellphone to send Danielle a text message. A moment later, Danielle's bedroom door opened, and Lily went inside.

"I thought for sure you'd be sound asleep by now," Lily whispered. She sat with Danielle on the edge of the mattress. After coming home from the police station earlier, Danielle had finally made her bed. She hadn't yet turned down the sheets and blankets for the night.

"I was hoping you'd come in here before you went to bed. We haven't had a chance to be alone since all of this happened."

"I can't believe they kept us apart all morning and wouldn't even let us talk to each other," Lily said.

"I guess they couldn't risk us comparing notes. After all, maybe the five of us killed Morris."

"Like one of those old mysteries, where all the suspects are guilty?"

"Pretty much." Danielle glanced around the room.

"You looking for Walt? Is he here?"

"No...I'm looking for Lucas."

"Lucas? What are you talking about?"

"I saw Lucas today. Walt saw him first. The second spirit I told you about. It wasn't someone connected to Peter's murder like we assumed. Just some bizarre coincidence."

"I don't understand. Lucas has been dead for over a year."

Danielle explained to Lily what she knew about Lucas's spirit, beginning when Walt first encountered him before Morris's body was found.

When Danielle finished, Lily said, "Oh my god, of all times for your deceased husband to show up...on Valentine's Day!"

"Technically speaking, he showed up on Friday the 13th," Danielle reminded her.

Lily started to giggle.

"What is so funny?"

"Sorry, I couldn't help it. Ironic in a twisted sick sort of way. Lucas showing up, sort of a Friday the 13th Valentine's Day surprise."

"You have a strange sense of humor," Danielle said with a sigh.

TWENTY-ONE

Dressed in her plaid pajama bottoms and oversized red T-shirt, Danielle sat in the center of her bed, her bent knees pulled up to her chest as she protectively wrapped her arms around them. Resting her chin atop her knees, she gazed across the dimly lit room. Lily had turned the overhead light off when she had left, but there was some moonlight coming through the bedroom window.

When coming upstairs earlier, Danielle had asked Walt not to come into her bedroom to say goodnight or chat. She suspected Lucas wouldn't appear again if he, or anyone else, was with her.

Unable to stifle a yawn, Danielle glanced over to the nightstand and looked at the clock. She had been sitting alone on the bed for almost thirty minutes.

"Lucas, can you hear me? Are you nearby?" Danielle asked out loud. "Please, let's get this over with. Tell me why you came so you can move on. This is unbearable, wondering if you're going to show up at any moment."

The room was silent. And then she heard it, soft pawing on the door.

"Oh, Max," Danielle mumbled, climbing off her bed. Walking to the door, she opened it, letting in the cat, who immediately began weaving in and out between her legs. She shut the door.

"For a while there, I thought you intended to hang out all night with Walt." Reaching down, she picked up the black cat and carried him over to the bed, placing him on the foot of the mattress. She pulled down the blankets and climbed under the bedding. Purring, Max strolled up the bed and curled up beside her.

"You have a cat," Lucas said. He stood next to the bed, looking down at her.

Danielle bolted to a sitting position. "You're here."

"Finding you alone has been a challenge."

Max lifted his head and stared at the apparition. A gurgling growl—one he normally reserved for expressing his opinion of other cats—replaced the purr.

Cocking his head slightly, Lucas looked inquisitively at the unhappy cat. "You don't like me."

Snatching up the snarling animal, Danielle climbed out of bed. "Sorry, Max, I need to talk to Lucas alone." After depositing Max in the hallway, she shut the door and faced her husband's ghost.

"I could understand what that cat was thinking," Lucas said in awe.

"Why did you come? Why now?"

Lucas glanced around the room. "I don't understand why you're here. Why Oregon? Why this house? Are you an innkeeper?"

"I own a bed and breakfast," she explained.

Lucas sat on the edge of the bed, looking up at Danielle. "Why a bed and breakfast? Why Oregon?"

"My great-aunt died and left me this house. I decided to turn it into a bed and breakfast," she explained.

"What about your marketing degree? What about our business?"

"I needed a change. I sold the business."

Abruptly, Lucas stood. "You sold it? How could you just sell it? We worked so hard; it was our dream."

"You weren't here anymore, Lucas. I needed to move on."

"But you were fully capable of running the business…of growing it into what we always imagined. You just walked away from all that we built?"

"Lucas, you walked away from us before I ever considered selling the business."

"You're angry with me. I understand. I suppose I deserve that."

"I've gotten over it. You can go now."

"I'm not ready to go, Danielle. I have too many questions. There are things I need to explain."

Weary, Danielle walked over to the loveseat and sat down. Lucas followed her. He stood before the unlit fireplace.

"I'm sorry I never truly believed you could see…ghosts. Is that what I am now, a ghost?"

"I suppose that's one definition. Some prefer spirit to ghost."

"Who's the one that looks like he just stepped out of an episode of *Boardwalk Empire?*"

"You mean Walt?"

"I think so."

"Walt Marlow, his grandfather built this house," Danielle explained.

"He's like me, isn't he? He's a ghost."

"Walt prefers the term spirit. But yes."

"Why is he here? Why hasn't he moved on?"

"Walt has his reasons."

"He was in your bedroom. I saw him cover you up."

"I guess he figured I was cold."

"I don't understand; how did he lift the blankets? I've tried to move things, but all I end up doing is tipping stuff over, making something move that I don't want to move."

"It's about harnessing your energy; but, Lucas, I don't believe spirits are supposed to stay on this plane—they're supposed to move on. You're supposed to move on."

"That's what Meghan said," Lucas mumbled.

"It sounds like your spirit got stuck after you died, which sometimes happens with a sudden, unexpected death. But now things have become clearer. You can focus on reality."

He frowned. "How do you know that?"

"Because that's what happens. That's what I've learned over the years. It's pretty obvious to me that after you came to terms with your death, you felt compelled to seek me out. Here I am. But there's really nothing for either of us to say—at least not now. I've moved on, and so should you."

"No, Danielle. Something is keeping me here. I can feel it. I can't leave yet. There's something I need to do."

Danielle considered his words a moment. "When Walt first saw you, he didn't know who you were. He thought you were in some way involved with Peter Morris."

"The man who was murdered downstairs?"

"How did you know his name?"

"He told me."

"What do you mean he told you? I don't believe Peter Morris could see or hear spirits."

"No. It was afterwards—after he stepped out of his body."

"You saw his spirit leave his body?" Danielle asked.

"I was trying to find you. I could sense this was where you'd be —somewhere in this house. But then I saw the two men in the front room, arguing—a man sitting in a chair, who I later learned was Peter Morris. And the other man, the killer."

"What were they arguing about?"

"I don't really know. I didn't care. They weren't talking very loud, they were whispering, but I could tell they were angry."

"Did you hear anything they said?"

"Not really. I wanted to find you. So I went through the rest of the rooms on the first floor. Before going upstairs, I went back to the front room. The men were still there."

"Was the light on?" Danielle asked.

"Only a nightlight. Just as the man walked behind Peter, he took out a gun."

"A gun?" Danielle frowned. "Morris wasn't killed by a gun."

"For a moment I thought he was going to shoot Peter, but then something caught his attention. Something sitting on the shelf. I didn't know what it was at first. But he slipped the gun back into his pocket and kept talking in a whisper. I couldn't hear what he was saying; I wasn't close enough. But I could tell Peter was laughing at whatever it was. I thought it was bizarre."

"Bizarre how?"

"Peter seemed oblivious to any danger. When the man pulled the gun out of his pocket, I was sure he intended to shoot Peter in the back. But then Peter laughed, and the man put the gun back in his pocket. I figured Peter must have said something that made the man change his mind. I was just about to leave and go upstairs to look for you when the man grabbed something from the shelf. It was a knife."

"It was the fishing knife, the one they found in the bathroom," Danielle murmured. "Chris's knife."

"It happened so fast, like the man knew exactly what he was doing. Peter never saw it coming. I just stood there and watched as he stepped out of his body and looked down at himself. His killer shoved the dead body with his foot, and it just fell onto the throw rug by the sofa. I thought for a moment he was going to use the rug to wrap up the body and dispose of it, but he just left the room."

"What did the killer look like?"

"There wasn't much light, but he was a stocky man about my age. I followed the killer out of the room and watched him go into the bathroom. Peter was still stumbling around his dead body, trying to figure out what had just happened."

"He hid the knife in the bathroom," Danielle whispered, speaking more to herself.

"When he came back out of the bathroom, I thought it was a good thing he'd left the knife behind, or there would be another dead body."

"What do you mean?"

"Just as he came back out of the bathroom, he slammed right into that woman."

"What woman?"

"I don't know. She's staying in a room upstairs with a man."

"Arlene?"

"I don't know if that's her name. She obviously knew the killer, seemed surprised to see him. She asked him what he was doing here."

"They knew each other?"

"He grabbed her by the arms, told her he was taking care of business, her business. And then ordered her to go back upstairs and go to sleep. Told her that in the morning she needed to remember to keep her mouth shut, because this would all come back on her if she wasn't careful, and it would ruin everything they were working to accomplish."

"What did she do?" Danielle asked.

"She ran back upstairs, after he kissed her."

"He kissed her?"

"Yes."

"Did they say anything else?"

"Not a word. She ran upstairs, and he left."

"What happened then?"

"I went back in the front room, where Peter Morris was still moaning over his body. A few minutes later, I heard someone walking in the front hall, and then I heard a door on the first floor close."

"That must have been Chris returning to his room. Did you go back out into the hall?"

"Not then. I stayed with Peter Morris for a while. I couldn't help but feel sorry for him. Eventually he told me his name, and I explained that he was dead. I remembered what Meghan had told me, and I suggested he move on. He just kept rambling, not making any sense. I got bored and eventually left him there and then went upstairs, looking for you."

"Did you ever see Peter Morris again?"

"No." Lucas smiled at Danielle. "Can we talk about us now?"

"What's there to say?"

"I still don't understand how the Danielle I knew would trade the life she had in California for this." He waved his hand, gesturing to the room around him.

"I guess neither of us knew each other very well."

"Downstairs, when I saw you earlier, with Walt and that other man…"

"Chris."

"This Chris, he could see me, couldn't he?"

"Yes. Chris can also see and hear spirits. Just like me."

"So he isn't dead? Like me and that other one?"

"No. Chris is very much alive."

"Who is he to you?"

"Chris is a friend. He's been staying at Marlow House."

"Lily's here too? Isn't she?" Lucas asked.

"Yes, Lily lives at Marlow House."

"I don't understand; did she take a teaching job here?"

"No, Lucas. Lily isn't teaching right now. She had some medical issues and had to give up her class. She's living here right now."

Lucas smiled. "One thing hasn't changed about you."

"What's that?"

"You're still taking in strays." Lucas vanished.

TWENTY-TWO

C losing her eyes did not help. She still couldn't fall asleep. The fact that Danielle hadn't slept the night before didn't make slipping off to dreamland any easier. Tossing the blanket and sheets aside, she sat up and dropped her feet to the cold floor. Her wiggling toes searched for her slippers and found them tucked just beneath her bed. She stood up and walked to the door, grabbing her robe along the way.

Slowly turning the doorknob, Danielle made a special effort to be quiet so as not to disturb the household. For a brief moment, she considered knocking on Lily's door; she needed to talk to someone. But there was no light coming from under the door, and she assumed her friend was already asleep. While Lily would probably be willing to talk, Danielle didn't want to wake the other guests. Since there was no light coming from any of the upstairs bedrooms, she surmised everyone was asleep.

Glancing toward the ceiling, she wondered if Walt was in the attic. She could always talk to Walt. Tiptoeing across the hall, en route to the attic staircase, she heard muffled voices. They came from Arlene and David's room. Pausing by their door a moment, she could hear arguing. What they were saying exactly, she couldn't hear. Yet she couldn't help but think about what Lucas had just told her about Arlene and Morris's killer.

Quietly continuing on her way, she headed down the hall and

then up the staircase leading to the attic, treading lightly on the wooden steps, cringing each time her slippered feet made the boards creak. At the top of the staircase, she found the door closed. Just as she reached out to take hold of the doorknob, the door swung open, seemingly of its own volition. But she knew that was not the case. Just as she entered the attic, the door slowly closed behind her.

"I heard you coming up the stairs," Walt said from his place by the attic window. Max sat on the windowsill, looking outside, his tail swishing back and forth.

"I tried to be quiet." Danielle walked to Walt.

"Max told me Lucas was here."

"Yes, he was." Danielle looked at Max, who continued to stare out the window, refusing to look in her direction. "Is Max mad at me?"

"Annoyed would be a more apt description," Walt told her.

Danielle reached out to stroke Max's neck, but he jumped down from the windowsill, ignoring her. He strolled away, eventually reaching the sleeper sofa, which he then jumped up on before snuggling down and closing his eyes.

"He really is annoyed," Danielle muttered.

"He's a cat. He'll get over it."

Danielle stood next to Walt at the window, looking outside to the darkness.

"Is he gone?" Walt asked.

"I assume you're talking about Lucas."

"Of course."

Danielle shrugged. "Gone for now, but for good? I've no idea."

"Why is he here?"

"That's what I'm trying to figure out. It seems spirits normally have a reason for sticking around."

Walt smiled in the darkness. "I suppose that's true."

"I wonder if maybe your original suspicion was correct."

"What's that?"

"Maybe Peter Morris is the reason Lucas showed up when he did."

Walt turned from the window and looked at Danielle. She continued to stare out into the dark night.

"Why do you say that?"

She let out a deep sigh and then proceeded to tell Walt everything Lucas had told her about what he had seen downstairs at the time of the murder.

When she was done, Walt asked, "Are you suggesting your guest Arlene is in some way involved in the murder?"

"According to Lucas, they knew each other. Good lord, he kissed her and sent her back upstairs."

"Yes, and to another man's bed. Odd, this generation of yours."

"I'll have to tell the chief; let him figure this out."

"Arlene did seem genuinely surprised to see a dead man in the parlor," Walt reminded her.

"True. And according to Lucas, she asked the killer what he was doing here. Maybe she had no idea he'd just killed Morris."

"If that's true, I wonder what she thought when she realized Morris had been murdered."

"I've a headache." Danielle groaned.

"Of course you do. You need your sleep."

"I've a favor to ask you."

"Anything," Walt vowed.

"Can you keep an eye on Arlene and David? Tomorrow morning I'll call the chief and let him know what I've found out."

"Okay. But you promise me you'll go back downstairs to bed."

"I might as well. I should stop worrying about Lucas suddenly appearing at any moment. It's likely he's moved on."

"Why do you think that?"

Danielle looked up at Walt. "His reason for being here was probably to witness the murder, and since he's passed the information on to me, he can go now."

"You don't honestly believe that, do you?"

"Why not? Why else would he be here? We really have nothing to say to each other."

"To begin with, I don't believe—and I don't think you do either—that spirits generally have clairvoyant powers, especially one who just realized the reality of his existence. I didn't even know who had killed me, so how can you imagine I could predict another person's demise and manage to be there to witness it?"

"That's true. But sometimes there are other forces involved. Something that made sure he'd be here at that specific time."

Walt laughed at the idea. "Other forces? Are we talking God, angels, what?"

Danielle shrugged.

"I find it implausible to imagine some higher being thought it a terrific idea to bring your deceased husband up to Oregon just to have him witness a crime and help you solve a murder."

"Then why is Lucas here?"

"Why do you think, Danielle?"

She didn't answer.

"You, of course," he answered for her. "I would say you and Lucas have some unresolved issues, and perhaps it's best for both of you to air them before he moves on—which may enable you to move on."

"I can't believe it; you were actually listening to what I had to say," Chris said from the doorway. Neither Danielle nor Walt had heard him enter the attic.

Walt groaned as Chris walked to them. "Is no room sacred in my house?"

"I'm just happy to see you were listening to me." Chris joined them by the window.

"You two talking about me behind my back now?" Danielle asked.

"What do you mean now?" Chris teased. "You've always been our favorite subject of conversation."

"When did you say you're moving out?" Walt asked.

"In the morning. I've already packed."

"That shouldn't have been too hard, considering everything you own fits into a pillowcase," Walt scoffed.

"I wouldn't say everything he owns," Danielle reminded him.

Chris turned his attention to Danielle. "Have you talked to Lucas?"

"He saw Peter Morris being murdered," Walt told him.

"Then he knows who did it?" Chris asked.

"I assume Logan Mitcham, since that's whose fingerprint they found out front," Danielle said.

"We could always see if your husband will agree to stick around for a lineup," Walt suggested. "I'm sure Chief MacDonald would appreciate the help."

"Lineup? Who would be in the lineup?" Danielle asked.

"Isn't that obvious? Mitcham…Chris," Walt explained.

"Me?" Chris frowned. "You know I had nothing to do with Peter's murder."

Walt shrugged. "So you say."

"Oh, stop that, Walt," Danielle chided. "You know Chris didn't kill Morris."

"I do?" Walt asked innocently.

"For one thing, when Lucas appeared in the library earlier, both you and Chris were there. Lucas asked me about Chris. If Chris had killed Morris, Lucas would have told me."

Walt shrugged. "Maybe. It's possible Lucas didn't get that close a look at him in the library. As I recall, your husband was only there a moment."

"Are you forgetting you woke Chris up? You seriously think he killed Morris and then went to bed and fell asleep?"

"Of course not. But you have to admit, it's rather amusing watching Chris get agitated." Walt smirked.

Danielle glanced over to Chris, who looked a little more than annoyed.

"What you want to do is slug me, don't you?" Walt taunted Chris.

"How did you guess?"

"Oh, stop, you two!"

"He started it," Chris grumbled.

"Walt just gets a little bored. You would be too, hanging around the same house for almost a century, never going out."

Chris almost reminded Danielle that was Walt's choice, yet instead said, "Fine. Why don't you tell me what Lucas told you about Morris's murder?"

After Danielle recounted Lucas's version of the murder, Walt said, "I told Danielle I'd keep an eye on Arlene and David while they're here."

"Strange, when I went to the bathroom to wash my hands of Morris's blood, Arlene seemed as if she was about to jump out of her skin. At the time, I assumed she was afraid of me—thought I'd just killed a man."

"If she really didn't know Mitcham had killed Morris when she saw him downstairs—assuming Logan Mitcham is the man Lucas saw—then she was probably freaking out at that point, realizing what he had done, and how she might be implicated in the murder," Danielle said.

"Maybe they planned to murder him, but she didn't know when Mitcham intended to do it," Chris suggested.

"But if she's part of this, then why kill Morris while she's staying here?" Danielle asked.

"Maybe it wasn't premeditated—at least at that moment. They were arguing; Mitcham took out his gun," Walt suggested.

"He just happens to have a gun?" Danielle asked.

"If it was Mitcham, he's a PI; so I imagine he always carries a concealed weapon," Chris said.

"Is that legal in Oregon?" Danielle asked.

Chris shrugged. "I've no idea. Of course, he didn't use the gun. What was the knife doing on that shelf, anyway? I didn't put it there."

"I don't know. According to Lucas, it looked like a spur-of-the-moment decision to use the knife instead of the gun," Danielle said. "I just keep wondering: was this premeditated, or did something happen during the argument that turned the situation lethal?"

"I'll be curious to see what MacDonald learns about your guest Arlene," Walt said.

"There's definitely something she's hiding," Chris agreed.

They were all quiet for several moments, considering the turn of events. Finally, Danielle broke the silence and said, "Now please explain what you meant when you said you were glad Walt finally listened to you?"

"He pointed out earlier that perhaps it might be good for you to take this opportunity and talk to your husband," Walt answered for Chris.

"Why? I don't see where we really have anything to say to each other. I've moved on; now he needs to do the same."

"Are you telling me that when he was killed in that car accident—and you found out about his affair—that part of you wasn't angry, not being able to confront him? To tell him how you felt?" Chris asked.

"Well…sure. But I've gotten over it."

"Danielle," Walt said softly, "take this opportunity; it might be your only one. Telling someone how we really feel can be liberating."

TWENTY-THREE

C hief MacDonald pulled up in front of the beach bungalow and parked his car. He sat there a moment and looked around. All was quiet. He hadn't been back to the modest beach house since that day in the fall when he had brought Danielle there to meet Will Wayne and confront the secret of the Gusarov family.

MacDonald knew Wayne had petitioned the court to become Karen's legal guardian and had won. The chief wasn't surprised. There was no other family member left to oversee Wayne's ex-wife's care, and while there was a considerable fortune attached to the trust fund paying for her expenses, Wayne had his own fortune and took legal measures to prove his motives were not monetarily motivated.

Fifteen minutes later, MacDonald sat in the bungalow's kitchen. It was not quite 9:00 a.m. on Valentine's Day.

"Karen is still sleeping," Will explained as he handed a mug of steaming coffee to the chief. "She had a rough night. Actually, the last few nights have been rough." Will took a seat at the kitchen table.

"Is it just you taking care of her?"

"Goodness, no. There're several excellent nurses and caregivers on staff; they rotate shifts. To be honest, I'm just here to oversee her care and make sure she gets what she needs." He picked up the cane leaning against the table and briefly tapped his leg. "I'm afraid I don't get around too well myself. I've discovered the dampness up here is not the best thing for my leg. I've been thinking about going back to Arizona."

"What about Karen?"

"I'm working on that. I'd like to take her with me if I can work everything out—legally. I'll set her up somewhere. Someplace close to wherever I land."

"You won't stay under the same roof with her anymore?"

Will shook his head. "No. When I first got here, she'd have occasional moments when she'd remember Bobby—that boy I used to be. Of course, she had no idea I was Bobby. But now, she's drifted off completely to another place. I realize I'm not getting any younger, and as long as I make sure she's properly cared for and I regularly check on her, then I think it may be time I move on."

"She's lucky to have you." MacDonald sipped his coffee.

"So tell me, Chief, why are you here?"

"Did you hear the news?"

"You mean about Peter Morris's murder?"

MacDonald studied Will. "I take that as a yes."

"I heard it on the radio yesterday. Almost called Danielle, but figured she was probably overwhelmed. Feel awful for her, having something like that happen right under her roof. Any leads on who killed him? According to the news, you hadn't arrested anyone yet."

"That's why I'm here." MacDonald set his mug on the tabletop.

Will let out a sigh and leaned back in his chair. "I suppose I'm not surprised."

"Why do you say that?"

"I have to assume Danielle told you how I hired a private investigator after receiving several anonymous calls telling me Morris was responsible for Isabella's death. I'm sure that would put me on top of the suspect list. But if Morris was murdered early Friday morning, as the radio said, I have an alibi. I was here all night with Karen and two nurses. Didn't get much sleep. Like I said, the last few nights have been rough."

"Can you tell me a little bit about the private investigator you hired?"

Will picked up his mug and took a sip of coffee before answering. "Logan Mitcham, what about him?"

"Did he find out anything about Morris in relationship to your daughter's death?"

140

Absently licking his lips, Will set his cup on the table and looked up into the chief's eyes. "He claimed to have evidence Morris had her killed."

"What evidence?"

Will shrugged. "I haven't seen the evidence yet. Not sure if I will."

MacDonald frowned. "Why do you say that?"

"I suppose I would have come to you eventually. But I wasn't quite sure what to do next," Will explained.

"I don't understand."

"After Mitcham told me he had evidence Morris killed my daughter, I asked to see it. But he told me I'd never get any satisfaction going through legal channels because Morris was so well connected. He suggested I have Morris killed. Said if Isabella was his daughter, that's what he'd do."

"He told you to kill Morris?"

"He didn't suggest I do it myself, told me he knew someone who could get the job done, but that it would cost me. I told him I wasn't interested in killing anyone, I just wanted to know the truth. He told me to think about it."

"What was the evidence?" MacDonald asked.

Will shook his head. "I don't know. He never gave me anything. This was on Tuesday. I considered hiring another private detective. I figured if Mitcham was right and Morris had Isabella killed, then someone in the coroner's office had to be involved. But I didn't want to call Mitcham back—even to ask him to turn over what he claimed to have so far. I felt very uncomfortable calling him because of his offer to find someone to kill Morris."

"But someone did kill Morris."

"Yes. But I didn't have anything to do with it."

"You said you were going to come to me?"

"Danielle urged me to talk to you, after I told her about the phone calls I'd received. She said you had no love for Morris and would happily put him away."

"But you didn't come to me even after Mitcham offered to have Morris killed."

"His offer to hook me up with a hit man threw me. But it's not like he offered to kill Morris himself. And this all happened just the other day. To be honest, I found myself more angered at the idea that someone in the coroner's office would take a payoff to cover up a murder. I kept asking myself, should I call another private investigator to look deeper into it, call Mitcham back and insist he turn over what he had, or call you?"

"What did you decide?"

"I didn't decide anything. Karen's gotten her nights and days confused, and we've been trying to get her to sleep at night, but she's been keeping us up, and then during the day, I'm wiped out. Which, to be honest, is one reason I've realized it might be time to get my own place again and let the professionals handle Karen at night. I really don't have the stamina."

"When was the last time you spoke to Mitcham?"

"That would have been on Tuesday, when he offered to find me a hit man."

"You haven't talked to him again?"

Will shook his head. "No."

"Do you have any idea where he might be?"

"I would assume you could find him at his office in Portland or his home. I can give you his office address and phone number, but I have no idea where he lives. If you ask him about his offer to find me a hit man, I'm sure he'll deny it."

"How did you happen to hire Mitcham?"

"One of Karen's nurses recommended him."

AFTER LEAVING THE BEACH BUNGALOW, MacDonald drove to the police station. On his way there, he called Brian, updating him on his interview with Will Wayne. When he arrived at the station, he found Brian and Joe sorting through the file boxes confiscated from Logan Mitcham's home and office. The private detective still had not been located.

"You told us to focus on any files on Will Wayne's case," Brian told the chief. "But there's really not much."

"What do you mean?" the chief sat down at the table with his men.

"Wayne was obviously one of Mitcham's clients," Joe explained. "But aside from a few notes explaining what Wayne wanted him to investigate, there's nothing about the actual investigation."

"Not nothing, exactly," Brian reminded him. "There's a copy of an invoice in the file, which Wayne apparently paid. But aside from that, nothing on what Mitcham found regarding Isabella's death."

"According to Will, Mitcham found evidence Morris had Isabella killed—but he never turned that information over to Will. Maybe he didn't keep case notes in paper files. Perhaps we'll find something on his computer," MacDonald suggested.

"That might be the case," Joe said. "But I glanced through his other files, and they all include detailed reports on the various cases he's worked on—notes on surveillances, photographs, all kinds of information. But there is absolutely nothing in Wayne's file."

"Maybe he has it with him," MacDonald suggested.

"Or perhaps he destroyed it," Brian said. "Maybe Wayne accepted Mitcham's offer to find a hit man."

"He didn't have to look very far," Joe said dryly.

"You're suggesting Wayne is covering for himself, throwing out the story of a hit man since I asked him about Mitcham?" the chief asked.

"If you hire a contract killer, and then the cops mention that man by name when discussing the murder, and you realize you've a motive and a connection to the hit man, then yes. It might be wise to toss something out there," Brian said.

"True, but as far as Wayne knows, the only reason I asked him about Mitcham was because he told Danielle about hiring him, and she told me after Morris was murdered and we started looking into people with motives to want the man dead."

"I doubt Mitcham realizes he left behind his fingerprint," Joe said.

The chief stood up. "Keep going through the files. Hopefully you'll find something that'll help us locate Mitcham."

The room's landline telephone began to ring. Brian answered it. When he got off the phone, he looked at Joe and the chief. "They found Mitcham's car."

"Just his car? Not him?" Joe asked.

Before Brian had a chance to answer, the chief asked, "Where?"

"Parked a couple blocks from Marlow House. In an alleyway behind a vacant house."

"How long has it been there?" MacDonald asked.

Brian shook his head. "None of the neighbors remember seeing it parked there yesterday."

143

MacDonald headed for the door. "Let me know if you find anything."

Just as MacDonald was about to walk out of the room, Joe said, "Well, this is interesting." The chief paused at the doorway and turned to face Joe, who held an open file in his hand.

"What is it?" MacDonald asked.

"Seems Will Wayne is not the only person we know who hired Logan Mitcham," Joe said.

The chief stepped back into the office. "Who else?"

"According to this file, Heather Donovan is one of Logan Mitcham's clients."

TWENTY-FOUR

D anielle had just stepped out of the shower when she heard, "Happy Valentine's Day, Danielle."

With a startled yelp, she snatched the towel from its rod, covering herself.

Lucas laughed. "Really, Danielle, you're my wife. No reason to be modest."

"I believe the term is widow," Danielle snapped. "What are you doing in here? I thought you left?"

"It's Valentine's Day. Surely you remember." He smiled.

"Yes, I know it's Valentine's Day. So?"

"Valentine's Day was always special for us. It was the day I officially asked you to marry me." He glanced at her hands. The only ring she wore was on her right hand—a gold setting with an aquamarine stone. Lucas frowned. "Where's your wedding ring?"

"I took it off after you died."

"What did you do with it?" he asked.

"I gave it back to your mother."

"Why would you do that?"

"It was your grandmother's ring. I thought it should go back to your family."

"It was yours, Danielle. Yours to keep. I gave it to you."

Danielle shivered and wrapped the towel tighter around her

body. "Could you please leave? I'd like to dry off and put my clothes on."

"Fine. But I think you're being silly. We can talk after you get dressed." He disappeared.

After dressing and pulling her hair into a French braid, Danielle waited in her room for Lucas to return. Thirty minutes went by. When he didn't appear, she went downstairs and found Joanne just coming out of the parlor.

Danielle eyed the mop Joanne carried. "Good morning, Joanne."

"I cleaned up in the parlor. There was still a little blood on the floor by the sofa, but I was able to get it up."

"Sorry you had to do that. I should have done it myself last night."

"No, don't worry about it. I can't even imagine how horrible it was for everyone, finding Peter Morris in there." Joanne glanced briefly over her shoulder, into the parlor. "Plus, I feel somewhat responsible."

"Responsible? What do you mean?"

Joanne rested the mop handle on the floor and looked down sheepishly. "I'm afraid I'm the one who left Chris's knife in the parlor. If I hadn't done that, then maybe whoever killed Mr. Morris would have vented his anger differently. Maybe just sock him in the nose. But to use a knife on him…"

"You put the knife in there?"

"I'm sorry. There was tape stuck in the window frame, and I needed something sharp and narrow to remove it with. I didn't want to use one of the kitchen knives, and I remembered Chris's tackle box on the back porch, and I figured there'd be a knife in there that would work. I didn't think I'd hurt the knife, and I was only going to use it for a minute and put it back. But then I got sidetracked when someone came to the front door. I set the knife down in the parlor and forgot about it. You have no idea how sorry I am."

"I think we need to tell Chief MacDonald this. I know he's been wondering how the killer got ahold of Chris's knife."

"I already did. Well, actually, I talked to Joe Morelli. He asked me to come in to the police station…I'm really sorry, Danielle. I know I shouldn't have borrowed Chris's knife without asking. If you…well, if you don't feel comfortable about me working here…"

Danielle wrinkled her nose and shook her head. "Don't be silly.

We've all done something like that before. I'm just happy you told Joe. I know he's had his eye on Chris for this murder, and since Chris's knife was the murder weapon…"

"Chris, I don't—"

Joanne's sentence was cut off when Chris walked into the entry hall and asked, "Did someone call my name?"

"Morning." Danielle turned to face Chris. "I now know how your fishing knife got into the parlor."

"I do too." Chris nodded toward the woman by Danielle's side. "Joanne explained when she got here this morning." He smiled.

"I already made some pancake batter," Joanne told them. "As soon as I finish up here, I was going to put the bacon on. Chris, you are going to have breakfast before you go, aren't you?"

"That's right, you're leaving this morning," Danielle said. "It's going to feel…well, different with you not here."

"Hey, you aren't getting rid of me that easy!"

"I was afraid you'd say that," Walt said when he appeared the next moment. Both Danielle and Chris flashed Walt a smile—Chris's being more a smirk than a smile.

"I stripped the sheets off and put them and my dirty towels in the laundry room," Chris explained.

"You didn't have to do that," Joanne told him. "But thank you."

"Hey, no problem." Chris grinned.

"Well, I better get breakfast on." Mop in hand, Joanne scurried down the hallway.

"I'm going to miss you," Danielle told Chris a moment later.

"I don't know why you're going to miss him. As he said, just because he's moving out, it doesn't mean we're getting rid of him," Walt reminded her. "And he's just down the street."

"That's right, Walt. And I won't just drop by to visit Danielle. I plan to come see you."

"Lucky me," Walt said dryly. He disappeared.

Danielle glanced around the entry hall. Walt was nowhere to be seen. She looked back to Chris and whispered, "You know, I think he's going to miss you. I believe he rather likes having someone more to talk to than just me."

"He has Max and Sadie—and even Bella, for the moment," Chris reminded her.

"True. But I've a feeling conversing with animals isn't quite the same thing as human contact."

"Perhaps…" Chris glanced around. "Is your husband's spirit still lurking in Marlow House?"

Danielle sighed. "I saw him this morning. I don't think he intends to leave until he says whatever he wants to say to me."

"If you sincerely want him to leave, then why don't you listen to him?"

"What, you think I want him to stick around?"

Chris shrugged. "Maybe. He was the man you once loved enough to marry. The two of you never had a chance to resolve your issues."

"Issues I wasn't even aware of until he died!"

"Which makes it worse. This is your chance, Danielle. Most people never have the opportunity to confront someone who has died. It's our unique gift."

"Gift or curse," Danielle muttered.

"I suspect you don't view your friendship with Walt as a curse."

"Well…no…"

"Then use your gift and talk to your husband—really talk to him. And it's not only for you; it's for him. He probably needs this more than you do."

"Since when did you start caring so much for my husband? You don't even know him."

Chris shrugged. "I've never been good at walking away from a spirit who needed my help."

Danielle studied Chris for a moment. "You mean like Anna?"

"To me, Anna will always be Trudy, but yes. Although, I have to confess, my motivation for helping her had more to do with wanting to get her out of my life. In the beginning I just wanted to help her —but when my efforts didn't seem to be going anywhere, she became more demanding, and after a while, I just wanted to find something—anything—to get her to move on."

"I can understand that."

"So what are you waiting for?" he asked.

"I don't think Lucas is going to come around while anyone is with me. He made that pretty clear earlier."

"Then go somewhere where you can be alone. I don't think anyone's in the library, and—" Chris glanced at his watch "—it'll be breakfast pretty soon; so I suspect the rest of the house will be in the dining room before long. Go."

"Fine…" Danielle sighed. "I'll see if he shows up there."

Five minutes later, Danielle sat alone in the library. She was about to call out Lucas's name when he appeared in the room, standing before the portraits of Walt and Angela Marlow.

"I know who he is." Lucas nodded toward Walt's portrait. "But who was she?"

"Angela Marlow. She was Walt's wife."

"Beautiful woman." He glanced from the portrait to Danielle. "Does her spirit haunt this house too?"

Danielle stood up and walked to Lucas's side. "No. In fact, she conspired to murder her husband."

Lucas arched his brows. "Really? And I thought we had some unresolved issues. What happened to her? Was she arrested? Why is her portrait still here? Didn't he want it removed after she tried to kill him?"

"He didn't know about it before he died. She and her brother planned to kill Walt, but then she died unexpectedly and her spirit returned to Marlow House, and she tried to stop her brother from carrying out their plan, but she wasn't able to intervene."

"He was murdered by his brother-in-law?" Lucas cringed.

"Yep."

"Loving family," Lucas muttered. "I wonder if there's a hell after this—when I finally move on, will it be to a heaven…or will my sins send me to hell?"

"I don't believe you're going to hell, Lucas. In Angela's case, she's stuck at the local cemetery."

Lucas frowned. "Why the cemetery?"

"Consider it a cosmic time-out. She's basically under house arrest. Her spirit isn't allowed to move on—nor can she venture outside the cemetery."

"What's Walt's story? What did he do wrong?"

"Walt? Why do you assume he's done something wrong?"

"He's still here. From what I gathered from Meghan, a spirit is supposed to move on—and you just said Angela Marlow can't because she tried to kill her husband. And I assume I couldn't move on earlier because I was so confused about what had happened—that was, until Meghan helped me come to terms with things."

"I suspect in Angela's case, she'd be moving on to a much warmer climate had she not tried to prevent Walt's murder."

"So there is a hell?"

Danielle shrugged. "I really don't know. I just know there's something more."

"Why is Walt Marlow still here?"

"He's not ready to move on yet. This was his home. He will eventually."

"Does this mean I can stick around too? That I don't have to move on if I don't want to?"

Danielle turned to Lucas and shook her head. "No. You need to move on, Lucas. You don't belong here."

"You're still angry with me, aren't you?"

Danielle sighed. "I don't know what I feel, Lucas."

"Fair enough." He turned back to the portrait and studied it a moment before asking, "What happened to our portrait, Danielle?"

"I gave it to your mother."

"I suppose I should be grateful you didn't burn it."

"The portrait meant a lot to your mother. Your death was hard on her."

"Was it hard on you, Danielle?" When she didn't answer, he said, "We need to talk; I need to explain."

Heather barged into the library. "Who are you talking to?"

Danielle glanced to her side. Lucas was no longer there.

"Good morning, Heather. I guess I must have been thinking out loud," Danielle lied.

Walking into the room, Heather stared a moment at the spot Lucas had been standing in. "You know, sometimes I really think this place is haunted."

Danielle glanced around uneasily. "Umm...why do you say that?"

"For a moment there, when I first walked into the library, I thought I saw a man standing next to you. Just a glimmer. And it's not the first time."

"Not the first time? Are you saying you've seen this man before?"

"No. But I've seen another man." Heather pointed to Walt's portrait. "That one."

"You've seen Walt Marlow?" Danielle squeaked.

"You know I saw Harvey—I even talked to him."

"Yes..."

"You did too. Sometimes, I think you like to pretend it all never happened."

"It's just something I'd rather forget," Danielle said.

"I suppose I can understand, considering you and Lily were almost killed in that fire. But I have a gift. I know I do."

"You say you've seen Walt Marlow…have you talked to him?"

"Now you're just making fun of me!" Heather snapped.

"No…I'm not, honest. But you talked to Harvey."

"Well, this is different. With Walt Marlow, it's just brief flashes. He's there one moment and then gone the next. Like with the one I just saw. I think I should probably use my oils."

TWENTY-FIVE

"Let's not," Walt said when he appeared in the library.
Curious, Danielle studied Heather's reaction, waiting to see if she could see Walt. Heather didn't appear to have an inkling his spirit lingered just a few feet from her.

"But I'll have to get the oils out when I come back," Heather said.

"Come back? Are you going somewhere?"

"I got a call this morning from Police Chief MacDonald; he wants me to come down to the police station again for more questioning. I'm afraid if I don't go now, he'll come here, and frankly, I would rather talk to him down there."

"Are you going to have breakfast first? I know Joanne is making it now."

Heather shook her head. "No. Would you mind telling her I won't be here for breakfast?" Heather glanced at the cellphone in her hand, checking the time. "I need to go."

"SHE REMINDS me a little like someone from the Addams family," Brian told MacDonald. The two men stood together in the room adjacent to the interrogation room, watching Heather Donovan through the two-way mirror. She sat alone at the table, absently surfing the Internet on her cellphone while waiting for someone to come in and interview her.

"She does, doesn't she?" MacDonald chuckled.

"What grown woman goes around wearing her hair in two ponytails?"

MacDonald studied Heather for a moment, noting her coal black hair pulled into low pigtails and the severe bangs cut straight across her forehead. He shrugged. "It rather suits her."

"Might as well get this over with," Brian said before leaving the room.

A few minutes later, Officer Brian Henderson sat across the table from Heather Donovan in the Frederickport Police Department's interrogation room.

"Thanks for coming down this morning," Brian said as he opened his folder and shuffled through its papers.

Heather turned off her phone and set it on the table. She looked across at Brian. "I figured it would be easier to do this down here instead of at Marlow House."

"It does make it easier on me." Brian smiled.

"What did you want to ask me?"

Brian looked up from his papers to Heather. "Do you know a man by the name of Logan Mitcham?"

Heather closed her eyes and let out a groan, slumping down in her chair. "I suppose he called you about me, right?"

"Why would Mr. Mitcham contact us about you?"

Heather sat back up straight in her chair and glared at Brian. "I imagine because I said that if I could strangle Peter Morris, I would! But that doesn't mean I stabbed the SOB, does it? Damn!" Heather angrily folded her arms across her chest and slumped back down in her chair. "Whatever happened to client confidentiality? I sure won't recommend Mitcham to anyone!"

"Why don't you back up a moment, Heather? Tell me how you happen to know Mr. Mitcham—and then you can explain why you told him you wanted to kill Peter Morris."

Sitting up straighter, she continued to glare at Brian. "Just because I said I wanted to strangle him doesn't mean I wanted to kill him. It's a figure of speech, for goodness' sake!"

"Once again, Heather—how do you happen to know Mr. Mitcham?"

Heather let out a sigh and leaned forward, resting her elbows on the table. "I don't know why you're making me say everything you obviously already know. But fine—I hired Mitcham to investigate Peter Morris."

"Why would you do that?"

Heather studied Brian for a moment. "You don't know, do you?"

"Go on."

Heather shrugged. "I hired him to look into Peter Morris and Earthbound Spirits in regards to Presley House, well, the property, anyway."

"What did Morris have to do with the property?"

"I found out my mother hadn't been paying the taxes on the property. After the house burned down, I assumed I still owned at least the lot, but I found out it had been sold for back taxes, and the new owner was Earthbound Spirits. I spoke to someone over at the assessors' office, and she told me on the Q.T. that something looked a little hinky about it, and she promised to look into it. I decided to hire someone to look into it for me, so I hired Logan Mitcham."

"What did he find out?"

"After charging me more than I could afford, he told me Earthbound Spirits hadn't done anything wrong. That when someone doesn't pay property taxes, that's what can happen. He told me it was nothing personal, that Earthbound Spirits acquires a lot of land this way."

"How did you happen to tell Mitcham you wanted to strangle Morris?"

"After he told me what he found, I got...well, I suppose I was upset. I really thought I would find out something that would help me get my property back. But according to Mitcham, there was absolutely nothing I could do about it. He told me I needed to simply move on. I suppose I didn't appreciate his advice. Told him I was pissed and that I didn't care if Morris took my land legally... that I still would like to strangle him."

"How did Mitcham react to your outburst?"

"Sort of got the feeling he was used to clients getting upset when he told them something they didn't want to hear. I don't know why he had to run to you the minute he found out someone killed Morris. I don't even see how that's ethical."

"After you got upset with the news, then what happened?"

Heather shrugged. "I left his office. Told him thank you for his help. Although I suppose, I probably said that a little snarky. But I was pissed at the time!"

"How did you happen to hire Mitcham?"

"Someone recommended him. Claimed he was the best one for my situation."

"Someone? Who?"

"I don't know."

"What do you mean you don't know? You don't know who recommended Mitcham?"

"Well, I don't know them personally."

"So what are you telling me, you walked up to some stranger on the street, asked them for a name of a good PI and they gave you Mitcham's?"

"Of course not," Heather scoffed. "It was online."

"You mean one of those referral sites, like Angie's List?"

Absently picking up her cellphone, she fidgeted with it as she explained. "No. When I found out who'd ended up with my land, I went online to see what I could find out about the cult. And it is a cult, you know. There had already been so much in the paper, what with Morris's right-hand man killing himself and confessing to a murder and other crimes. It didn't take long to find out I wasn't the only one with a gripe with Earthbound Spirits."

"How so?"

"I came across a forum on cults, and there was an active thread all about Earthbound Spirits. I joined the forum and started talking to other people there, exchanging experiences. That's when I met CultCurious."

"CultCurious?" Brian asked.

"Yeah. That's his handle. Or her. Not really sure. He sent me a private message. Told me if I was really serious about going after Morris, I needed to hire Logan Mitcham. Said he was a PI who was already looking into the group, wanted to bring them down, and he'd probably appreciate any new ammunition that would help do that. Said he probably wouldn't even charge me. Of course, he was wrong there."

"Wrong?"

"It wasn't free. But I really wasn't looking for a free private detective, just one who'd be best for my case. I'd hoped Mitcham would be it."

"Do you think he did a poor job?"

Heather shrugged in defeat. "Probably not. It just wasn't what I wanted to hear. I wanted him to tell me Morris had done something illegal and that he could prove it, and I could get my property back. But that's not what he told me. And since he's not a fan of Earthbound Spirits, I have to assume had he found anything I could've used against the group, he would have told me. But still, to tell you about me is really jerky."

Brian was about to ask another question when Heather angrily tossed her phone aside and looked across the table at Brian. "Did he give you all his clients' names?"

"What do you mean?"

"Did Mitcham hand over his client list, all those poor people who have a legitimate grudge against Earthbound Spirits? While I didn't kill the man, I'm not crying over his death. He hurt many people. I don't think any of those people deserve to be harassed by you!"

"Heather, I've no intention of harassing anyone."

"Boy, I'm going to give Mitcham a piece of my mind, and when I go online again, I'm going to let everyone know what a betrayer he is!"

"First of all, Mitcham did not say anything about you. In fact, we haven't even talked to him."

Heather frowned. "I don't understand. You knew I'd hired him."

"He's a person of interest. We're trying to locate him. We came across an invoice he made out to you, which is how we knew of the connection."

She stared dumbly across the table a moment before asking, "Are you saying Mitcham never said anything to you about me threatening to strangle Morris?"

Brian nodded. "Like I said, we haven't spoken to him. But we're trying to contact him. Do you know where we might be able to find him?"

Heather shrugged. "I met him at his office. Do you have that address?"

"Yes. Did he ever mention any other place he likes to go? Maybe a favorite restaurant where he meets with clients? A hobby he mentioned in passing? Something?"

"No. Sorry. I just met with him twice. Once when I hired him and the second time when he told me what he'd found. Or should I say, hadn't found."

"The night of the murder, when Chris stepped out of the parlor, when he was with Morris, you told Chris Danielle was looking for him."

"I thought she was."

"But you admitted you didn't actually talk to her. That you heard her call out from the kitchen."

Heather shifted in her chair. "Yeah, what about it?"

"Danielle wasn't in the kitchen. But Chris left to find her… leaving you alone with Morris."

Heather shook her head in frantic denial. "No…I didn't tell Chris that to be alone with Morris! I honestly believed I heard her cry out from the kitchen. Sometimes…well, sometimes I hear things…well…and see things…that other people don't."

"I'm not sure what you're getting at."

Heather leaned forward and whispered, "I think Marlow House is haunted."

"Haunted?"

"I've seen Walt Marlow on a few occasions."

"Umm…have you shared this with anyone?" Brian asked.

"Actually, I told Danielle this morning. Of course, she doesn't believe me. I could tell."

"Let's forget about…ghosts…for a moment. Why don't you tell me again what happened between you and Morris after Chris left him with you?"

"Nothing happened between us. Maybe he didn't do anything illegal to get my property, but I still didn't want anything to do with him. I didn't want to talk to him. But I certainly didn't kill him."

"What did you do, exactly?"

"After I told Chris about Danielle looking for him and how she might be in the kitchen, I admit I expected it to speed up the goodbye."

"Speed up what goodbye?"

"Between Chris and Morris, of course. Haven't you ever noticed when you walk someone out to leave, they linger on and on with inane conversation until you want to just shove them out the door? I figured with Chris knowing Danielle was looking for him, Morris would just leave."

"But it didn't work out that way, did it?"

TWENTY-SIX

D anielle was about to step into the front lobby of the
Frederickport Police Department when Heather stepped
outside. Heather paused and looked at her before stating, "You
didn't mention you were coming down here."

"Thought I'd stop by and see if there was any news on the
murder investigation."

"Are you sure you didn't just come down here to find out why
they wanted to talk to me again?"

Danielle frowned. "No. Why would I come all the way down
here to ask that when you're living at Marlow House?"

Heather shrugged. "Well, your friend Police Chief MacDonald
isn't here. Or at least, I didn't see him."

"I thought that's who called you."

"It was. But I spoke to Officer Henderson." Heather pushed by
Danielle. "I'm out of here. Going to grab some breakfast."

"Bye…" Danielle said lamely, watching Heather make her way
to the parking lot. After a moment, Danielle gave her head a little
shake and made her way inside the building. After being buzzed in
to the inner offices, she came face-to-face with Joe Morelli.

"Happy Valentine's Day, Danielle," Joe greeted her.

"Morning. Any breaks on the case?" she asked.

"Nothing I can really share at this time. But hopefully, we'll have
something we can tell you."

"Is the chief here?" she asked.

"The chief won't be able to tell you any more than me," Joe told her.

Danielle smiled. "I just wanted to say hi," she lied.

"I was hoping you might have changed your mind about going out with me tonight."

"Thanks, Joe. I appreciate the offer, but with everything that's going on right now, I can't even think about going out."

"Morning, Danielle," Brian greeted her, walking to where she stood with Joe.

"Hi, Brian. I see you talked to Heather again this morning."

"She told you?" Brian asked.

"Earlier, she mentioned the chief asked her to come down, and I just ran into her on her way out. But she didn't say why you wanted to talk to her again."

"Just routine." Brian shrugged. "Rechecking our facts, that's all."

Danielle smiled. "I was wondering, is the chief here?"

Brian told her he was in his office at the same time Joe reminded her the chief wouldn't have anything new to tell her. She smiled at both officers and then politely excused herself and made her way to the chief's office.

"She does make herself at home around here," Brian observed dryly.

"I should probably tell her to wait out front while I check with the chief." Joe started to follow Danielle when Brian reached out and grabbed him by the arm. Joe paused and looked back at the other officer.

"Don't waste your time, Joe. The chief will see her. You know it. I've no idea what's with those two. If it wasn't for Carol Ann, I'd swear they've got something going on."

"Oh please, the chief is hardly Danielle's type," Joe scoffed.

"You're right. I imagine Chris Glandon is more her type."

"THIS IS A SURPRISE," the chief greeted Danielle when she entered his office, closing the door behind her. "We just had your—what is Heather Donovan, your boarder or guest? She was just here."

"I suppose she qualifies more as a boarder," Danielle said as she sat down. "I just ran into her outside. She mentioned earlier she was on her way down here. So anything new?"

The chief glanced down at the stack of papers on his desk and gave them a little shove. "I don't know. But whenever I turn around, I find someone else connected to Logan Mitcham."

"You don't mean Heather?"

"Apparently she hired him to look into Morris and Earthbound Spirits, something about them getting ahold of her Presley property."

"Are you saying Earthbound Spirits is the new owner?"

"You know about it?"

"I knew she lost it for back taxes. I had no idea Earthbound Spirits was the new owner. She left that part out."

"Apparently, Earthbound Spirits has picked up a number of properties because of unpaid property tax."

"According to Heather, she suspected the new owner had done something illegal to get ahold of the property; that's why she talked about hiring a private detective. But I didn't realize she'd hired someone. I sort of had the impression she didn't have the money."

"She hired someone all right—Kelly Bartley's neighbor. Yet according to Heather, Mitcham claimed Morris didn't do anything illegal. Earthbound Spirits apparently got the property fair and square."

Danielle leaned back in the chair. "I suppose there is a first time for everything."

"So why did you stop by? Just to see why we wanted to see Heather?"

Danielle smiled. "Not particularly. Though that's just what Heather suggested. No, the real reason I want to see you this morning is to tell you something I learned last night. Actually, it's someone else with a connection to Mitcham."

"Who?"

Danielle leaned toward the desk. "You know how I told you about Max seeing Arlene go downstairs after Heather went up to her room for the night?"

"Yes. I've been hesitant about bringing her back in for more questions. At least, not right now. I suppose I could say someone claimed to have seen her come downstairs, but who? I'm sure everyone has compared notes by now."

"According to my sources, after stabbing Peter Morris, the killer

—a man—stashed the knife in the bathroom. Just as he was leaving the bathroom, he ran into Arlene, who had just come downstairs."

"She saw the killer?"

"Not only did she see him, she knew him. Knew him enough that he kissed her before he told her to go back upstairs to bed, shortly before he left."

"You're saying Arlene Horton was part of the murder?"

Danielle leaned back in her chair and crossed her denim-clad legs. "I'm not sure I'd say she was part of the murder, exactly. According to Lucas, she seemed genuinely surprised to find the man downstairs."

"Lucas? Your deceased husband?"

"Yeah…" Danielle sighed. "Lucas is still hanging around. He witnessed the murder."

"What does he say happened?"

Danielle repeated what Lucas had told her. When she was finished, she and MacDonald sat in silence for a few moments, considering the new information.

"We know David has a tie to Peter Morris. He's a Hilton. The youngest grandchild of Helen Hilton, who left her estate to Earthbound Spirits."

"And one of the grandchildren involved in the lawsuit against the cult," Danielle added.

"Hilton has the motive…" the chief muttered.

"There is obviously a tie between Arlene and Mitcham. But if there is something romantic between those two, why is she sharing a bed with David?"

The chief smiled. "Sounds interesting. How long are they staying? I'm a little concerned about them still being with you. It may not be safe, but until I can find something—other than testimony from a ghost or cat…"

"Don't worry about our safety. Walt promised to keep an eye on both of them. But I have this gut feeling that they aren't killers."

"Maybe not, but Mitcham is still missing, and it was his fingerprint we found at your house."

"Have you talked to Will yet?" Danielle asked.

"Yes. Which now, considering what Heather told me, makes me even more confused about the players in all this." The chief leaned back in his chair, crossing his arms over his chest.

"How do you mean?"

"According to Wayne, Mitcham found evidence Isabella was murdered, which I know is false."

"How do you know that?"

"Because I looked into it again and had someone else review the medical records, and there is no doubt Isabella died of natural causes. Yet according to Wayne, Mitcham offered to hook him up with a hit man—to kill Morris. Because, according to Mitcham, Morris was so well connected he'd get away with the murder."

"You aren't suggesting Will hired Mitcham to kill Morris, are you?"

"No. According to Wayne, he was more interested in finding out who in the coroner's office was involved in the cover-up, but he backed away from Mitcham after the offer. Plus, the PI never handed over any of the information he claimed to have uncovered. So basically, he expected Wayne to simply take his word for it."

"Why would Mitcham lie about something like that?" Danielle asked.

"I just hope your friend didn't hire Mitcham to kill Morris and just told me all that to throw me off, in case Mitcham screwed up— which he did—and left a clue that would lead us to him."

Danielle shook her head. "I just can't believe Will would hire a hit man."

"You don't have kids, Danielle."

"What does that have to do with it?"

"If someone hurt one of my boys like that—I honestly don't know what I'd do. In fact, I don't even like to think about it."

"No...Will Wayne is a good man."

"I'd like to think I'm a good man too. But when it comes to someone hurting one of my kids—well, anything is possible. It's not as if Peter Morris was a particularly likable man. He had a history of bilking vulnerable people out of money, and if Wayne honestly believed he had Isabella killed, it wouldn't surprise me."

"So why haven't you arrested him yet?"

"Aside from the fact I keep tripping over other people connected to Mitcham who also have motives, I think it would be premature. I really don't want to repeat your cousin's murder investigation."

Danielle knew what he was talking about. Several people, including herself, were arrested for Cheryl's murder before the real killer was arrested.

Danielle listed off the current suspects. "So far, there's Heather,

Arlene—David, if you consider his connection to Mitcham through Arlene and his history with Earthbound Spirits—and then there's Will."

"You forget Kelly."

"Kelly? Sure, she's his neighbor, but she didn't have a reason to kill Morris."

"Sure she did."

"What are you talking about?" Danielle asked.

"What's our agreement, Danielle?" the chief asked.

Danielle let out a sigh. "What you tell me in confidence about an ongoing case cannot go any farther than you and me unless you give me permission to tell someone like Lily or Walt. And I'll be your spiritual informer."

"Spiritual informer?" The chief smiled.

"Or is it spiritual snitch?" she asked.

"Okay…whatever…but for now, you need to keep this between us. If Kelly happens to tell you herself, pretend like it's the first time you've heard it."

Danielle frowned. "Heard what?"

"Kelly believes Peter Morris was responsible for her roommate's suicide. Not much different from Cleve's suicide, yet in this case, it was primarily about money."

"Money?"

"The young woman had an inheritance from her grandmother. She was troubled. Morris convinced her to move on to paradise— and oh, by the way, leave me your money so I can continue to help other girls like you."

"Damn…" Danielle shook her head in disgust. "We should be giving Logan Mitcham a medal instead of finding him so we can throw him in prison."

"I know how you feel, believe me."

"So now what?" Danielle asked.

"Now I'd like to learn more about the connection between Mitcham and Arlene. I'd also like to figure out how Hilton plays into all this."

"It's interesting how all roads seem to lead back to Mitcham. But how did all these people happen to hire the same private detective? What are the odds of that?"

TWENTY-SEVEN

Chief MacDonald sat with Brian Henderson and Joe Morelli in his office, discussing the Morris murder. Danielle had left fifteen minutes earlier. MacDonald felt frustration in not being able to share what he knew about Arlene and Mitcham. But how could he possibly tell his men a ghost over at Marlow House happened to see the killer kiss Arlene?

"Did Danielle have anything new that might help us?" Joe asked.

"Not really." The chief closed the file folder he had just been sorting through and tossed it on his desk.

"Does Danielle still have a full house?" Joe asked.

"I understand Chris Johnson moved out this morning."

"It's about time."

Ignoring Joe's comment, the chief said, "I think we need to take a closer look at Arlene Horton and David Hilton. After all, we know Hilton has a history with Morris, one he didn't disclose in our interview."

Brian thumbed through a file, reviewing his notes. "While I agree we need to take a closer look at everyone, I think the ones we need to focus on right now are those with a direct tie to Mitcham. Heather was the last one to see Morris alive—and she admits to hiring Mitcham. Kelly has a motive, connection to Mitcham, and she admits to being outside the house around the time of the murder."

"If Heather hired Mitcham to kill Morris, why do it where she's staying?" Joe asked. "I think the one with the most compelling motive is Will Wayne."

"I'd like to find out more about how Wayne happened to hire the same private detective as Heather," Brian said. "Maybe there's some connection between Heather and Wayne."

"Talk to the nurse who supposedly recommended Mitcham to Wayne. See what she knows," the chief told him.

CAROL BARNES SAT ALONE in a booth at Pier Café, waiting for Officer Brian Henderson to join her. She glanced at her watch. They had agreed to meet at the café. It would allow Carol time to grab something to eat before she had to be at her appointment.

The server was just bringing Carol her lunch when a man wearing a police uniform entered the café. Assuming he was Brian Henderson, she waved him over to her table.

"Are you Carol Barnes?" the officer asked when he reached her table.

"Yes. Are you Officer Henderson?"

"Yes. I appreciate you meeting with me on such short notice," Brian said as he took a seat across from her.

Carol looked apologetically at the plate of food before her. "I hope you don't mind, but I ordered myself something to eat. I've an appointment in an hour and missed breakfast."

"That's fine." Brian removed a small notepad from his pocket. "Please eat. We can talk while you have lunch."

The server who had brought Carol's food returned to the table. She looked at Brian. "Would you like to order something?"

"Just coffee, please."

When they were alone, Carol asked, "So how can I help you?"

"I understand you referred Logan Mitcham to Will Wayne," Brian began.

"The private detective?" Carol picked up her sandwich.

"Yes. How do you know him?"

"Oh, I don't know him. Never met him before." Carol took a bite of her sandwich.

"If you've never met him, how did you happen to refer him to Mr. Wayne?"

"As you probably already know, I'm one of the nurses who works with Mr. Wayne's wife, Karen." Carol set her sandwich back on her plate. "I suppose, technically speaking, she's his ex-wife. But considering how good he is to her, she might as well be his wife. I've gotten to know Mr. Wayne. We've spent a lot of time talking. When he told me about his daughter and the phone calls he received..." Carol paused a moment and looked up into Brian's eyes. "Do you know about the phone calls?"

"Are you referring to the anonymous caller who claimed Peter Morris had Isabella killed?"

Carol nodded and took a quick bite of her sandwich. A moment later she said, "I was at the house when he got one of the calls. He was pretty upset. I asked him what was wrong—if there was anything I could do. The poor man, he just broke down. You have to understand, it can be very stressful taking care of a loved one with Alzheimer's, even when you have help, like Mr. Wayne does. It's emotionally draining. And then to learn someone might have murdered his daughter."

The server brought Brian his coffee and then left the table. Brian asked Carol, "Did you ever suggest he go to the police?"

"I did at first. But he felt no one would listen to him if he didn't have some tangible proof. After all, the coroner's office ruled his daughter's death was from natural causes."

"So you recommended Mitcham?"

"Yes, considering the circumstances, I felt Mr. Mitcham was the best choice for him."

"How is that? I thought you said you had never met Mr. Mitcham before."

"Someone on the chat board recommended Mitcham. Told me if I wanted to hire a private detective to investigate Earthbound Spirits, he was the only one to use—because he'd been investigating Earthbound Spirits for a number of years, helping people whose family members got sucked into the group."

"What chat board?"

"I suppose I should explain." Carol placed her partially eaten sandwich back on her plate and took a sip of water. "I used to work at the hospital, and one of the other nurses got involved with Earthbound Spirits. I'd just moved into the area and had never heard of them before, so when Cora started talking about them, I was curious. I'm not a churchy person, and some of the things she told me sounded interesting."

"Are you saying you got involved with Earthbound Spirits?"

Carol let out a short laugh and shook her head. "Heavens no! But I'll admit I was intrigued. Not curious enough to go to one of the rallies Cora tried to get me to attend, but I wanted to know more about them. So I went online. That's when I came across the forum on cults and an ongoing discussion about Earthbound Spirits."

Brian remembered what Heather had told him. "Someone on the forum mentioned Mitcham?"

"Not on the forum, exactly—but in a private message. No one on the forum uses their real names. But one of the regular posters—someone who goes by CultCurious—sent me a private message. I'd been discussing Cora on the forum, but I never mentioned her name or where she worked, just that I was concerned about her after reading what everyone was saying about the group."

"What did CultCurious say in the private message?"

"He told me if I wanted to help my friend, or if her family needed some way to get her away from the group, I should contact Logan Mitcham. I figure everyone has a right to whatever wacky religion they want to follow. So I told CultCurious thanks, but that I had no intention of contacting the private investigator. But then later, when Mr. Wayne told me about his daughter and his concerns, I remembered the private message and gave Mr. Wayne the private investigator's name."

"Do you still frequent the forum?" Brian asked.

"No. I surfed around on the site for about a week and chatted there for a couple of days. But then I switched jobs and didn't see Cora again. That was about six months ago." Carol shrugged. "I didn't think too much about Earthbound Spirits after that."

"And you remembered Logan Mitcham's name?"

"Heavens, no." Carol laughed. "I told Mr. Wayne about the private detective I'd heard about, and then I logged back into the chat room. I'd never deleted my private messages, so it was fairly easy to pull up the old message with the detective's name."

"BOTH HEATHER DONOVAN and Will Wayne found Logan Mitcham through the same chatroom. In both instances someone with the handle CultCurious recommended Mitcham," Brian told Joe and MacDonald as the three men sat in the break room, eating lunch.

After Brian detailed his interview with Carol Barnes, Joe set his burger on a napkin and picked up his cellphone. He opened a browser and ran a quick search. Looking up to Brian, he asked, "Did you find out the name of this forum or chat room? The one CultCurious hangs out in?"

After Brian gave Joe the website's name, Joe asked, "Why hasn't Kelly Bartley mentioned this chat room?"

The chief looked over at Joe. "Why would she? She met Mitcham because he's her neighbor."

"Or so she says." Joe popped a French fry in his mouth.

"What do you mean?" Brian asked. "We know he lives down-stairs from her."

"Kelly claims to be researching Earthbound Spirits for the exposé Ian's working on. If that's true, then she has to be familiar with this website—it's one of the first links that come up when I did my search on Earthbound Spirits and complaints."

The chief shrugged. "She probably knows about the website, but the fact that she didn't mention it doesn't really have a bearing on the case."

"How do you figure that, Chief?" Joe asked. "Kelly claimed she had no idea Mitcham was a private detective working on cases trying to uncover dirt on Morris and his group. Who's to say she wasn't given Mitcham's name when she posted on the group, just like Heather and the nurse?"

"What makes you think she posted on the forum?" the chief asked.

"Come on, seriously? There is no way she missed this website, and since she's researching the group, what better place to hook up with others who have stories about Earthbound Spirits than this forum? Which means she'd be asking questions."

"Let's say she has posted on the site; there's no reason to jump to the conclusion that CultCurious sent her a private message like he did with several others," the chief reminded him.

"I agree, but it doesn't mean we shouldn't look into it." Joe studied the chief for a moment. "I don't get you, Chief, this isn't like you. I'd think you'd be the first to check out Kelly's browser history, see if she had more of a connection to our missing PI than just being his neighbor."

"You're thinking she may have hired him to kill Morris?" Brian asked.

"I think it's something we need to look into." Joe popped another French fry into his mouth.

The chief sat quietly at the table, thinking about what Danielle had told him earlier about Arlene Horton. That was the real reason he felt Joe's focus on Kelly was wasted energy. He was about to ask Joe just how did Kelly know Morris was going to be at Marlow House, when he realized the same question could be asked of Arlene. Of course, according to Danielle, her husband's ghost claimed Arlene seemed surprised the private detective was at Marlow House. With a groan, MacDonald pressed the heel of his right hand against his forehead.

"You all right, Chief?" Brian asked.

"This case is giving me a headache."

PAGE AFTER PAGE filled the laser printer's tray while Ian stood, smiling down at the machine. Lily walked into his home office, carrying two cups of coffee. She handed him one and then took a sip from the remaining cup.

"So this is it?" she asked.

"The article, anyway. I need to go through it and approve the editor's changes," he explained.

"I can't wait to read it. I know Danielle's really anxious to. Are you going to make us wait until the article comes out in the magazine?"

"Maybe it would be better if you didn't read the article and wait until the book comes out in a couple months," Ian teased.

"Yeah, right, like that's happening." Lily laughed. "I intend to read both the article and the book."

Ian wrapped his arm around Lily's shoulder and gave her a quick squeeze. "I appreciate your support."

"Hey, this story was my idea. I'm just thrilled you thought it was a good one. This is kind of an extra Valentine's Day gift—the article version of the Emma Jackson story back from the editor."

Ian gave her cheek a quick kiss. "Does that mean I don't need to give you anything else for Valentine's Day?"

Playfully nudging him with her elbow, she said, "I don't think so."

"Umm...guys..." Kelly interrupted a moment later. Ian and Lily looked to the doorway, where Kelly stood. "I don't think I can leave today."

"That's fine, Kelly." Ian studied his sister for a moment. "Is something wrong?"

"I just got a call from Brian Henderson. They want me to come back in. They need to ask me more questions," she said dully, her eyes filling with tears.

"Kelly, maybe I should go with you," Ian suggested.

"Do you think I need a lawyer?"

TWENTY-EIGHT

D amp and frigid, the sea breeze intensified, morphing into a robust gust that dislodged Danielle's braid. Brushing errant strands behind her ear, she hurried to the front door, pulling the jacket tight around her body. Before she had time to knock on the door, it swung open. Without a second thought, she rushed inside the beach bungalow.

Chris slammed the door closed behind her. "Not the best day to move."

"It's freezing out there! The wind just came out of nowhere." Danielle shivered. She immediately walked across the room and looked out the back sliding-glass door. The house boasted an unobstructed view of the ocean. "I sure wouldn't get tired of this view."

"It's really something, isn't it?" Chris asked, standing beside her. "I'd offer you some hot coffee or something, but I haven't gone to the store yet."

"That's okay, I'm coffeed out." No longer shivering, she glanced around the room. "You know, this furniture isn't bad."

"The place has everything—fully furnished, linens, pots, and pans."

"Not everything. It doesn't have coffee." Danielle grinned.

"You said you didn't want coffee."

"Oh, I'm just teasing. I've already exceeded today's coffee quota. But you know, a house is not a home until there's food in the fridge."

"Like I said, I haven't gone to the store yet."

"You need minions, Chris. You can afford them."

"Minions?" Chris laughed.

"Sure. To do all your mundane tasks, like clean your house and buy your groceries."

Chris cocked his brows. "Do you have minions?"

"I have Joanne. But I really wouldn't call her a minion."

"And then there's Lily."

Danielle laughed. "I think Lily and I take turns being each other's minion—one day it's her; the next it's me."

"Very democratic of you." Chris grinned. He then asked seriously, "Did you talk to the chief yet?"

"Yeah. I stopped over there this morning right after I left the house."

"Have you been there all this time?"

"No. I had some errands to run. Thought I'd stop by here before heading back home. Hope you don't mind."

"Don't be goofy. You're always welcome. So what did the chief say?" Chris led the way over to the leather sectional facing the sliding glass door. They both sat down.

"I think he would've been happier if I'd had something more tangible on Arlene aside from according to my dead husband."

Chris leaned back in the sectional, propping one of his legs over his opposing knee. "He'll have to take what you have. I'm just glad Joanne admitted to putting my knife in the parlor. I still think your pal Joe would love to hang this one on me."

"I don't know what Joe's problem is."

"I do," Chris said under his breath.

Danielle flashed Chris a reproving smirk. "Oh please, I've had my issues with Joe, but I don't believe for a minute he would ever try to hang a murder conviction on someone over jealousy."

"He arrested you for murder," Chris reminded her.

"I know. How can I forget? You and Walt keep reminding me. But Joe arrested me because he sincerely believed I'd killed my cousin. He didn't arrest me out of spite because he was jealous."

"So you do admit he's jealous?"

"Well—" Danielle sighed "—he does keep asking me out for Valentine's Day. I'd really hoped he and I would just move onto a friendship phase and he'd stop trying to rekindle our nonexistent romance."

"You could have simply told him you already had a date for Valentine's Day." Chris flashed Danielle a boyish grin.

She smiled. "If my life wasn't so complicated right now—between a murder in my parlor, a houseful of suspects, and Lucas's spirit rambling around Marlow House—I might be tempted to take you up on that Valentine's Day date. How about a rain check?"

"I'd like that."

They sat in silence for a few moments until Chris finally asked, "So what's next in the investigation, do you think?"

"I know they're still trying to track down the private detective."

"Do they think he's taken off?"

Danielle shrugged. "I don't know. It sure looks like he's the one who killed Morris. After all, it was his fingerprint, and Lucas saw a man kill Morris. I have to assume that man was Mitcham. The chief hasn't been all that sharey with me on the details. I just know they're still looking for him. So I have to assume they're watching his condo and office."

"I really don't like the idea of Arlene and David staying at Marlow House. When are they leaving?"

"They paid for the entire weekend. I expect they'll take off tomorrow by noon. Not sure what their plans are tonight. We're not offering anything for dinner like we did over Christmas."

"I'll just feel better knowing they're no longer there, especially since you and Lily are alone, with me here now."

Danielle laughed. "Hardly alone. We have Walt, and he's promised to keep an eye on them. And don't forget Heather."

"Heather? She's not on my list of favorites after she tossed me under the bus."

"I have to admit she did seem quick to point the finger at you when the cops were looking for a murder suspect."

"We're forgetting someone else you have over there…"

"That's right. Lucas." Danielle sighed.

Chris started to say something when the doorbell rang. He jumped up from the couch and headed to the door.

"I come bringing pizza!" Adam announced when Chris opened the front door. "And champagne!" Adam held a pizza box in one hand and a bottle of champagne in the other. As he entered the room and Chris shut the door, Danielle stood up from the sectional to greet him.

"I saw your car out there," Adam told Danielle as he walked

into the kitchen and set his housewarming gifts on the kitchen counter. "I almost didn't come in."

Danielle stood by the kitchen sink, watching Chris open the box of pizza. She glanced to Adam and asked, "Why wouldn't you come in?"

"Well…you know…" Adam looked from Danielle to Chris, back to Danielle, a smirk on his face while wiggling his eyebrows.

"Oh…" Danielle scowled. "Always with the dirty mind."

"I'm starved," Chris told them, snatching up a slice of pizza and taking a bite.

Danielle studied Adam for a minute. "Just how do you do that?"

"What?" Adam tucked a napkin under a slice of pizza and handed it to Danielle. "Have an active imagination?"

"No. Wiggle your eyebrows like that." She took a bite of the pizza, still looking at Adam. Once again, his dark brows wiggled.

"It's a gift," Adam said with a dramatic sigh. He took a slice of pizza for himself.

"Please tell me you brought beer," Chris said, picking up the bottle of champagne and looking at it.

"Actually, I did. It's still in the car. I'll be right back." Still holding his slice of pizza, Adam dashed outside.

"Wow, you're a demanding client. The guy comes with pizza and champagne, and all you say is where's the beer?" Danielle teased.

"It is all about priorities, Danielle. Priorities."

When Adam returned with the beer a few minutes later, he sat with Danielle and Chris at the kitchen table.

"I really do want to thank you for bringing the pizza and beer— and the champagne." Chris took a swig of beer.

"I figured the pizza and beer were to celebrate your new home. The champagne is for another celebration." Adam lifted his can of beer in mock salute.

"I got it?" Chris asked.

Danielle glanced from Adam to Chris. "You got what?"

"The Gusarov Estate," Adam explained. "They accepted his offer."

"Well, that's great!" Danielle lifted her can of beer. "Congratulations."

"Thanks. I haven't even been in it yet."

"Want me to take you over there today?" Adam offered.

"I just hope the place isn't haunted," Danielle murmured as she took another sip of beer.

Adam stood up. "Funny, Danielle." Tossing his napkin onto the table, he headed for the bathroom.

When Adam was out of earshot, Chris asked, "Haunted? Are you trying to be funny?"

Danielle wrinkled her nose and cringed. "Well, actually…when I agreed it would be a great building for you, I didn't stop to consider it's always possible…well…"

"Possible what?"

"Stoddard was murdered there. Of course, he never haunted his own place; he decided to torment me instead. And after he realized I wasn't responsible for his death, well, I'm pretty sure he moved on…but still…" She took another sip of her beer.

"You saying Stoddard's ghost might be at the estate?"

Danielle considered the possibility for a moment. Finally, she shook her head. "Nah, probably not. After all, I don't remember seeing his ghost there—just Darlene's."

"Darlene? His wife?"

"Yeah, but you don't have anything to worry about there. She's busy haunting Pilgrim's Point."

Chris glared at Danielle. "If you got me to buy a haunted house…"

Danielle smiled. "Nah, I'm just teasing you. It's not haunted." She took a quick gulp of beer and thought, *I hope it's not haunted.*

When Adam returned from the bathroom a few minutes later, Danielle changed the subject. "Hey, Adam, you know your friend Arlene, the one staying at Marlow House?"

"Sure, what about her?" Adam sat back down at the table.

"Any idea how long she's been with David?"

"You asking because of his last name?" Adam asked.

Danielle shrugged. "What are the chances, Helen Hilton's grandson being at Marlow House the same time Peter Morris is murdered?"

"I'd assume the police have talked to him already."

"Honestly, I have no idea." Danielle sighed.

"I know it's a bizarre coincidence. And frankly, I know zip about this Hilton guy other than reading about the family when the lawsuit was going on. But that was a number of years ago, and if a guy has the patience to wait around before killing the man who screwed his family out of a fortune, I'd have to assume he'd have a better alibi. Something other than I was sleeping upstairs."

"What about Arlene?"

"What about her?"

"Did she have any grievances against the group?"

Adam frowned at Danielle. "Where's this coming from?"

"She's just trying to cover all the bases," Chris offered. "Adam, you have no idea how stressful all of this has been. Waking up to find a dead body in the next room tends to make one paranoid."

"I'm not paranoid," Danielle muttered.

Chris patted her hand. "You know what I mean."

In response, Danielle rolled her eyes at Chris.

"Maybe Arlene had some issues with the group, but she'd never hurt anyone. I know her better than that," Adam insisted.

"How well do we really know anyone? Especially casual friends," Danielle asked.

"We weren't casual friends," Adam confessed.

"When you said she was someone you knew when dating Isabella, I assume she was a casual friend. So you and Isabella were close to Arlene?"

"Not exactly." Adam set his beer can on the table. "Arlene and I had a brief affair back when I was dating Isabella."

Chris paused mid-sip. Still holding the can of beer by his mouth, he looked at Adam, who was now looking from Danielle to him. Before taking a swig of beer, Chris said, "Hey, don't look at me. Who am I to judge?"

"Oh…" Danielle cringed. "Sorry, I didn't mean to pry."

"Sure you did." Adam flashed her a half smile. "Isabella and I were having some issues—she was getting deeper and deeper into Earthbound Spirits. I needed someone to talk to; Arlene was there. One thing led to another."

"Was that when you two broke up?" Danielle asked.

Adam shook his head. "No. I stayed with Isabella. But we broke up not long after that. She never knew about Arlene. And I didn't see Arlene again until Thursday morning."

TWENTY-NINE

"Ian, you and Lily need to wait out here while Joe talks to your sister," the chief explained when Ian, Lily, and Kelly arrived at the Frederickport Police Department.

"Is Kelly under arrest?" Ian asked just as Joe stepped into the room.

"Under arrest?" Kelly gasped.

Joe frowned at Ian. "Why would you ask that?"

Ian reached out and gave his sister's hand a gentle squeeze. "I just don't see why I can't sit in with her while you question her."

"Ian, this really will go much quicker if you just let Kelly go in with Joe," MacDonald said.

"If I'm not under arrest, does that mean I can just leave now?" Kelly asked, sounding more confident than she had looked just moments earlier.

"Yes, I suppose so," the chief said. "But I really hope you don't do that."

"Okay," Kelly said, no longer holding onto Ian's hand. "I'll talk to Sergeant Morelli, alone."

"You sure, Kel?" Ian asked.

"Yeah, I'll be fine."

"I WANT to thank you for coming back in," Joe said after he closed the door and gestured toward the table.

"I just want you to know, if I don't like your questions, I'll get up and leave. Do you understand?" Kelly took a seat.

Joe tossed his notebook onto the table and looked at her for a moment before sitting down. "I'd say that's rather a shift in attitude compared to when you first walked in the door."

"I just don't like being bullied," Kelly said primly.

"I don't believe anyone has bullied you, Ms. Bartley."

"Ms. Bartley? What happened to Kelly?"

"I was under the impression you might take offense to an informal greeting."

"Just because I'm not going to let you bully me, you don't have to pretend you don't even know me."

Joe let out a weary sigh. "I'm not pretending anything."

"I know all about that two-way mirror." Kelly nodded toward the mirror. "I also know how you arrested Danielle for her cousin's murder, when she was innocent."

"I regret any pain I caused Danielle, and I believe she knows that. I'm not here to pass judgment on you, Kelly; I simply want to ask you a few questions."

"Fine. Because I didn't have anything to do with Peter Morris's death. Just because I didn't like the man doesn't mean I killed him. Heck, there are lots of people I dislike, and I've never killed any of them."

Joe smiled. "I'm happy to hear that."

He pulled out his cellphone and opened his browser window. "Could you please tell me if you're familiar with this website?" He showed her his cellphone.

Leaning forward, she looked closely at the small monitor. "Why sure, that's the website on cults. They have a thread about Earthbound Spirits."

Joe set the phone down. "So you're familiar with the site?"

Kelly shrugged and visibly relaxed. "Sure. Is that why you brought me in here, to ask me about that website?" She leaned forward again. "Oh…I get it. You want to use it to locate people who had it out for Peter Morris. I bet you'll find a bunch."

"Is there a reason you didn't mention the website when you spoke to us earlier?"

Kelly frowned. "Why would I do that? You didn't ask me for a list of websites. I told you I did research for Ian. You knew he was doing an exposé on Earthbound Spirits."

"Does this mean you're familiar with CultCurious?"

"Oh, CultCurious. Yeah, he's a regular on there."

"Have you two ever exchanged private messages?"

"No, never. But I'm pretty sure he has with other posters."

"Why is that?" Joe asked.

"Every once in a while someone will post something like *thank you, CultCurious* or *you're the best, CultCurious.* But it's never something in response to a previous post, so I have to assume it's in response to something they talked about in private."

"What kind of things did you post about on the board? I assume you posted there."

"At first, I mainly read it. The different members share their stories—you know, about how some friend or relative got sucked into the cult. Or how someone they knew turned over all their money to Earthbound Spirits. Stuff like that."

"Did you ever post?"

"After a while, when I wanted to ask a question. I didn't really share on the board."

"You never discussed your friend Candice?"

"Yes, but never publicly, only in private message."

"Why only in private message?"

"Anyone can join that site and read what people are posting. I was there to find others who'd been hurt by Morris's group. I wasn't there to vent or find support. When I messaged someone from the group, I was always up front with them. I let them know I was working on a story about the cult. And then I would share a little bit about Candice's story, without getting into specifics. I just wanted them to know I understood. That way they were more inclined to share."

"Did anyone ever suggest you hire a private detective?"

Kelly frowned. "You mean someone like Mitch?"

Joe paused and studied Kelly. "I thought you didn't know what he did for a living?"

"Danielle told me after you talked to me the last time. She recognized his name and told me Will Wayne had hired someone by that name to investigate Peter Morris."

"Well...did anyone?" Joe asked.

Kelly frowned. "Did anyone what?"

"Suggest you hire a private detective to help you with the article."

Kelly shifted uncomfortably in the chair, fidgeting with her purse.

"So someone did suggest you hire a private detective? Someone did mention Mitcham to you? Is that it?"

Kelly let out a sigh. "No, of course not."

"Then what is it?"

"I guess I sort of gave some of them the impression I was a private detective—after all, I was researching Earthbound Spirits. I didn't say that exactly, but a couple people sort of got that idea."

"Was this on the open board or in a private message?""

"Only in the private messages. So you see, why would they suggest I hire someone if they assumed that's what I did for a living?"

"Did you ever have any contact with CultCurious?"

Kelly shook her head. "I told you I never exchanged messages with him. And I don't remember ever responding directly to any of his posts. Although, a couple times he responded to mine."

"How do you know CultCurious is a male? Or do you?"

"I don't really. I suppose it could be a girl. Why are you so interested in CultCurious?"

"I really can't say at this time."

"I do remember one thing," Kelly said hesitantly.

"What?"

"Once I was in a private chat with one of the regulars there—JoJo45—and she told me CultCurious had asked about me in a private chat. I guess he wanted to know what my deal was, since I'd ask questions on the board, but never shared any stories."

"Did he share his stories?"

Kelly shook her head. "No, not really. After JoJo45 told me what CultCurious had asked her about, I asked her the same question about him. Which, now that I think about it, is probably why I think of CultCurious as a guy because JoJo45 referred to him that way. Anyway, according to JoJo45, CultCurious had been an Earthbound Spirits member, but soon became disillusioned with the group. She never said that anything particularly bad had happened to him. He never claimed to lose a bunch of money or anything."

"So JoJo45 was a woman?"

Kelly smiled. "Yeah. I know because during one of our private chats, she shared how she was a new grandma."

"What was your handle?"

"Mine? KellyB."

LILY STOOD UP. "I'll be right back."

Cellphone in hand, Ian remained seated, silently surfing the Internet. Without looking up, he mumbled, "Okay."

Lily's first stop was the chief's office, but he wasn't there. Walking down the corridor of the inner offices of the police department, she got a few inquiring glances from staff members, yet no one asked her where she was going or who she was looking for. She found Chief MacDonald in the break room, pouring himself a cup of coffee.

"Hey, Chief," Lily greeted him when she entered the room.

"How did you get in here?" he asked.

"Your security sucks."

The chief smiled. "You come to say goodbye?"

"Not until Joe's done with Kelly."

"He is. Kelly left the interrogation room a few minutes ago." The chief took a sip of his coffee.

Lily frowned. "I didn't see her."

"I heard her ask Joe where the bathroom was. She was probably in there."

"Were you in the interrogation room with her and Joe?"

The chief smiled and took another sip.

"Oh, I get it. What's with you guys? A bunch of voyeurs."

The chief laughed.

"What was all this about? Why are you dragging Kelly down here when it's Arlene you should be interviewing?" Lily asked in a whisper.

"Danielle told you?"

"Yes, before she left this morning. Told me about Lucas and what he saw."

"Damn, it must be insane living at Marlow House."

Lily rolled her eyes. "You have no idea."

"About Arlene, you have to understand, I can't very well drag her down here based on something Danielle's dead husband told her."

"Does that mean you're just going to ignore it and harass poor Kelly?"

"Don't be dramatic, Lily. No one is harassing Kelly. And your boyfriend—and his sister—did mislead us during the first interviews."

"I know. Ian regrets that. But you have to understand, it's his job."

"Yes. And I have my job. I've a murder to solve, one that happened under your roof."

"Don't you think I know that? What about Arlene? For goodness' sake, she kissed the man who killed Peter Morris!"

"According to Danielle, he kissed her."

"Whatever." Lily shrugged.

"Don't worry, Lily, I'm not ignoring Arlene. For the moment I'm just trying to assemble as much information as I can."

"Any word on that Mitcham dude?"

"No. He still hasn't shown up."

Lily's phone began to buzz. She looked at it. "It's Ian; he's waiting out front with Kelly."

"I imagine you want to get out of here. It is Valentine's Day."

"Yeah, Ian had planned something romantic at his house, but it looks like he'll have a houseguest for another night—thanks to you."

"I'm sorry, Lily."

"Yeah." Lily shrugged. "You and Carol Ann doing anything special for Valentine's Day?"

"We have a late dinner reservation and a babysitter set up for the kids."

"Well, have fun."

"You too, Lily."

THIRTY

C hief MacDonald remembered a time when investigating a suspect didn't involve sitting in front of a computer, searching through social media sites. When he first started in law enforcement, the small community he worked for at the time didn't even have Internet access. While he would normally assign someone from his office to search for information on a person of interest, he felt this particular job was best left to him, considering he was unable to share with his people what he knew about Arlene Horton.

Focusing his attention on the computer monitor, he reached for his coffee cup and then took a sip. The cold coffee made him cringe. Instead of spitting it out, he reluctantly swallowed and set the mug back onto the desk, shoving it aside.

Turning his attention back to the search, he clicked one more time, only to find an answer to one of his questions: *Did Arlene Horton have a personal grudge against Peter Morris?*

"Damn," he muttered to the silent room. "That's a pretty good motive for murder."

MacDonald didn't stop there. He continued the online search, moving next to the chat website that Kelly, Heather, and Carol had used. It was almost 4:00 p.m. on Valentine's Day when he turned off his monitor and called Brian and Joe into his office.

"I've finished reading through the postings on the cult watch website," Joe announced when he and Brian entered MacDonald's office. "Kelly was telling the truth, no back and forth between her handle and CultCurious." Both Joe and Brian took a seat.

"I haven't gotten far in tracking down the identity of CultCurious," Brian added. "But I created a profile there, chatted it up a bit with a few people—they're all talking about Morris's murder. CultCurious hasn't posted since Wednesday morning."

"Did you notice the handle JusticeNow?" Joe asked.

Brian nodded. "Yes. I was going to mention it. JusticeNow's story sure sounds like the one Kelly told about her roommate."

"Kelly never said anything about her friend's sister being a member on the forum, and JusticeNow was a pretty active member. I can only think of one reason why Kelly wouldn't mention it: because she's JusticeNow," Joe suggested.

"You think Kelly created two handles?" Brian asked.

"Seems all three of us have been surfing the same site." The chief picked up a stack of papers on his desk and shuffled through them, making two piles.

"You too?" Joe asked. "I rather thought you'd be heading out early. You don't normally work on Saturday, and it is Valentine's Day. Don't you have something special planned with Carol Ann?"

"A late dinner. I've plenty of time to make it. But first, we need to stop at Marlow House."

Brian frowned. "Marlow House? We? As in the three of us?"

The chief looked at Brian. "I think you should be there."

"What's this about?" Joe asked.

"I've been taking a closer look at Arlene Horton," the chief explained.

"Arlene Horton? You talking about Hilton's girlfriend?" Joe asked.

The chief nodded. "It appears we didn't take a close enough look into her background. Of all our suspects—"

"Arlene is a suspect?" Brian interrupted. "Maybe Hilton's accomplice."

"Of all the persons of interest, Arlene has the most compelling motive," the chief explained.

"More compelling than Will Wayne? He believes Morris killed his daughter. I can't imagine a better motive," Brian said.

"What about Kelly? If she had a second handle, then she lied to us about talking with CultCurious on the site. By the back and forth between those two, it's obvious JusticeNow and CultCurious exchanged private messages."

"Let's put Kelly on the back burner for now," the chief said. "As for Wayne, I agree his motive trumps Arlene's, even if Isabella died of natural causes. Because Wayne doesn't know that," MacDonald said.

Joe frowned. "Then why do you say she has the most compelling motive?"

"More compelling when you consider she was at the scene of the crime," the chief explained.

"True, but Kelly was just across the street, and she initially lied to us about being outside the house around the time of the murder," Joe reminded him. "And she has a reason to hate Morris."

"Perhaps, but I think we need to take a closer look at Arlene Horton." He then went on to explain Arlene's motive for killing Morris, while handing each man a stack of the papers.

"I don't understand," Joe muttered. "I checked out Arlene's background. She's an only child, grew up in Vancouver, Washington. Her father is the deacon of their church, where she's an active member."

The chief arched his brows. "So?"

"But her father is a deacon," Joe repeated.

Brian rolled his eyes at his partner. "Oh please, Joe, the chief is right. So? You don't think a churchgoing man can have secrets?"

Joe thumbed through his papers. "This is not exactly a secret," he muttered. "Not if Arlene posted all this stuff on her Facebook page...which I obviously missed."

"In your defense," the chief said, "those posts are over two years old."

Joe tossed the papers on the desk and looked up. "What made you go back that far?"

"Just a hunch." It wasn't exactly a lie, MacDonald told himself.

Still holding his papers, Brian leaned back in the chair and looked across the desk at MacDonald. "What now?"

"I obviously want us to talk to her again. But I don't want to do it down here."

"Why not?" Joe asked.

"For one thing, I'd like a certain element of surprise. At this point, she figures we totally missed her connection to Morris. If we drag her down to the police station, it'll give her time to second-guess what we might ask her. Plus, stopping by and telling her we just need to ask a few questions will seem less threatening. She'll assume we're asking her as a witness, not a suspect."

"I'd like to hear Hilton's explanation for withholding his family's connection to Morris," Joe added.

"I also suspect Arlene and Hilton aren't quite lovers," the chief added.

"Why do you say that?" Joe asked.

"If you'll look at page three of the conversations I printed out from the forum, I've a feeling Arlene and Hilton hooked up on that site. I can't be a hundred percent sure, but if you read it, my guess, Arlene's handle is NeedAnswers and Hilton's is FortuneLost666."

Joe retrieved his papers from the desk while Brian shuffled through his, looking for the pages in question. After finding them and reading through the exchange, Brian said, "You know, it really wouldn't surprise me to find out those two are posing as lovers."

"This sure sounds like it could be them," Joe muttered as he continued to read.

"Brian, why wouldn't you be surprised?" the chief asked.

"Because when we were called to Marlow House the night of the murder, they were all wearing nightclothes. Arlene was dressed in a floor-length, flannel nightgown, not an inch of skin showing. Not exactly sexy night wear for a romantic weekend with a lover."

"Well, it has been cold," Joe suggested.

Brian laughed. "Maybe, but I doubt that was the only reason for wearing flannel. Unless, of course, Hilton has some sort of flannel fetish."

Joe tossed the papers onto the desk.

"More I think about it, it makes sense," Brian added.

With a sigh, Joe said, "Maybe so, but how did they know Morris was stopping at Marlow House? From all accounts, it was a spur of the moment visit. Morris was already parked outside when he called Chris Johnson and told him he was going to stop over."

Brian tossed his papers with Joe's and stood up. "What we do know is—that fingerprint belongs to Logan Mitcham, and according to what the lab told us today, the blood belonged to Morris. So it's a safe bet someone hired Mitcham to kill Morris. According to Wayne, Mitcham offered to set him up with a hit man, and it's pretty clear the hit man he was talking about was himself."

"Maybe Arlene and Hilton did team up together and hired

Mitcham to kill Morris; they both had a motive to want the man dead," Joe said. "But why even bother coming to town? Isn't that the point of hiring a hit man, to keep a distance between yourself and the crime scene? And why kill Morris under the same roof as the people who paid for the hit? And how in the hell did they time everything, getting Morris to Marlow House?"

Brian sat back down. "Maybe it was a crime of opportunity. Logan Mitcham is a private detective. He was probably trailing Peter Morris."

"What, and this is some colossal coincidence?" Joe asked. "He follows Morris to Marlow House, where, three—no, four, if you count Chris—people have motives to kill Morris, happen to be staying. Oh, and let's not forget Kelly Bartley, she also has a motive, and she was just across the street. Our killer conveniently finds a murder weapon waiting for him in the parlor, which he considerately leaves behind so we don't have to keep searching for it."

"Well, now that you put it that way…" Brian slouched back in his chair. "It would sure be a hell of a lot easier if we could track down Logan Mitcham and see what he has to say."

"Hopefully, we'll have him in custody shortly, but in the meantime, we have two people we can talk to."

"You know, now that I think about it, if Horton and Hilton really had nothing to do with any of this, wouldn't they have just left yesterday?" Brian suggested. "Good lord, someone was just murdered where they're staying, and the killer is still on the loose."

"You have a point," Joe agreed. "Nothing like spoiling the mood of a romantic weekend than finding a man butchered downstairs."

"They probably figured if they left too soon, people would get suspicious, while an innocent person wouldn't even consider that; they'd just want to get the hell out of Dodge," Brian speculated.

"WHY HASN'T HE CALLED?" David asked, pacing the bedroom he shared with Arlene.

"I told you we should just leave. Can we please just leave?" Arlene pleaded.

"Just because Peter Morris is dead, it doesn't mean this is over. Earthbound Spirits' corruption needs to be exposed."

"David, don't you understand, with Peter Morris dead—this changes everything."

"Why?"

"For one thing, don't you think someone is going to start looking at us?"

"They haven't so far. And anyway, we had nothing to do with his murder."

"Maybe not, but we sure as hell had a reason to want the man dead!"

"That's why we need to keep the appointment," David insisted. "I bet anything someone from Earthbound Spirits killed him. It's an inside job. A power play. Who's next in line with him dead? That faux religious nonprofit controls a fortune in assets."

Walt lounged on the bed in David and Arlene's room, watching them argue. It was the first time they'd said anything of interest—anything that remotely alluded to the murder. He continued to listen until Arlene left David to take her shower and dress for wherever they intended to go for dinner.

Danielle was just entering the front door when Walt appeared in the entry hall. "You've been gone all day," Walt greeted her, sounding somewhat annoyed. "Where have you been?"

Glancing around, Danielle asked in a whisper, "Where is everyone?"

"Joanne is in the kitchen. Lily is over at Ian's. I've no idea where Heather is—I just know she isn't here—and our lovebirds are up in their room. Well, more accurately, David is in their room, and Arlene is in the shower."

Danielle nodded to the parlor. "Let's talk in there."

"I think I found out something about your lovebirds," Walt said after Danielle shut the parlor door. He took a seat on the sofa and watched as Danielle sat in the chair across from him.

"What's that?"

"First, I don't believe they're lovebirds. I don't even believe they're close friends."

"Really?"

"One thing they do share: they both hated Peter Morris and they both want to see Earthbound Spirits taken down."

"That doesn't surprise me, considering Hilton's family. And we already know Arlene has some sort of personal relationship with the killer."

"She may be involved with the murder, but I don't think David is. One thing I do know, if either of them had something to do with the murder, they're keeping that fact from each other."

"Why do you think that?" Danielle asked.

"When I was listening to them, David kept reiterating how they weren't involved in the murder, while Arlene kept asking him if they could go home now. She does not want to be here."

"Why are they here? Innocent or guilty, I expected them to check out early."

Walt glanced up to the ceiling. "According to David, they're supposed to meet someone. That's why they're still here."

"Meet who?"

Walt shrugged. "They didn't mention his name. Only that they were waiting for his phone call. David seemed to think it was more important to meet him now that Morris was dead, while Arlene seemed to think now that Morris was dead, there was no reason to meet him."

"I suppose if—" Danielle stopped talking when she heard the doorbell.

Before answering the door, she peeked outside the parlor window. "It's the chief. He's with Joe and Brian."

THIRTY-ONE

W hy didn't David listen to me? Arlene asked herself. If he had, she wouldn't be sitting alone with Police Chief MacDonald in Marlow House's library. Combing her fingers through her damp hair, Arlene wished she had used her blow dryer before coming downstairs to get a cup of hot tea. Finding the three police officers standing in Marlow House's entry didn't surprise her, considering what had happened the day before. What did surprise her was finding herself alone in the library with the police chief while David was in another room with the other two officers.

"Will this take long?" she asked. "I really would like to finish getting ready. David and I have a reservation, and I still need to fix my hair. It is Valentine's Day, and well…that is why we came for the weekend."

"Really? Is that the only reason?" the chief asked.

Releasing hold of a damp curl, Arlene dropped her hand to her lap. "What do you mean?"

"Is there a reason you failed to mention your connection to our victim?"

Arlene stared blankly at the chief. "I have no connection to Peter Morris."

"Maybe not directly. But your brother certainly did."

Dejectedly dropping her head, she looked down at her lap and then closed her eyes. "You know."

"Yes. Why didn't you tell us Cleve Monchique was your brother?"

After releasing a heavy sigh, she lifted her head and met MacDonald's gaze. "Everything happened so fast."

"Were you involved in the murder of Peter Morris?"

"No!" Arlene adamantly shook her head. "I had nothing to do with his death! I was as surprised as anyone to see him lying on the floor—obviously murdered. No, absolutely not!"

"So why didn't you tell us Cleve was your brother?"

Arlene shrugged. "I never lied. I answered all your questions. I was afraid if I told you about my brother...I didn't want to get involved."

"I'm surprised you stayed and didn't leave after the murder. I know if I was on a romantic vacation and something like that happened, I'd check out early."

"I wanted to," Arlene muttered. She looked down to her hands, which now fidgeted nervously in her lap.

"Why did you and Mr. Hilton really come to Frederickport?"

"We told you...just a holiday..." Arlene whispered.

"I think it's time you be honest with me. After all, David is in the other room with Officers Morelli and Henderson, and I'm certain they'll convince him to explain why the two of you really came here. We also know about Helen Hilton."

"Am I under arrest?" she asked.

"No."

"So I'm free to go?"

"Yes. But that doesn't mean I can't decide later to bring you in for questioning—at the police station."

DOWN THE HALL in the parlor, David Hilton stiffly perched on a chair facing Joe and Brian, who sat together on the small sofa. David's eyes were unable to keep from looking at the floor, where just the day before the grizzly sight of Peter Morris, his throat slashed, sprawled before the sofa.

"Do we have to do this in here?" David asked.

"Does it bother you, knowing Peter Morris was killed in here?" Brian asked.

David shifted nervously in his chair. "I've never seen a dead person before. And certainly never one who'd been attacked like that. Hard not to think about it." He looked up into the officer's face. "Why am I here?"

"Can you explain why you never disclosed your past differences with Peter Morris?" Brian asked.

"I assume you mean the lawsuit against Earthbound Spirits."

"Yes. Don't you think that's something you should have mentioned?" Joe asked.

"Why? It's public knowledge. I didn't hide my name. Figured if you wanted to ask me something about it, you would."

"So you're saying you weren't concealing—by omission—the grievance you had with Peter Morris and his organization?" Joe asked.

"If you're implying I had something to do with his death—that I was hiding the fact our family was bilked out of our rightful inheritance by those con men to cover up my motive for wanting the man dead, you're totally off base. I didn't want to see Morris dead. I wanted to bring the SOB down and hold him accountable for all the damage he's done to countless people."

"People like Arlene's brother?" Brian asked.

David visibly tensed for a brief moment and then relaxed and leaned back in the chair, his gaze never leaving the officers. "You know that too." Absently combing his fingers through his hair, he said, "Arlene didn't have anything to do with Morris's murder either."

"But you both had a motive to want the man dead," Brian reminded him.

"Like I said, we didn't want him dead. We wanted to hold him accountable. I wanted to see the SOB taken off to prison. I imagine right now, the current powers-to-be at Earthbound Spirits are hailing this as some celebration—their beloved leader has been released from this world and moved onto paradise. It reinforces their sick message, that even if something horrible happens—like your throat gets slashed—there is reason for celebration, providing you embrace the teaching of Earthbound Spirits. And oh, by the way, don't forget to leave us your money."

"Why don't you tell us why you and Arlene really came to Marlow House."

"I MET DAVID ONLINE," Arlene explained. "This was about nine months ago. "I was trying to find out more about Earthbound Spirits. We met on a forum. He told me about his grandmother, how she'd been brainwashed by the group."

"Your brother was involved with Earthbound Spirits for a number of years; had you looked into the group prior to this?"

"Not really. I didn't even know Cleve was my brother until about ten years ago when his mother told him she'd gotten pregnant from a married man, and the father he thought was his, wasn't. His world sort of fell apart, and he tracked down his biological father —my dad."

"How did that work out?"

"Mother already knew about the affair and the child. When Cleve found that out, I think it bothered him more than had Dad kept it a secret. I always felt that in Cleve's mind he wanted to imagine himself this love child—the baby my father bitterly gave up to save his marriage and protect the child he already had—me."

"I'm not sure why that scenario would matter one way or another."

"Since Mother already knew about the affair and obviously forgave Dad, Cleve didn't understand why Dad hadn't made any effort to be in his life. And when he met Dad, well, my father's not the most affectionate of men."

"Did they ever come to terms with each other? Have some sort of relationship?"

"No. Not really. But after I learned about Cleve, I reached out to him. Both of us had grown up believing we were an only child, but we weren't. We had each other."

"From what I read on your Facebook page, it didn't seem like you saw him a lot."

"Ahh...so that's how you figured this out. Well, they say we should be careful what we post online." Arlene smiled sadly. "No, we didn't see each other much, but we kept in contact. When he first started getting involved with Earthbound Spirits and he told me about it, I got the feeling he was acting out—joining a cult to spite Dad."

"Why would that spite your father?"

"Dad's pretty involved in his church. I think Cleve saw that as hypocritical, my father the Christian deacon who denied his own bastard son for most of that son's life."

"Did you try to get your brother away from the group?"

Arlene shook her head. "Not at first. At first, I thought it was harmless. After all, what he shared with me seemed pretty innocuous. I figured, if it made Cleve happy. But then, when we would see each other, I noticed he'd changed. He started working for them, and something about his entire demeanor seemed off to me. I suppose, if we had seen each other more frequently, in person, I would've tried to do some sort of an intervention. As it is, I was too late."

WALT FELT LIKE A BADMINTON BIRDIE, bouncing between the parlor and library, listening in on the interrogations. Although, he imagined if Danielle were to ask the chief if Arlene and David were being interrogated, he would tell her they were simply being questioned and either one could leave if they wanted to. At least, that was the impression MacDonald and his men conveyed to Danielle's two guests.

So far, Walt had learned Cleve was Arlene's half brother. He was tempted to pop out for a moment and tell Danielle that tidbit, but he was afraid he'd miss something. He also learned Arlene and David were not romantically involved. That did not surprise Walt. Since keeping a closer watch of the two, not once had he been forced to vacate their room due to amorous activity. In his day, if you checked into an inn with a lovely young woman, most of that time was spent involved in activities requiring far less clothing. He didn't imagine things had changed that much since he had been alive.

With a wave of his hand, Walt summoned a cigar and silently puffed as he listened to what David had to say.

"We were supposed to meet someone in town tonight. That's the real reason we came to Frederickport," David finally confessed.

Joe glanced around the room and took a sniff. With a frown, he dismissed the sudden scent of smoking tobacco and focused his attention back on David. "Who were you meeting?"

"A private detective we've been working with, trying to find the evidence to bring down Earthbound Spirits once and for all."

"The detective's name?" Joe asked.

"Logan Mitcham. He has an office in Portland."

Brian and Joe exchanged quick glances before Brian asked, "When is this meeting to take place…and where?"

"It's tentatively set up for tonight at 7:00 at the pier." David glanced at his watch. "But he was supposed to call us to confirm that everything was still on. If you believe we had something to do with Peter Morris's murder, I suppose you could come with us, talk to Mr. Mitcham. He'll be able to confirm that's the reason we're in Frederickport—not to kill anyone."

"Why stay at Marlow House? Why come to Frederickport at all?" Brian asked.

"Mr. Mitcham told us he'd uncovered some damning information on the group, something that would guarantee jail time for all those at the top of the Earthbound Spirits food chain. But he had one more piece of paper to get his hands on, which he could only do this afternoon. We planned to meet tonight, where he'd turn over all the evidence, which we were then going to hand over to the local police department. To you."

"And you haven't heard from him?" Joe asked.

David shook his head. "No. And that concerns me, in light of Peter Morris's murder."

"How so?" Brian asked.

"I assumed he would have contacted us right after learning of the murder. After all, we were all working together to bring Morris down, and Morris was killed at the same place we're staying."

"WHY DID you decide to stay at Marlow House?" the chief asked Arlene just as Walt returned to the library.

"Logan suggested Marlow House. He told us Danielle Boatman disliked Peter Morris, that she saw him for what he really was. And that she was friends with you. He assured me Danielle was someone we could trust and would help us. Once we had the evidence we needed, we planned to go to Danielle and then to you."

"Why not give the evidence directly to the police?"

"Logan explained he'd tried to do that before—with another one of his clients whose son got involved with the group at the Astoria branch. But the authorities in Astoria just blew them off. Logan thought we'd have more of a chance being taken seriously if someone you trusted brought you the evidence."

"It sounds like you and Logan Mitcham got pretty close," the chief noted.

Arlene stood up. "I've told you everything. I'd like to go now."

"No, you haven't told me everything. You didn't tell me about seeing Mitcham at Marlow House just after he murdered Peter Morris. You didn't tell me how he kissed you and told you to go back upstairs."

THIRTY-TWO

W alt hadn't expected MacDonald to just blurt out what Danielle had told him. After all, if Arlene called his bluff, he had no way to substantiate his claim. By her startled gasp and the way she fell back into the chair and broke into sobs, Walt was fairly certain Arlene wasn't in any shape to call anyone's bluff. The young woman was crumbling right before his eyes.

"I didn't know he killed Peter Morris," Arlene sobbed. "I didn't even know Morris was dead until we heard Heather scream and we came downstairs."

MacDonald let Arlene cry and made no effort to calm her. He watched as she finally got a grip on her emotions and stifled her sobs. Using the back of her hand to wipe away tears, she looked up at MacDonald. "I swear; I had no idea he'd killed Morris."

"Are you saying when you all found Morris the next morning, you didn't know what had happened?"

"I couldn't believe Logan would do something like that. I figured there had to be some explanation. I wanted to talk to him, but he wouldn't answer my phone calls."

"How long were you and Logan lovers?" MacDonald asked.

She shook her head. "We weren't. I mean, that one time…but it was just once. I told him we had to keep it professional, and I thought he understood."

"When was this?"

"About two weeks ago." Arlene stood up and walked to the desk. She removed several tissues from their box and then returned to her seat.

"So what happened that night?"

"I came downstairs to get something to drink when I heard noise coming from the entry. I thought maybe it was one of the cats. But it was Logan. To say I was surprised to see him was an understatement. He kissed me, told me he was taking care of things for me, and then he told me to go back upstairs."

"You didn't think it was a little odd, him showing up at Marlow House in the middle of the night? From all appearances—as if he'd broken in?"

"I was so startled to see him I just did what he told me to. And when I was going upstairs the only thing I could think of was that he was there for me—checking on me. He knew I was there with David, that we were staying in the same room. Heck, he'd practically arranged it. He knew there was nothing between David and me—I just assumed—well, he had feelings for me. That our one night meant more than I realized. I was a little afraid at the thought, that he would just show up like that, yet a part of me—there was something romantic about it."

"What did you think when you saw Morris's body?"

"I...I...I don't know. At first, I thought it had to be some sick coincidence, that Logan being here had nothing to do with Morris's death. And then...then I started wondering if he'd killed Morris for me." Arlene broke into sobs.

When she calmed down again, MacDonald asked, "What does David know about any of this?"

"David has no idea Logan and I ever...I mean...I never told anyone."

"Does David know about you seeing Mitcham here?"

"No. The next day, after we left the police station, I just wanted to go home. I needed to think and figure this all out. He has no idea Logan may have killed Morris."

MacDonald arched his brows. "May have? Do you seriously have any doubt who killed Peter Morris?"

"I keep thinking there must be some explanation for Logan being here. Maybe he was trailing Morris. Maybe he saw who murdered him. Maybe he's in danger now too."

"I NEED SOME MAKEUP," Danielle muttered. Standing before the bathroom mirror, her reflection stared back at her. Methodically, her fingers unwove the braid. Dark circles visibly shadowed the area below her eyes.

Lily was staying across the street at Ian's. Kelly had been too frightened to return to Portland, not while her neighbor was still at large. The three intended to stay in for a homemade dinner and movie, certainly not the romantic evening Ian originally planned for Valentine's Day. They had invited Danielle to join them, but she had declined.

If it hadn't been for Walt, Danielle would never have known what Arlene and David had said during their recent interviews. She understood why MacDonald didn't go into detail with what they had learned; it wasn't possible with Joe and Brian listening in. The two would never understand why MacDonald was so candid with a civilian.

What she did know—thanks to Walt—was that Arlene and David had agreed to go with the police and help them locate Logan Mitcham. This meant they would be flanked by undercover police when showing up for their 7:00 p.m. appointment at the pier. Danielle wondered if the private detective would actually show up.

While Arlene and David were being interviewed, Danielle received a text message from Heather. She wouldn't be coming home for the night and wanted to make sure Danielle fed Bella.

It was the first night without Chris in the house—which seemed odd. He had moved into Marlow House about eight weeks earlier and had immediately fit in—even with Walt. Perhaps Walt complained about Chris, but Danielle was fairly certain Walt was going to miss the good-natured man, who, like herself, could see and hear spirits.

"I always loved when you'd unbraid your hair. I wish you'd wear it down more," Lucas told her.

Startled, Danielle turned around and came face-to-face with her husband's spirit. She had no idea how long he had been standing behind her, watching. Why would she? A spirit's image had no reflection.

"How long have you been standing there?"

"A while. You look tired. I don't think running a bed and breakfast is a good idea. It's dangerous. I'm sorry I left you. We had such a good life together."

"Lucas, you left me long before that car accident."

"We need to talk about that," Lucas said. "But it's Valentine's Day. Can't we have at least one night together where we just shut the world out? Where we go back in time, like it used to be—just you and me."

"We can't go back in time."

"We could pretend. Just for one night. And it is Valentine's Day —our day."

Instead of a response, Danielle's gaze moved over Lucas. He looked exactly as she remembered—with his perfectly coiffed dark hair, reminding her a little of the guy on the evening news—his tanned skin, as if he'd spent the day at the beach or in a tanning booth—chiseled features and tailored clothes.

It seemed as if he had been away for more than fourteen months. In some ways, it felt like fourteen years. She then realized, even if it had been fourteen years, he would still look the same— exactly the same. How peculiar that would be, she thought, if the man she once married remained at Marlow House, and as each year went by, her face and body aged, as people do—while Lucas's image remained trapped in time, the oldest version of himself in life. For some reason, that thought horrified her.

And then she thought of Walt. The same could be said of Walt. How will I feel when I'm fifty and Walt still looks as if he's in his twenties?

"Danielle, are you all right?" Lucas asked. He reached out to touch her hand, but his moved through hers as if it was air.

Before she could answer his question, her cellphone began to ring. When she picked up the phone from the counter to see who was calling, Lucas vanished.

THE PHONE CALL was from Chris. He was downstairs, debating if he should ring the bell or not.

"I think you still have your house key," Danielle said when she led Chris into the living room. He carried a sack, and by the smell, Danielle suspected he had brought Chinese food.

"I'd never just use it without your permission."

"Then why didn't you give it back?" Walt asked when he appeared the next moment.

"Evening, Walt," Chris greeted him cheerfully. Looking at Danielle, he said, "I called Lily, and she told me her and Ian's plans had changed; they stayed in with Kelly. When I asked her what you were doing, she said you had stayed home alone and didn't think you'd planned anything for dinner. Thought I'd save you from a peanut butter and jelly sandwich." He handed Danielle the sack of food.

"I never eat peanut butter and jelly. Only peanut butter and mayonnaise."

Chris cringed. "You really did need to be saved!"

Danielle chuckled. "Thanks, Chris, that's really sweet of you."

"Yes, he's a peach," Walt grumbled, taking a place by the fire. He watched Danielle unpack the food on the coffee table.

When a lit cigar appeared in Walt's hand a moment later, Danielle looked up at him and asked, "Walt, would you mind smoking after dinner?" She wrinkled her nose. "Smoking and food really don't go together."

"I wouldn't know about that," Walt grumbled. His cigar vanished. "It's been a few years since I enjoyed a good meal."

"Where is everyone?" Chris asked as he took a seat.

"Heather sent me a text message saying she wouldn't be back until tomorrow night. No idea where she went. She didn't say."

"I imagine you'll be glad when she moves back home," Chris said.

"Why?" Walt asked. "Even when they move out, they just come back."

Danielle flashed Walt a smile and took a seat by Chris. "Be nice, Walt. It's Valentine's Day. Let's all try to get along."

"Where's—" Chris glanced around "—your husband?"

"Oh please, do not call that man her husband," Walt scoffed.

"I'm not sure I'd call him a man," Chris quipped.

Narrowing his eyes, Walt glared at Chris. "What is that supposed to mean?"

"Well, technically speaking..."

"Oh, stop, you two! I've had a really crappy week. Can we all please stop with the digs?"

"I'm sorry," Walt and Chris mumbled at the same time.

"As for Lucas..." Danielle looked at Chris. "I was talking to him when you called. He seems to just pop in for a few minutes and then goes—where he goes exactly, I've no idea."

"I noticed David Hilton's car wasn't out front. I assume he and Arlene went out to dinner."

"Oh…David and Arlene…" Danielle then went on to tell Chris all that had happened since she had last seen him that afternoon.

"YOU KNOW, technically speaking, Chris got his way," Walt told Danielle later that evening after Chris had gone home. He stood with her in the kitchen while she shoved the trash from their take-out dinner into the garbage can.

"Got his way how?"

"I know he asked you out for Valentine's Day."

"How did you know that?"

Walt shrugged.

"I wouldn't really call take-out Chinese in my living room with Chris a Valentine's date. After all, you were with us."

Walt smiled. "Yes. I know."

"Who are you talking to?" David asked from the kitchen doorway. Danielle looked up from the trash can and saw David and Arlene standing in the hallway, looking into the kitchen. She hadn't seen them come in.

"Umm…I was talking to myself. Did they take Logan Mitcham into custody?"

David shook his head. "No. He didn't show up."

"Still no word on where he might be?"

"None." David said curtly. "I was wondering, would you rent me the room Chris was using? If there're no sheets on the bed, I'll be happy to put them on myself."

"Looks like they've decided to end their lovers' charade," Walt observed before waving his hand to summon a lit cigar.

THIRTY-THREE

Holding his forehead in the palm of his hand, Adam impatiently motioned for the server to come to his table. He had just sat down a moment earlier.

"What's the hurry, Adam?" she asked, order book in hand.

"Get me a Bloody Mary," he groaned.

"Rough night last night?" she teased.

"Just shut up and get me one."

The waitress didn't seem offended by his retort. Instead, she walked away chuckling.

Outside the restaurant, Bill Jones tossed his cigarette butt to the sidewalk before pushing through the front door. With a newspaper in hand, he glanced around, looking for Adam.

"Damn, you look like hell," Bill told Adam when he reached his table.

"You should see what it looks like inside here." Adam motioned to his forehead. "A hell of a lot worse."

"That bad? What did you drink, anyway?"

"The question should be what didn't I drink?"

Bill chuckled. "What was the occasion? I know, you were drowning your sorrows. No Valentine's Day date." Seeing the waitress coming toward them, Bill turned one of the two clean coffee mugs on the table right side up in its saucer.

The waitress reached their table, carrying a coffee pot in one hand and a Bloody Mary in the other. She set the cocktail in front of Adam. "Here's the dog that bit ya." After filling Bill's cup with coffee, she told them she would be back in a minute to take their order.

"Thanks," Adam said before taking a swig.

"Feel better?" Bill asked when Adam set the drink down.

"No. But I'll tell you this, I wasn't drowning my sorrows, I was celebrating. And it was worth every bit of this headache." Pain shot through Adam's right temple, making him cringe. "Or...maybe not." He took another sip of the drink.

"Oh, that's right, you had that closing yesterday. On the beach cottage."

"Something better." Adam grinned.

"Better than a closing? Never thought I'd hear you say that."

"I had an accepted offer—on the Gusarov Estate."

Bill let out a low whistle. "Holy crap. That'll be some commission!"

"You're telling me. This is turning out to be a great year."

"Where did you get the buyer?"

"Same one who bought the cottage."

"Boatman's friend, huh?" Bill set his mug on the table and opened the morning paper. "Can't believe there was a murder at Marlow House. That Boatman is a magnet for trouble."

"Danielle's all right." Adam nursed his drink.

"I'm sure you're thinking that about now, considering she's the one throwing all this real estate business your way."

"I used to think she was pretty ditzy, but..."

"Ditzy?" Bill laughed. "The woman leaves the television on to keep her neighbor's dog company."

Adam shrugged. "Lots of people treat their pets like people."

"She's a space cadet."

"Well, she could've hung our butts for breaking into Marlow House, and all she did was make us fix the window."

Bill peered over the paper. "Who fixed the window?"

"Okay, so you fixed it. But I helped pay for it."

"Whatever..." Bill shrugged and continued to read the paper.

"Anything new on the murder?" Adam asked.

"Says here they're looking for a person of interest. Some private investigator. Logan Mitcham."

"Never heard of him." Adam took another sip of his cocktail.

"They got a picture of him."

"Let me see." Adam reached for the paper.

"No one I recognize," Bill said after turning the paper over to Adam.

"Damn, I do." Adam said.

"Really? Where do you know him from?"

"I don't really know him. But he works for Peter Morris."

"You mean he worked for Peter Morris." Bill smirked.

"Yeah, whatever. I wonder if they're looking at him for the murder or just for information?"

"Doesn't say. Just says person of interest."

"YOU DON'T LOOK VERY GOOD," Danielle said after she opened the front door for Adam Nichols later that morning.

"Yeah, I've heard that before," Adam said.

"Come on in. Want some coffee?"

"Might as well. Unless you have any tomato juice and vodka."

"Out celebrating last night?"

"How did you know?" He followed her into the kitchen.

"Just a guess."

Ten minutes later, Adam sat with Danielle at the kitchen table, drinking his second Bloody Mary of the day while Danielle poured cream into her coffee.

"I read the paper this morning, about the cops looking for Logan Mitcham. Wondered if you knew what was up with that."

"Why, do you know him?" Danielle sipped her coffee.

"Not personally. Didn't know his name until I read the paper. Just that he worked for Morris."

Danielle paused mid-sip and stared at Adam. "What do you mean he worked for Morris?"

"Just that. I saw him a few times with Morris. And I was told he worked for him."

"Worked for him, how?" Danielle frowned.

"That's sort of what I wondered. I read this morning, he's a private investigator. Wondered why a private investigator would be working for Morris."

"Interesting," Danielle murmured. She looked up at Adam. "Have you said anything to Arlene about this?"

"Arlene? No, why? What does she have to do with Mitcham?"

"Well, for one thing, you told me you and Arlene knew each other back when Isabella was involved in Earthbound Spirits. Wondered if Arlene ever saw Mitcham with Morris."

Adam frowned. "I doubt it. Why?"

Danielle stood up. "Come on, Adam, we need to go to the police station."

"Police station, why?"

"Come on, before Arlene comes downstairs."

"THIS DOESN'T MAKE SENSE," MacDonald murmured. He sat in his office with Adam and Danielle.

"I really don't know what this is about, Chief. I was minding my own business, nursing a hangover, when I saw this guy's picture in the paper. Figured Danielle would know the story, and I foolishly stopped by Marlow House to ask. I should've known better," Adam grumbled. "She drags me down here."

Ignoring Adam's rant, MacDonald asked, "Are you sure he worked for Morris?"

"Pretty sure. I don't think Isabella would have lied to me about it."

"Isabella told you?" the chief asked.

"Yeah. A couple times we ran into Morris in Portland. He was with the guy from the paper. The second time we ran into him, I asked Isabella who he was. She said he worked for Earthbound Spirits. I figured he was some accountant or something."

ARLENE WAS LOADING her suitcase into the trunk of David's car when Danielle and Adam returned from the police station. Adam silently watched Arlene as Danielle pulled the Flex into the driveway.

"So the little romantic weekend comes to a close," Adam murmured under his breath.

"Not sure how romantic it all was. David slept downstairs last night." Danielle put her car in park.

"Trouble in paradise?" Adam asked.

"I don't mean to be gossiping about my guests, but I'm sure all of this is going to come out in the newspaper anyway."

Adam frowned. "What do you mean?"

"David and Arlene didn't come here for some romantic weekend. They were here to meet a private detective who was supposed to hand over evidence on Earthbound Spirits."

"Damn...and then Morris was murdered."

Still sitting in the car, Danielle looked over at Adam. "Why didn't you say anything about Arlene being Cleve's sister?"

Adam leaned back in the passenger seat and closed his eyes. Resting a wrist over his forehead, he mumbled, "No more gin for me."

"You aren't answering my question."

Opening one eye, Adam turned his head and peered at Danielle. "I didn't see the point. All it would do was get the cops to spend all their time focusing on Arlene and Hilton instead of looking for the real killer. Look what happened to us when Cheryl was killed."

"Didn't you for a moment wonder if either Arlene or David was involved?"

"I don't know Hilton, but Arlene? No way. And obviously the cops must agree with me or she wouldn't be packing up to head out of town right now."

"The police probably figure they know where to find her."

"So what happened to the evidence they came here for?"

"The man who was supposed to bring it to them was the private eye whose picture was in the paper this morning. So, no, they didn't get their evidence."

"Logan Mitcham? But he worked for Morris. Are you saying he turned on his boss?"

"Oh yeah. And when he turned, he really turned."

"Are you suggesting..."

"The cops have evidence that Mitcham may have killed Peter Morris," Danielle told him.

"Damn..." Adam shook his head. "What kind of evidence?"

"I can't say, but that's the real reason they're looking for him."

"And Arlene was working with him?"

"She and David hired him to look into Earthbound Spirits. I doubt she knew he worked for Morris."

"Damn..." Adam unhooked his seat belt and opened the car door.

Just as Danielle got out of the Flex, she noticed Arlene coming down the driveway.

"Danielle!" Arlene called out. "David and I are..." She paused when she saw Adam getting out of the red Flex.

"Hello, Arlene," Adam greeted her.

"Adam...hello." Arlene looked from Adam to Danielle. "I just wanted to tell you David went to fill up the car with gas, and when he comes back, we're going to finish bringing the rest of our things to the car and take off."

Before Danielle could respond, Adam asked, "Danielle, do you mind if I talk to Arlene alone?"

Danielle glanced warily from Adam to Arlene. "Umm...okay... I'll be in the house."

"I KNOW why you were really in Frederickport," Adam told Arlene. The two sat on the porch swing in front of Marlow House.

"The entire weekend was a disaster." Arlene groaned.

"Sorry. I understand the private detective you hired has disappeared."

"Yeah, and they think he's the one who killed Morris."

"Why do they think that?" Adam asked.

"Because...well...for one thing...I saw him in Marlow House around the time of the murder." Arlene then went on to explain her encounter with Mitcham prior to the murder, leaving out the part about their brief affair and his parting kiss.

"There's also something else," Arlene confided. "Something I haven't told the police yet."

"There's more?"

Arlene nervously licked her lips. "Logan told me the only way we would ever bring Earthbound Spirits down was if we got more people to start looking into their criminal behavior."

"I can understand that."

"He told me we needed a high-profile case—that's when he suggested I call Isabella's father and tell her Morris had her killed."

"Isabella died of natural causes."

Arlene shook her head. "According to Logan, he had evidence proving Morris had her murdered."

"If that was true, why didn't this Logan guy just go to the police himself?"

"Because the coroner's office was in on it. And Isabella's father has money. He'd be able to get the right people to listen to him."

"So what did you do?"

"I called Mr. Wayne several times to try to get him to look into it."

"Do you believe your brother killed Isabella?"

"No!" Arlene shook her head adamantly. "Cleve refused to kill her, that's what Logan told me! I could never have called Mr. Wayne had I thought my brother was responsible. I...I don't know what I would've done."

"Did you tell Wayne who you were?"

Arlene shook her head. "No. I made up a story about how I was a member of the group and afraid. Logan thought Mr. Wayne would believe my story if he visited a website we frequented—one that discusses some of the things Morris's group has done to hurt other families. I kept forgetting to tell him about the website." Arlene shrugged. "But I don't think it really mattered. I got the feeling he believed me."

THIRTY-FOUR

O verhead, the dark clouds threatened to bring another day of rain to Frederickport, Oregon. After parking her car in front of the beach house, Carol Barnes grabbed her purse from the passenger seat and prayed she would make it to the front door before the rain started falling. Just as she reached the gate, she noticed the mailbox was open, and it wasn't empty.

"Someone forgot to get the mail yesterday," Carol muttered as she snatched the envelopes from the box.

"Morning, Carol," Will Wayne greeted her when the nurse came through the front door a few minutes later. He sat on a recliner, remote in one hand and a cup of coffee in the other as he watched television.

"How did Karen do last night?" Carol walked over to Will.

"She finally had a good night."

Carol handed Will a stack of mail. He frowned and asked, "What's this?"

"No one brought in the mail yesterday."

Setting his coffee cup down, he took the envelopes from her. "Now that I think about it, you're right." Will chuckled. "Wondered what you were doing bringing in mail on a Sunday."

Slipping her purse's strap from her shoulder, she hung it on the coat rack. After removing her jacket, she hung it with her purse. "Is Karen up?"

"Yes. Connie's in her room with her." Wayne set the remote on the table with the coffee cup and began flipping through the stack of mail. Most of the envelopes appeared to be junk mail except for one envelope addressed to him. There was no return address.

Now alone in the living room, Will tossed the junk mail onto the end table. Tearing open the envelope addressed to him, he found a letter inside—not handwritten, but printed, as was its envelope. He began to read.

"Will Wayne, I know you paid to have Peter Morris killed for what he did to your daughter. If you want me to keep your secret, you will now have to pay me…"

Crumpling the letter in his hands, Will took a deep breath. After sitting there a moment in thoughtful silence, he uncrumpled the sheet of paper and continued reading. It told how much money the blackmailer expected and where and how to deliver the funds.

"I'M sorry I ruined your Valentine's Day," Kelly told Lily. The two women sat together at Pier Café, while Ian was back at the house reviewing the edits on the Emma Jackson story.

"Aww, it's all right." Lily picked up her cup of hot chocolate and took a sip, leaving behind a faint whipped cream mustache. "I don't blame you not wanting to go back to your place as long as Mitcham is on the loose."

"I suppose I could have gone back to my friend's in Astoria." Looking Lily in the eyes, Kelly tapped her upper lip. Lily smiled and then picked up a napkin, wiping off the whipped cream.

"Like I said, it's fine. I had a good time last night."

Kelly chuckled. "Yeah, watching movies with your boyfriend and his little sister. What a great way to spend your first Valentine's Day together."

Lily smiled and took another sip of her hot cocoa.

"But I'll confess, Lily. I really did not want to go back to Astoria. I felt safer staying with my big brother. Does that sound silly?"

"Given the situation, no."

"How do you feel about staying at Marlow House after the murder?"

Lily shrugged. "I'll feel much better when they catch the guy. But I feel pretty safe over there."

"I don't know." Kelly shook her head. "Things Ian has told me about Marlow House makes me wonder if it's cursed."

Lily laughed. "Cursed? Why would you say that?" *Haunted maybe, but not cursed.*

"Ian told me about the home invasion. Danielle and Joe could have both been killed."

"True, but they weren't."

Kelly toyed with the rim of her water glass, glancing from it to Lily. "Umm…what's the deal with Joe and Danielle?"

"The deal? What do you mean?"

"I know they used to date."

"They went out a few times after we first moved here. But nothing came of it. Mostly because Joe thought she murdered her cousin."

"But they worked through that, didn't they? I mean, they seem to be friends now. She invited him to her Christmas party."

Lily studied Kelly for a moment. "Why all the questions?"

Nibbling her lower lip, Kelly looked up at Lily. "You have to admit, he's awful cute."

"When I first met him, I thought he was pretty hot. He has that sexy Italian thing going for him. But…"

"But what?"

Picking a spoon up from her napkin, Lily absently stirred her cocoa. "Oh, Joe is nice enough. He just never really saw Danielle."

Kelly frowned. "What's that mean?"

"I guess it just means Joe was never right for Danielle, that's all."

"She seems pretty close with Chris. Are they together? I asked my brother, and he told me to ask Danielle."

"Sounds like your brother. Hmm…are they together? I get the idea they're dancing around the possibility. Now he's a hottie!"

"Yeah, I suppose." Kelly sipped her water.

"You suppose? Lord, I'm always saying that boy could be an underwear model."

Kelly frowned. "Is he cuter than my brother?"

Lily smiled. "Not to me."

The server brought their burgers, and when she left the table, Lily asked, "So what's your deal. You interested in Sergeant Morelli?"

"Well, I was, until he hauled me down to the police station a second time."

"Technically speaking, it was the chief who had you come in for questioning."

"But still, it was Joe who interviewed me. And I hated when he called me Ms. Bartley."

Lily grinned. "That is your name."

"It's just so hard to find a good guy." Kelly sighed.

The café door opened and in walked Heather Donovan. Lily noticed her immediately while Kelly continued to stare dreamily into space, her thoughts occupied elsewhere.

"Heather looks like she slept in her clothes," Lily murmured under her breath.

"I saw your car out front," Heather said when she reached them. Without being asked, she sat down in one of the empty chairs at their table.

"So what did you do for Valentine's Day?" Lily asked. "Danielle mentioned you didn't stay at Marlow House last night."

"It'll be nice to move back to my own house, where people aren't keeping tabs on every move I make," Heather snapped, grabbing a menu from the middle of the table.

"Hey, I'm sorry. I didn't mean anything by it," Lily countered. "Just wondered if you did something fun."

"Do I look like I've been having fun?" Heather asked.

"Wow, don't bite my head off."

Heather let out a sigh. "I'm sorry, Lily. I've just had a really crappy week."

"This has been pretty crappy all around," Lily agreed. "You want to talk about it?"

"You know that guy who was in the paper this morning? The one they call a person of interest in Peter Morris's death?"

Lily and Kelly exchanged glances before Lily said, "Yeah, the private investigator."

"He was my freaking private investigator!" Heather seethed.

"You hired Mitch?" Kelly asked.

Heather frowned at Kelly. "Mitch? You know him?"

"Well, I know him as Mitch. He lives in the condo below mine."

"Really?" Heather narrowed her eyes. "Do the police know?"

"Sure they know," Lily answered for Kelly. "If they're looking for him, don't you think they know where he lives?"

Heather stared at Kelly. "Doesn't mean the police know you live in the same building as him."

"They know," Kelly said quietly. "That's why I'm staying at my brother's. I don't want to go home until they find him."

"So you know him?" Before Kelly could answer, Heather said, "I guess that's a silly question since you called him Mitch. So are you two friends or something? Why are you afraid to go back to your place? Is he dangerous? The paper didn't say anything about him being dangerous."

"No, I don't know him very well. I didn't even know he's a private detective or that his last name is Mitcham."

"Why did you hire him?" Lily asked.

"To look into that issue with Presley House and Peter Morris."

"What did Peter Morris have to do with Presley House?" Lily asked.

"I guess I never told you. Earthbound Spirits is the new owner of the property. They're the ones who got their hands on it after my mother failed to pay the property tax."

"No kidding? Why didn't you ever say anything to Ian about it? You know he's researching Earthbound Spirits for illegal activities," Lily asked.

"It wouldn't have helped Ian's story anyway. As it turned out, everything was handled legally. Not really what I wanted to hear. But what can I do about it now?"

"Even if everything was handled legally, I can see where you'd still be pissed. Pretty easy to hold a grudge against someone who just walked in and took advantage of the situation when you were obviously vulnerable," Kelly noted.

"What is that supposed to mean?" Heather snapped.

Kelly shrugged. "Nothing. I mean…well…that's just what Peter Morris did best, take advantage of vulnerable people for his own profit."

"Well, I suppose the joke's on him." Heather chuckled.

"Why, because he's dead?" Lily asked.

"No…although that way too." Heather laughed. "What I meant was, I guess the joke is on Earthbound Spirits. You see, according to the insurance company, I was no longer the owner of the Presley Property when it burned down, something neither of us were aware of at the time. So they aren't obligated to pay the claim. And while Earthbound spirits got a great deal for a house on the property—the bare land is worth less than what they paid for it. Not to mention, the site still needs to be cleaned after the fire. From what I understand, the current property owner is obligated to do that, and since they never purchased home owner's insurance for it, they're basically screwed."

THIRTY-FIVE

Perched atop a stack of boulders along the Oregon shoreline, Mitch glanced up at the gray clouds. They blocked the afternoon sun and promised rain. Fortunately, the inclement weather detoured visitors away from the beach, which he hoped would allow him time to properly dispose of the body.

The fact that it wasn't raining and his jacket was dry made it not just bearable to be outside on a dreary February afternoon, it made it quite comfortable. Mitch rarely got cold, and he counted that as a blessing, especially since he had been hiding out along the beach for what seemed like an eternity, trying to figure out how to get rid of the body.

He loathed double-crossers, ignoring the fact that Peter Morris would probably have good cause to accuse him of that infraction. However, Mitch really didn't care what Peter Morris thought of him. Morris deserved whatever he got.

Standing up, he dusted off his slacks and made his way down the rocky mound. The body was not far away, tucked safely under some shrubbery. His first thought was to drag it to the ocean and let the sea take care of things, but he was afraid it would simply wash up on shore in a few days.

When he reached the body, he stared at the bullet hole in the man's gut.

"That must have hurt," he murmured, and then he looked at the man's eyes, which gazed vacantly up to the gray sky.

Staring down at the man in fascination, Mitch tilted his head first to the right and then the left, as if a slight change in angle would make some significant difference in what he was seeing.

"How did you get yourself in this mess?" Mitch asked the corpse. He then laughed and said, "Oh, I remember, you were being greedy!"

Mitch leaned down to the body, preparing to grab the man by his ankles, when he paused. "Maybe if I fill your pocket with rocks. You think that might keep you in the water?"

The corpse remained silent. Mitch stood up and looked around, wondering where he might find rocks small enough to stuff into the man's pockets and down his pants. Although, he wasn't sure that would weight the body down sufficiently to keep it in the ocean.

It was then he heard it—voices. Mitch was no longer alone on the beach. Without a second thought, he raced for cover, seeking refuge amongst the shrubbery. Peering out from his hiding place, he spied the people attached to the voices: two teenage girls.

Smiling, Mitch thought, I can easily take care of them. I already have one body to dispose of, what's two more?

He watched and waited as the two unsuspecting girls walked toward the corpse still hidden from their view. They chatted with each other, laughing and giggling, each oblivious to what lay just a few yards away.

Engrossed in their teenage banter, neither girl was aware of Mitch, who hunkered down behind a bush they had just walked by. His plan was to wait until they stumbled upon the corpse before jumping from his hiding place and taking them both down. It would be easy. After all, he doubted either one weighed more than ninety pounds, and their surprise at finding a body along the beach would make it even more difficult for them to react to the situation in a manner that might actually save their lives.

The little blonde saw it first. Her scream jolted even Mitch. The next moment, the other girl joined in and started screaming. Mitch slunk out from his hiding place. They had no idea he was right behind them as they looked down at the dead man, whose blank eyes stared into their terrified faces.

CHRIS STOOD at his kitchen counter, unloading groceries. Just as he set a gallon of milk in the refrigerator, he heard pounding on his back sliding door—pounding and shouting. Shutting the refrigerator, he walked to the door. Standing just outside were two teenage girls who looked as if someone wielding a chainsaw was on their heels.

Quickly he unlocked the door. The moment he did, the two girls practically flew inside, both shouting hysterically. It took him several minutes before he could calm them down enough to learn what had happened.

"He's dead!" the petite blonde sobbed. "And he looked right at me!"

"Who's dead?" Chris asked.

"We found a dead body on the beach. It's all bloated and gross and his eyes are open!" the other girl told him.

"I want you both to sit down," Chris ordered. He immediately locked his door and picked up his cellphone. A moment later, he had the Frederickport Police Department on the line.

When he was off the phone, he looked at the girls. "The police want you to wait with me until they get here. Did you see anyone near the body or on the beach?"

Both girls shook their heads. "Just the dead guy," the blonde said.

"Maybe you'd better call your parents and let them know what's going on and where you are. By the way, my name is Chris Johnson."

WHEN CHRIS OPENED his door ten minutes later, Brian Henderson was on his front porch.

"What's this about a dead body?" Brian asked.

Chris looked over Brian's shoulder. He didn't see any other officers.

"You came alone? Don't you need the coroner or something?"

"I was in the neighborhood, so I told them I'd take the call. Let's see what we really have. You told the dispatcher you didn't see anything, some girls did?"

Chris opened his door wider. He stepped to one side, giving Brian room to enter.

"The girls are inside. They showed up at my back door, screaming their heads off. Claimed they found a body on the beach."

Brian entered the house, first wiping his feet on the mat. He glanced around. "So this is your new place?"

"I just moved in yesterday."

"Nice. Right on the beach too. Plus, not too far from Marlow House."

Chris ignored Brian's comment and led him to the girls.

Without waiting for the rest of the officers to show up, Brian had the girls lead them to the spot where they claimed to have found the dead man. Chris trailed along. When they got a few hundred yards from the spot, the girls stopped and pointed in the direction of the body. They refused to budge another foot.

Chris saw the man hiding in the bushes. He was about to shout out to Brian when something stopped him. It was the way the man's hand moved through the foliage. Instead of saying anything, Chris ignored the man lurking nearby and walked with Brian to where the body lay.

Hands on hips, Brian looked down at the corpse and let out a sigh. "If I'm not mistaken, that's our missing private detective. Sure looks like him."

"Logan Mitcham?"

Brian pulled a clean handkerchief from his pocket and kneeled by the body. Covering his hand with the handkerchief, he gingerly removed the man's wallet.

"I'm going to kill you for bringing them here!" Chris heard a male voice shout. He turned and watched as the man from the bushes jumped from his hiding place and lunged at the teenagers. Neither girl was aware of his presence and continued to whisper amongst themselves.

When the girls ignored him, he turned his attention to Brian and Chris. "What are you doing? Put that wallet back! It doesn't belong to you!" the man wailed.

After opening the wallet and looking over the dead man's identification, Brian stood up. "It's Mitcham all right. Looks like he's been dead a while. But the coroner will be able to tell us more."

"Can we go now?" one of the girls called out. She held a cellphone in her hand. "My mother just texted me. They just parked by Mr. Johnson's house."

"I'd like to get both of your statements first." Brian looked at Chris. "Would you wait here with the body, make sure no one disturbs it? I want to walk the girls back, and the rest of my people should be pulling up around now."

Chris was about to answer when he paused a moment, watching in fascination as the man from the bushes stood nose to nose with Officer Henderson. The man scrunched his features into an ugly scowl and shouted, "I said put that wallet back!"

"Well?" Brian asked impatiently, waiting for Chris's response.

"Sure," Chris waved his hand toward his house. "I'll wait here. Feel free to use my kitchen table if you need someplace to take the girls' statements."

"Thanks." Brian turned from Chris.

"What is wrong with these people?" the man shouted.

Chris silently watched Brian and the girls head back to his house. When they were out of earshot, he looked at the ranting man and said, "You're Logan Mitcham."

Mitch startled and swung around to faced Chris.

"You can see me," Mitch said.

"Yes."

"Why were they ignoring me? They acted like they couldn't even see me."

"Because they can't," Chris explained.

"Don't be ridiculous," Mitch snapped. Impatiently, he combed his fingers through his shortly cropped hair.

Chris wandered over to the body and looked down. "Do you know who that is?"

Angrily walking to Chris, Mitch looked down at the body.

"I just know it's his fault I'm in this mess."

"So who is he?" Chris asked again.

A flicker of confusion crossed Mitch's face. "I'm not really sure."

"Doesn't his face look a little familiar?"

Mitch shook his head.

"Why did you kill Peter Morris?" Chris asked.

Mitch's face broke out into an evil smile. His eyes narrowed and he looked over at Chris. "So you know about that?"

"Sure."

"I could kill you right now before that cop comes back."

"I'm not the only one who knows," Chris told him. "All the cops know you slit Morris's throat. You left your fingerprint on Marlow House's front gate."

"Big deal. I could have left my fingerprint there any time."

"Oh, did I mention it was a bloody fingerprint? Morris's blood."

"Doesn't prove anything. Everyone wanted him dead. If anyone knows that, I do."

"I wouldn't worry too much about being arrested for Morris's murder."

Mitch eyed Chris suspiciously. "Why do you say that?"

Chris nodded down to the corpse. "Because that's you."

Thunderstruck, Mitch stared down at his corpse.

"Why don't you tell me who killed you?"

Mitch vanished.

"WHAT DO you mean you left Glandon with the body," Joe hissed under his breath. He stood with Brian in the front entry of Chris's beach house while another officer took statements from the teenage girls.

"Johnson, not Glandon," the chief reminded him. He had just walked up behind Joe and caught his comment.

"What's the problem?" Brian asked. "I didn't want to leave the body unattended, and I needed to get a statement from the girls. They told me their folks were here to pick them up, and I was afraid they'd just take off and not wait. Both of them are pretty shaken."

"Are you implying Chris had something to do with Mitcham's murder?" the chief asked.

"We know Mitcham probably killed Morris. And we know Morris was blackmailing Johnson. Maybe Johnson hired Mitcham to do the job and then decided to get the hit man out of the way so it wouldn't come back to him."

"What, and leave the body a short distance from his new beach house?" the chief asked.

"Maybe he was getting ready to dump it in the ocean when the girls showed up."

"Stop trying so hard to pin this on Johnson," Brian snapped. "It's not like you, Joe."

"I'm just saying—"

"I hear what you're saying," Brian cut him off. "And I don't like it; plus it makes no sense. You haven't seen the body yet. It's been dead for a couple days. If he were going to dump it in the ocean, he would have done it already. And according to the girls, he was nowhere around the body when they found it. They went running to the first house they could find, and that happened to be Chris's. And by the looks of things in the kitchen, he had just come back from the grocery store. Didn't even have time to put all the groceries away when the girls showed up. What killer takes time to buy groceries before disposing of a body that's lying out in the open not far from his back door?"

THIRTY-SIX

"This is a surprise," Danielle said after she opened the front door and found Chris and MacDonald standing on the porch together.

"The chief said I could tag along," Chris explained.

"Sounds interesting." Danielle opened the door wider and showed them in. Together they went into the parlor.

"Where're your guests?" the chief asked as he took a seat on one of the chairs facing the sofa.

"Arlene and David left about twenty minutes ago. She said you told them they could."

"I know where I can find them." MacDonald removed his baseball cap and tossed it on the empty chair next to him.

"Lily went to a show with Kelly, and I guess they ran into Heather at lunch, so she joined them." Danielle sat down on the sofa.

"Heather hanging out with Lily? What, did hell freeze over?" Chris asked.

Danielle flashed Chris a smile and then looked at the chief. "So what's up?"

"We found Logan Mitcham, or rather, Chris found him."

"Chris found the killer?" Walt asked as he appeared in the room, a lit cigar in his hand.

"I didn't find him. The girls did," Chris corrected.

"What girls?" Danielle asked. "Where was he?"

MacDonald wrinkled his nose and took a sniff. He looked around. "Is Walt in here with us?"

"Yes, he just popped in," Danielle explained.

"Hello, Walt," the chief said with a grin.

"That's so weird," Chris mumbled. He moved toward the empty place on the sofa next to Danielle, but Walt vanished from his spot by the desk and appeared in the next moment, sitting on the sofa where Chris was headed.

Glaring at Walt, Chris moved instead to the desk and sat down.

"Would someone please explain where you found him. Is he under arrest?" Danielle asked.

"He's dead," Chris told her.

"Dead?" Danielle looked from Chris to the chief.

"His body was found on the beach not far from Chris's place. Some teenage girls found it."

"Hmm, by your place?" Walt looked over at Chris and smiled. "What have you been up to?"

"Funny, Walt." Chris rested his elbow on the desk. "I'd just come back from the grocery store and these two hysterical girls start pounding on my door. They both had cellphones, but at that point they weren't in any position to use them."

"According to the coroner, it looks like he was out there for a few days," the chief explained.

"Those poor girls," Danielle muttered. "Any idea how he died?"

"Someone shot him. I asked him who killed him, but he didn't say."

"You saw him?" Danielle asked.

"His spirit was still hanging around. Not a particularly nice guy, by the way. I seriously think he would've killed one of us if he was capable of harnessing his energy."

"Oh, that's lovely," Danielle said under her breath.

"Considering the way he slit Peter Morris's throat, that doesn't surprise me," the chief said.

"Are you certain he killed Morris?" Danielle asked.

"He didn't deny it when I told him I knew he killed Morris. He said I couldn't prove it, and he even threatened me. Mitcham was in that state where the spirit doesn't quite grasp the fact he's dead. He was looking right down at his dead body—staring himself in the eyes—but it just didn't seem to click with him that the body was his."

"So he didn't tell you anything?" Danielle asked.

"Not really, aside from confirming what we already suspected. He killed Morris."

"Now what?" Danielle asked.

"Brian and Joe are on their way to Portland to search his office and condo more thoroughly. The last time Brian went, the search warrant was limited. But now that Mitcham's dead, he's our new victim, and we won't have the same limitations. Hopefully they'll find something."

"I know Kelly didn't want to go home, with Mitcham still at large. I suppose she can go back to Portland now," Danielle said.

MacDonald stood. "I just thought I'd stop by and let you know what's going on."

"But we still have a killer on the loose." Danielle stood up.

"Two murders in one week. Not sure about my new neighborhood." Chris was only half teasing. He followed Danielle and the chief out of the parlor while Walt remained behind, silently smoking his cigar.

"Chief, what about Earthbound Spirits' offices?" Danielle asked when they got to the front door.

"What about them?"

"Have you searched them yet? Or Peter Morris's home? Maybe you'll find something there. You just said now that with Mitcham dead, you can go back, and I assume do a more thorough search because he's now a victim."

With his hand on the doorknob, MacDonald looked back at Danielle. "Searching Mitcham's home and office is not the same. Mitcham rented the condo in his own name, he wasn't married, lived alone, and he doesn't share his office with anyone. But with Peter Morris, Earthbound Spirits owns the offices, and even the house Peter Morris lived in is owned by Earthbound Spirits."

"Does this mean you can't search any properties owned by Earthbound Spirits? After all, the man was murdered."

"Yes, he was, Danielle. But so far, we haven't been able to convince a judge to give us a warrant. Earthbound Spirits' attorney is arguing our purpose for wanting a search warrant has nothing to do with finding Morris's killer, but about going on a witch hunt to find something to tarnish the image of the organization Peter Morris founded."

"Does this mean you aren't going to be able to get one?"

"No. It just means it's taking us longer than we'd like." The chief looked at Chris. "You want a ride back to your place?"

"Nah, I can walk." Chris glanced to Danielle. "I thought I'd stay and talk to Danielle a few minutes."

After the chief had gone, Chris stood alone with Danielle by the front door.

"I was wondering; how's everything been going with you and Lucas? Is his spirit still lingering?"

Danielle looked around the entry hall. "Yeah, I think so."

"You think so?"

"It's been pretty crazy around here—having a murder in the house tends to do that."

Chris smiled. "Yeah, tell me about it."

"Lucas only seems to come around when I'm alone—which hasn't been happening much."

"Is he still here?" Walt asked when he appeared the next moment.

"It was nice seeing you too, Walt."

Walt smiled and then grew serious. "Chris, do you have any idea who might have killed that palooka Mitcham?"

Chris shrugged. "I have no idea. I wish he'd said more when I saw him."

"Do you think he moved on?" Danielle asked.

"Either that, or moved on with his body."

"I just don't like the idea of a killer moving through our neighborhood," Walt said.

Chris couldn't resist saying, "What do you care? You're dead."

Walt narrowed his eyes. "I was talking about Danielle and Lily."

"What about me?" Chris teased. "Don't you worry about me?"

"I suppose I do. But only because I'm afraid if someone kills you, you might decide to move back into Marlow House."

Chris reached for the door. "I know when I'm not wanted."

Danielle smiled. "You don't have to leave."

"I really have to get back to my house. I went to the store today and never finished putting my groceries away."

"Okay, I'll let you know if I hear anything," Danielle promised.

Chris gave her a nod, and as he went to pull open the door, Walt called his name. Turning to face the ghost of Marlow House, he heard Walt say, "Be careful."

DANIELLE SAT in the library with Max curled up on her lap. She absently stroked the cat's black fur as she listened to his loud purr and watched the fire flicker in the hearth. Walt had taken a book from the library and had retreated to the attic. Reading in the library wasn't practical with guests in the house. Books seemingly floating in midair might not be good for business.

She contemplated going into the kitchen and making herself something to eat when she heard the front door open and the sound of paws clomping over the wood floor, heading in her direction. In the next moment, Sadie raced into the living room, her eye on Danielle's lap. Max heard the dog coming and immediately jumped up, greeting the golden retriever with a hiss. But Sadie was too much for the feline, and she easily dislodged the cat from his perch, taking his place.

Danielle let out a grunt and found herself laughing as Sadie bathed her face in dog kisses. Disgusted, Max sauntered over to the fireplace and curled up on the throw rug.

"Sorry about that," Lily said when she entered the room.

"I swear, sometimes Sadie thinks she's a lapdog." Danielle patted the large canine, trying to get her to calm down. Sadie awkwardly circled Danielle's lap, her tail happily thumping against Danielle's chest, as she attempted to make herself comfortable. With another grunt, Danielle gently shoved Sadie down while still giving her reassuring pats. Resigned to a spot on the floor, Sadie curled up by Danielle's feet.

"So Ian's driving to Portland with Kelly?" Danielle had recently talked to Lily on the phone, updating her on the missing private detective.

"Yeah. Kelly wants to go home and get some of her things. While she feels better knowing Mitcham isn't a threat, we have no idea who killed him. In some ways, I think she's more afraid. At least before, when she thought Mitcham was the lone killer, she knew who to look out for."

"I suppose I can understand that. If whoever killed Mitcham happened to be at Marlow House at the time of Morris's murder and knows Kelly looked in the window, who knows what he—or she —might imagine Kelly witnessed. That's assuming they happen to find out Kelly was over here that night, and since Carla is the one who saw her, I imagine half the town already knows."

"At least Carla didn't know who she saw exactly. Anyway, Ian's going to drive down with Kelly so she can pick up some of her stuff, and they'll come back in the morning. Since she works online, she can do that anywhere. But just between you and me, it seems a little nuts because both murders happened near Ian's house. So if it was me, I'd probably feel just as safe in Portland. But don't tell anyone I said that."

"I won't. Why didn't you go with them?"

"I've a dentist appointment in the morning, remember? They'll be back tomorrow night." Lily smiled and then looked to the doorway with a questioning frown. "I didn't see Heather's car out front. Do you know where she is?"

"Heather called after I talked to you on the phone. She went to Vancouver to stay with friends."

"When I left her after the show, she didn't say anything about going to Vancouver."

"Speaking of the show..." Danielle smiled mischievously. "Did you see Fifty Shades of Grey? I know it just started playing at the theater."

Lily laughed. "Umm...no. The idea of sitting through a movie like that with my boyfriend's little sister, not to mention Heather... no, thanks. That ain't happening."

Danielle laughed and then redirected the conversation. "I've a hunch Heather decided to take off again when she learned there was another murder in the neighborhood. I'd called her right after I talked to you about them finding Mitcham's body. And then she called back fifteen minutes later, saying not to expect her tonight."

"Didn't she even stop by to take a shower or change her clothes?" Lily asked. "This afternoon she looked like she'd slept in her clothes."

"No. But I figure she probably stopped by her house and grabbed what she needs. I don't think she brought all of her clothes with her when she moved in here. According to her, they've stored most of her things—what she didn't have to get rid of—in the garage. There wasn't any mold in there."

Lily glanced up to the ceiling. "Where's Walt, by the way?"

"Reading in the attic. Bella's up there with him. But I might as well tell him to read down here since everyone's going to be gone. Oh...there is also Lucas."

Lily glanced around the room. "Lucas is still here?"

"I think so. He briefly showed himself this morning and then vanished."

"I still can't believe he's here. And why is he here?"

"To be honest, I can't wrap my head around it. And frankly, I would rather not deal with it. I had put all that behind me; I wish he'd just move on."

"Well, have you talked to him? I mean really talked to him? Asked him why he's here?"

"From what I understand, he's been in some sort of ghost limbo since he died, hanging out in a building near the site of the accident. He just recently came to terms with the fact he's no longer alive, but instead of moving on, which is the natural progression, he decided to find me."

"There must be a reason."

"Yeah, well, that's sort of what Walt and Chris says too. They both tell me I need to resolve whatever issues Lucas and I have so both he and I can move on."

"Sounds like a good idea to me."

"I thought I had moved on. Anyway, he never sticks around long enough for us to have a real discussion."

Lily stood up. "One thing about living in Marlow House, it's never ordinary. I'm going to go up and take a shower."

Danielle glanced down at the sleeping golden retriever. "I assume Sadie is staying with us?"

"If that's okay."

"Sadie is always welcome. I'm sure Walt would love to see her."

Opening his eyes, Max lifted his head and looked over at the sleeping dog. As soon as Max's gaze set on Sadie, the dog's tail began to thump, but her eyes remained closed while her chin rested soundly on her front paws.

THIRTY-SEVEN

The rain clouds had vacated the Portland sky. It promised to be a sunny Monday morning. Wearing fuzzy pink slippers and casually dressed in blue sweatpants and sweatshirt, Kelly wasn't going far; just to her car to grab something she had forgotten to bring in the night before.

When she reached the bottom of the stairs, she noticed the door to Mitch's place was ajar, and she could hear voices coming from inside. Her first impulse was to flee up the stairs to her own condo, where Ian was, but when she looked over to the parking lot, she saw the Frederickport police car.

Curious, she walked over to Mitch's open doorway and peeked inside. Sitting on Mitch's sofa were Brian Henderson and Joe Morelli sorting through several file boxes.

"Some businesses keep a second set of books; Mitcham obviously kept a second set of client files," Kelly heard Brian say.

Not wanting to be seen, she stepped out of the doorway's view, listening.

"Talk about someone playing both sides," Joe said. "Looks like that tip the chief got about Mitcham working for Morris was spot on. Over the last few years Morris paid Mitcham a small fortune to investigate potential members and their families."

"If Mitcham wasn't so meticulous in his record keeping, there wouldn't be a paper trail. Looks like he was always paid in cash," Brian noted.

Nervously, Kelly nibbled on her lower lip, her ear close to the partially opened doorway.

"Considering what he was being paid, between Morris and the clients who hired him to spy on Morris, I wonder what he did with his money," Joe said.

"By his credit card records—all those trips to Vegas and the Indian casinos—and the pile of lottery tickets in his trash can, I'd say Mr. Mitcham had a gambling problem."

"Well, look here…" Kelly heard Joe say. She was tempted to peek into the doorway, but kept herself out of sight.

"Apparently, Kelly Bartley was one of Mitcham's assignments. According to the notes in this file, Morris got wind of the exposé Ian was working on, and Morris paid him to move into her complex to spy on her."

Keeping perfectly still, Kelly found herself holding her breath and closing her eyes, not wanting to be discovered.

"Bingo," Brian said. "Apparently, someone did hire Mitcham to kill Morris. And you'll never guess who."

Kelly opened her eyes and listened.

"JusticeNow. Talk about working both sides."

WHILE HE MAY HAVE RETIRED his cowboy boots for the rainy season, Will Wayne still clung to his cowboy hat. The Western persona he had created those many years ago had become a part of who he was. As a gentleman does, he had removed his hat the moment he entered the front lobby of the Frederickport Police Department. He carried his cattleman hat in one hand and his cane in the other, using it to help steady his way.

The woman from the front desk led him to the chief's office after informing her boss of his arrival. She left him alone in the office with the chief, who sat behind the desk.

"Please sit down," MacDonald said after standing up and greeting Will.

When both men were seated, Will reached into his jacket's inside pocket and removed an envelope. "I received this in the mail." Leaning forward, he placed the opened envelope on the desktop and pushed it toward MacDonald. "It came on Saturday, but I didn't see it until yesterday."

MacDonald leaned forward and picked up the envelope, looking at it as he flipped it from side to side. "What is it?"

Will nodded toward the envelope in MacDonald's hand. "Just read it."

With a curious frown, MacDonald removed the letter before tossing its envelope to the desk. Leaning back, he unfolded the sheet of paper and began to read.

Will thought the room unbearably quiet. Considering the amount of time MacDonald spent reading the letter, Will was certain the police chief had read and reread it numerous times.

Finally, MacDonald refolded the sheet of paper and gently placed it atop the envelope on his desk. He looked at Will. "Do you know who sent this to you?"

Will shook his head. "I keep thinking it had to have been Logan Mitcham, because he's the only one I ever discussed killing Morris with—and he brought up the conversation, I didn't. But this morning, I heard the news about the police finding Logan Mitcham's body and that it had been on the beach for a few days; so it couldn't have been him."

"Well, it could have been sent by Mitcham. We think he was killed sometime Friday after Morris was murdered. Whoever mailed this to you could have mailed it on Friday if it arrived on Saturday."

"I didn't hire a hit on Peter Morris; I need you to know that."

"Why are you bringing me this?"

"I...I want to be upfront with the police. Complete disclosure. At this point, I don't know if Isabella died of natural causes or not, but even if I thought Morris had her killed, I would never do something like hire a hit man. What good would that do? Earthbound Spirits would still be here, living on after Morris was gone. Taking advantage of other vulnerable people. Remove Morris, and someone else just replaces him."

MacDonald picked up the letter. "I appreciate you bringing this to me. I'd like to keep it."

"Certainly."

THE MOMENT DANIELLE walked into the police chief's office, MacDonald looked up and set his cellphone on his desk.

"I was just getting ready to call you," he told her. "What did you do, sneak past the front girl?"

"I'm curious: if Joe was sitting at the front desk, would you ask me if I slipped by the front boy?"

MacDonald chuckled. "Point taken."

"Anyway, your security is really slipping around here." Danielle sat down.

"That's what Lily told me. Speaking of Lily, have you talked to her?"

"Talked to her? Just this morning at breakfast, why?"

"Have you spoken to her within the last thirty minutes?" he asked.

"No. She's at the dentist, having a root canal."

"Kelly is missing," he announced.

Danielle frowned. "What do you mean Kelly is missing?"

"Brian and Joe spent last night and most of this morning going through Logan Mitcham's office and home. They came across some information that they needed to question Kelly about. But when they went to her apartment, she wasn't there. According to Ian, when he got out of the shower this morning, she was gone. But she didn't take her purse or cellphone. Just her car keys."

"Gone?" Danielle stood up abruptly. "Has she been kidnapped? Did Mitcham's killer grab her?"

"According to one of the neighbors Brian talked to, they saw Kelly getting into her car and driving off about the same time Ian says he was in the shower."

Danielle sat back down. "But why would she just leave without her purse or phone? Without telling her brother where she was going?"

"I've no idea, and neither does Ian. I also had a visit from Will Wayne this morning." MacDonald picked up Will's letter and tossed it across the desk to Danielle. "He brought me this. Says it came in the mail over the weekend. Insists he never hired a hit man."

Danielle quietly picked up the letter and began to read. When she was done, she looked across the desk at MacDonald and frowned.

"When I interviewed Will after Morris's murder, he told me Mitcham offered to hook him up with a hit man, but Will insists he told him he wasn't interested. And then he gets this blackmail letter a few days after Morris's death."

Danielle didn't respond immediately. After considering all the recent events, she said, "None of this makes sense. Have Brian and Joe found anything useful in Portland?"

"They found information that confirms what Adam told us. Mitcham had been working for Morris. He was hired to investigate potential members. I guess he had quite an extensive file on both you and Chris. According to Mitcham's notes, Morris had written you off and refocused his attention on Chris. He also got wind of Ian and Kelly's investigation. Apparently, he moved to that condo specifically to be near Kelly and spy on her."

"Kelly…where is Kelly?" Danielle murmured.

"Hopefully, she just ran to the grocery store or something, and there's a simple explanation."

"Are they any closer to figuring out who killed Mitcham? Do you think this person was working with Mitcham to kill Morris, or was Mitcham killed in retaliation for killing Morris?"

MacDonald leaned forward, resting his elbows on the desktop. "This is what they've pieced together so far. It looks like Mitcham was working exclusively for Morris, getting paid well for investigating possible donors. But then Earthbound Spirits started having some money issues."

"Money issues?"

"Things started falling apart right after Christmas, after Cleve killed himself. Not sure what happened exactly, but Earthbound Spirits' funds weren't where they were supposed to be."

"Are you saying there was missing money? Someone was embezzling?"

"That and some poor investments. Even before Cleve's death, wealthy members started backing away from the group. Donations stopped."

"Maybe they realized it was a scam?"

"Perhaps. Funds were tight for Morris; he couldn't really afford Mitcham anymore, but he couldn't afford not to use him. So they made a deal. Mitcham would be compensated for whatever donations he helped facilitate. He would no longer be paid up front, but by a percentage of the donation after it came in."

"So basically, he was working on commission."

"Exactly. But it appears that after the first of the year, things started to change. Up until that point, Mitcham had been hiring himself out to people who had a grievance with Earthbound Spirits. He sold himself as someone who wanted to take the cult down. But the truth was, he was feeding false information to his clients."

"Up until that point, so something changed?"

"Not only did he start giving his clients the real dirt on Earthbound Spirits and Morris—he fed them false negative information. Like with Will Wayne. The notes Joe and Brian found in Wayne's file verify what I thought all along. Morris had nothing to do with Isabella's death."

"So Mitcham lied to Will."

"It seems as if Mitcham realized the tide had changed for his boss—the gravy train was about to come to an end. According to his notes, he was going to do something that would be his big payday, and he could retire."

"What was that?" Danielle asked.

"That's the problem. I'm not really sure."

"If it was to murder Morris and then blackmail Will for it, the money demand in the letter isn't really something he could retire on," Danielle noted.

"Not unless the blackmailer considers that the first installment."

"But unless he has something to prove Will hired the hit man, it seems like wasted energy. I would think if he had anything, Will wouldn't have brought you the letter."

"True—unless Wayne is the one who killed Mitcham. Since finding Morris's body, Mitcham's house and office have been under surveillance. There was no way for the killer to get in and destroy any evidence. Bringing me this letter might be Wayne's way of making himself look innocent if we happen to find something incriminating."

Danielle stood up. "I just don't see Will hiring a hit man and then killing him."

"When I spoke to Wayne the first time about Mitcham, it was after Morris was killed. Consider this: Mitcham does the hit for Wayne and then immediately goes to Wayne and blackmails him. Instead of paying Mitcham, Wayne kills him. Wayne doesn't know Mitcham carelessly left behind a bloody fingerprint. When I show up after the murder and start asking questions about Mitcham, Wayne tosses out the story about Mitcham offering to set him up with a hit man. His way of throwing us off, just like with this letter."

"If Mitcham blackmailed him in person, and Wayne killed him, what about the blackmail letter? Why send a letter?"

"Maybe Mitcham didn't send the letter—maybe Wayne wrote it himself," the chief suggested.

Danielle began pacing back and forth in front of the desk. "No. That doesn't make sense."

"I admit it has some holes," MacDonald conceded.

"Like Swiss cheese." Danielle took a deep breath and exhaled. "This is freaking driving me nuts. There is only one thing to do."

"What's that?"

"I need to talk to Logan Mitcham."

THIRTY-EIGHT

The first thing Danielle noticed was the distinct odor, a combination of chemicals and death. It made her nose twitch. The smell got stronger as she made her way down the hallway. MacDonald assured her there was no one at the morgue; they had all gone out for lunch. However, she could hear voices just beyond the doorway. Someone was here—and they were shouting or simply arguing loudly. Either way, she knew they were just inside the room she was about to enter.

Steeling her courage, she approached the door, reached out, and gripped its handle. She would normally take a deep breath to calm herself, but that was not an option. She had no desire to drink in more of the noxious fumes than was absolutely necessary.

The moment she opened the door, her fears were confirmed. While she knew the bodies of both Peter Morris and Logan Mitcham were still at the morgue, she had hoped the only spirit still lingering would be Mitcham's. He was the only one she needed to talk to.

For whatever reason, they both remained, and judging by the angry verbal exchange, they were unhappy with each other. She wondered if that was why they were both still here—Mitcham had followed his body to the morgue before Morris had time to move on, and seeing each other, the two had clashed, keeping them both grounded to this plane while they riled at each other.

Or perhaps…neither one cared for an extremely hot climate, which Danielle suspected would be their next stop after this one.

The two spirits stopped shouting at each other the moment Danielle walked into the room. She had made the decision before opening the door to pretend not to see them. Since their death, both had been surrounded by people who could not see them, such as police officers and members of the coroner's office, so she didn't imagine they would find her inability to see them unusual.

"What's she doing here?" Morris asked.

Ignoring both spirits, Danielle walked over to a chair and sat down. She took out her cellphone and pretended to be surfing.

"Looks like she's waiting for someone," Mitcham said.

Morris quickly lost interest in Danielle and turned his attention back to Mitcham. The two men began shouting at each other again. If she had hoped to learn anything from their exchange, she was sorely disappointed. While they confirmed what she already suspected—the private detective had murdered Peter Morris—she learned nothing new.

After ten minutes, Danielle had had enough. If the smell didn't make her throw up, the shouting was sure to make her head explode. Annoyed, she stood up, shoved her cellphone into the back pocket of her jeans, and faced the men.

"Shut up!" she shouted at the top of her lungs. "You two are driving me freaking nuts! Just shut up!"

Both spirits froze, their screaming silenced. Slowly, they turned to face her.

Danielle smiled smugly and sat back down, primly crossing her legs. "Perhaps we can now have a civil conversation?"

"You can hear us?" Mitcham asked. "Like Glandon. He heard me."

"Ahh…you recognized Chris, did you?" Danielle smiled. "Yes, he's like me. We can see spirits."

"Why can't anyone else see us?" Morris asked.

"Umm…maybe because you're dead?"

"You don't have to be so snotty," Mitcham grumbled.

Danielle laughed. "Seriously?" She pointed to Morris. "This one talks people into killing themselves for money, and you kill people for money. So how's it feel, guys, being dead? All cracked up to what you'd thought it would be?"

"Why are you here?" Morris asked.

"I want to know who killed your friend here. We already know who killed you."

"He's not my friend," Morris snapped. He glared at Mitcham and asked Danielle, "And how do you know who killed me?"

"Your PI here left his fingerprint behind—on my fence. A bloody fingerprint, your blood."

"I'm glad he's dead. I just don't want him here!" Morris shouted.

"So who killed him?"

"I know why he died." Morris laughed.

"Oh, shut up," Mitcham snapped.

"Go on," Danielle said, now crossing her arms across her chest as she watched the two agitated spirits pace the room.

"It was greed!" Morris shouted.

Mitcham laughed. "Greed? You're accusing me of being greedy? You, who couldn't wait for someone to die of natural causes to get ahold of their money?"

"How did greed get Mr. Mitcham here killed?" Danielle asked.

"He had this brilliant scheme," Morris said sarcastically. "He wanted to convince all those people who had once hired him to investigate me to hire a hit man and take me out. Of course, they wouldn't know he was the hit man."

"Wait a minute," Danielle said. "From what I understand, Mr. Mitcham here, while on your payroll, initially told most of those folks he couldn't find anything on Earthbound Spirits."

"So?" Mitcham asked. "I told them I couldn't find anything that would stick in a court of law, which just made them more frustrated —it should've made them more willing to seek justice in another way."

"Are you saying more than one person hired you to kill Morris?"

Morris laughed. "Logan's plan didn't go quite like he thought it would, which rather pissed him off. Although, he did get one person to bite."

"So? I could've still made them pay!" Mitcham insisted.

"And how was that?" Danielle asked.

"With Peter murdered and what I had on my clients, I'm sure I could have gotten money from most of them."

"Are you saying you intended to frame them for Morris's murder?"

"Sure, I had enough evidence to convince the police to arrest more than one of my clients. What they would end up paying for legal fees would be far more expensive than what I was asking."

"So who killed you?" Danielle asked.

Mitcham glared at Morris. "The same client who paid me to kill Peter."

NERVOUSLY NIBBLING HER LOWER LIP, Kelly stood on the front porch of the Bradford Estate. She glanced down at her slipper-clad feet. "I didn't think this out very well," she muttered to herself. Awkwardly, she ran the palms of her hands over her sweatshirt, as if that would, in some way, make her more presentable. Before getting out of her car, she had tried to straighten her hair, but she didn't have a brush or comb with her. Had she taken time to grab her purse before impulsively driving off, she wouldn't just have a comb, but some makeup as well.

Resisting the temptation to simply turn around, head back to her car, and go home, Kelly rang the doorbell. A few minutes later, Baily Bradford opened the front door. Like Kelly, she hadn't dressed for the day, but Baily's silk lounging suit looked far more glamorous. She wore her long blond hair pulled up into a feminine twist held in place by a rhinestone-encrusted comb.

"Kelly?" Baily said in surprise, her gaze looking her up and down. "What are you doing here?"

"I need to talk to you; it's important."

"Are you okay?" Once again, Baily looked her up and down. "Has something happened?"

"May I please come in?"

Baily shrugged and opened the door wider. "Sure, I guess."

Kelly followed Baily into the living room. The house had belonged to Baily's parents—to Candice and Baily's parents. But now, everything belonged to Baily. Kelly remembered Candice telling her the house had twenty bedrooms. Kelly always wondered why a family of four needed twenty bedrooms.

"Are you alone?" Kelly asked, nervously taking a seat.

"As alone as I ever am in this house." Baily glanced up to the ceiling for a moment. "Marie is upstairs somewhere, cleaning something."

"I need to talk to you about Peter Morris."

Baily's face broke out into a smile. "He's dead. Isn't that wonderful?"

"Well...umm...yeah...I suppose...You heard he was murdered?"

Baily wandered over to the coffee table and picked up a cigarette from a crystal dish. "Of course. It's been all over the news." After lighting the cigarette and taking a puff, she looked at Kelly. "Mother would have an absolute fit if she knew I was smoking in the house. Oh, she wouldn't give a crap that smoking might give me cancer; she just wouldn't want the smoke to get into her Persian rugs." Baily took another drag and smiled again. "But Mother is dead, just like Peter Morris. Of course, no one killed Mother—although I was tempted on more than one occasion, especially after I found out she did nothing to revenge Candice's death. It was more important for Mother to keep up appearances. Unfortunately, by the time I found out, Mother was already dead. So I suppose it all worked out."

"The police believe Logan Mitcham killed Morris," Kelly explained.

"Logan Mitcham? Never heard of him."

"He was a private detective."

"Was?" Baily took another puff.

Kelly nodded. "Someone killed him. They found his body Sunday, in Frederickport."

Baily shook her head and made a tsk-tsk sound. "Sounds like a bad week for Morris and his killer."

"The police are looking for Mitcham's killer."

"I really don't see why you're telling me all this. I'm glad Morris is dead—I imagine you're glad too. The bastard was responsible for my sister's death. But since I didn't kill him, none of this concerns me. Although, I am a little curious. Do you have any idea why the police believe this Mitcham guy killed Morris?"

"They found a bloody fingerprint at the scene of the crime. The blood was Morris's, and the fingerprint was Mitcham's."

Cigarette in hand, Baily cocked her head to one side and considered what Kelly had just told her. Finally, she shook her head and smiled. "Rather careless of him, wasn't it?"

"But the thing is, because of that fingerprint, the police know who killed Morris."

"So? What do I care?"

"The police are going through all Mitcham's files, looking for who hired Mitcham to kill Morris."

Walking back to the coffee table, Baily leaned over and smashed out her cigarette in an ashtray. "Who says anyone hired Mitcham to kill Morris? You said he was a private investigator, not a hit man."

"Baily, they know who hired Morris."

"Why are you telling me this?"

"They know JusticeNow hired him to kill Morris. He wrote it in his file."

Baily shrugged and picked up a fresh cigarette. "I don't know what you're talking about."

Just as Baily was about to light the cigarette, Kelly said, "I know you're JusticeNow."

Baily paused for a moment, then lit the cigarette. "I don't know anything about a JusticeNow."

"I understand why you did it. Morris ruined so many people's lives. But they know, and you need to be prepared. You need a lawyer, now. Tell them you had a breakdown, anything. But don't let Morris destroy you like he did Candice."

"Kelly, I think you're acting a little crazy. I really don't know what you're talking about. I don't know who this JusticeNow is. It has nothing to do with me."

"I recognized you on the forum. I went there too. You're Justice-Now. You talked about your sister, what Morris had done."

"I'm sure my sister wasn't the only one that man destroyed."

"Maybe not, but I know that's your handle. Logan rented the condo below mine. The police were there this morning. They didn't know I was there and I overheard them. According to what I overheard, Mitcham made a note that JusticeNow hired them to have Morris killed. I know they've been on that website. I told them about it."

"You told them about me?"

Kelly shook her head. "Not that you posted on that site. I never told them anything about you going on there. But I recognized you. I didn't see the point in dragging you into all this. I didn't think you had anything to do with it. But when I overheard them this morning—"

Baily had been taking cigarettes from the crystal bowl and fishing matches from a silver box sitting next to it, so Kelly didn't pay any attention when Baily opened the wooden box on the coffee table—not until Baily retrieved a small revolver and pointed it in her direction.

Letting out a gasp, Kelly asked, "What are you doing?"

"They can go to that website all they want. But I never once mentioned my real name—to anyone on the site. Only to Logan, and he's dead now. It seems you're the only one alive who knows my secret."

"My god…what did you do, Baily?"

"I did what my parents should have done years ago when they found out Morris's part in Candice's death."

"You killed Logan Mitcham."

"I didn't have a choice. The deal was I would pay him half up front and give him the balance when the job was done. He told me where to meet him. But when I got there and gave him the rest of the money, he told me that was simply the first installment. He intended to blackmail me. What he didn't know was I never meet strange men at night without this." Baily waved her gun and then aimed it back at Kelly.

"What are you going to do?" Kelly found herself trembling.

"I don't have a choice. You're the only one who can link me to JusticeNow."

Kelly shook her head. "That's not true. Mitcham kept files on his clients. It's only a matter of time until the police find your file, and I'm sure he made a note of your real name."

Baily smiled. "Logan was so foolish. After I shot him, I went back to his car. Do you know what he had in his trunk? He kept a file box with all the clients he intended to blackmail. I took the files with me. Burned them. Those clients should thank me."

"Please don't do this, Baily!"

THIRTY-NINE

"I don't believe you made her do this!" Chris angrily railed at MacDonald. Hands on hips, he looked from the chief, who sat behind his desk, to Danielle, who had just returned from the morgue.

"He didn't make me do anything; it was my idea. And how did you know I was here?"

"I stopped by your house. Walt told me you'd come down to the police station to check on the status of the case. You know, Walt's not going to be happy with you when I tell him."

"I don't get it. What did Danielle do that was so wrong? You talked to Mitcham's spirit at the beach," MacDonald asked.

Chris faced the chief. "Seeking out spirits—especially potentially hostile ones—can be as dangerous as using a Ouija board."

MacDonald looked from Chris to Danielle. "Is that true?"

Danielle shrugged. "I think that might be overstating it a bit." She sat down.

"How did Harvey and Stoddard work out for you?" Chris asked.

"Okay, I agree, they were annoying."

"Annoying? Walt told me how Harvey almost got you killed and Stoddard tried to!"

Danielle frowned. "You and Walt have sure been chatting it up a lot lately."

"And even if they aren't dangerous, if they want something from

244

you, it can be the devil to get them to leave you alone. Look at Trudy! She wouldn't give me a moment of peace until I did what she wanted."

"Okay, okay, you've made your point." Danielle sighed. She looked up at Chris and flashed him her sweetest smile. "And we really don't have to tell Walt about this, do we?"

Chris's only response was a noncommittal grunt.

"Anyway, they're gone now. Why don't you sit down?"

Begrudgingly, Chris took a seat.

"What do you mean gone?" MacDonald asked.

"When I first walked in, they were doing a lot of yelling—at each other. I managed to get a little information out of them, but then, Mitcham looked at Morris and told him he didn't intend to spend his eternity haunting a morgue with Morris, and he just —was gone."

"Where did he go?" MacDonald asked.

Danielle shrugged. "I assume he tried to move onto wherever he's supposed to go, which, as I always say in cases like this, may not be somewhere he really wants to go."

"What about Morris?" Chris asked.

"After Mitcham left, Morris said there was nothing left for him here, and he just faded away. Personally, I think he did the fade thing for dramatic effect. Unlike Mitcham, who, when he decided he was outa here, just vanished—poof—like a magician in a disappearing act."

"You said you learned something?" the chief asked.

"Mitcham figured so many people hated Morris that it would be easy to get them to hire a hit man. Imagine having a dozen people paying you for the same hit. Of course, all the clients think they're the only one, which is important, because he intended to blackmail the clients after he took their money for the hit."

"Are you saying more than one person paid him to kill Morris?" Chris asked.

"I guess hating someone doesn't necessarily mean you're willing to have them killed. Only one of Mitcham's clients hired him to kill Morris. That's the one who killed him."

"Will Wayne claimed to be blackmailed," the chief muttered, speaking more to himself.

Danielle shook her head. "I don't think Will is the one who hired the hit. Mitcham intended to blackmail all his clients who hated Morris, figuring at least some of them would pay up. My bet is he mailed Will that letter right after he killed Morris and before he met with the one client who'd hired him for the hit. If you go to Mitcham's other clients who had a grudge against Morris, you'll probably find they received the same blackmail letter."

"THIS DOES NOT FEEL RIGHT. Kelly has been gone for more than an hour," Ian told Brian and Joe. "Even if she had just grabbed some cash and run out to the store to pick up milk, she would have been back by now." The three men stood downstairs, inside Mitcham's condo. Brian's cellphone began to ring. Seeing it was the chief calling, he excused himself and went into the other room to answer the call.

"Hey, Chief. Kelly still hasn't shown up."

"Brian, I think your hunch was right. If Mitcham was paid to kill Morris, the person who paid for the hit is the same person who killed Mitcham."

Brian glanced to the doorway leading to where Ian and Joe waited. "If that's true, it looks like she may have panicked and fled. But I don't think she'll get that far without her purse or phone."

After finishing his call, Brian returned to Ian and Joe. "Ian, when Kelly was researching Earthbound Spirits for you, she regularly visited a cult watch website."

"Yeah, I know. What about it?"

"She had two separate accounts on that website."

Ian frowned. "What do you mean? She didn't have two accounts."

"Yes, she posted as KellyB and JusticeNow," Brian told him.

Ian shook his head. "Kelly wasn't JusticeNow, Baily Bradford was."

"Baily Bradford?" Joe asked.

"Yeah. I thought Kelly told you about her roommate."

"She did, but what does that have to do with this Baily Bradford?" Joe asked.

"Baily is Candice's sister."

"Why didn't Kelly tell us about JusticeNow?" Joe asked.

"Why would she? There were dozens of posters on that site with grievances against Morris. And Kelly was never a hundred percent certain it was Baily, she never interacted with her on the site, but she did read all her posts, which was why she was fairly certain who it was."

"It's true," Joe mumbled. "There were never any postings between KellyB and JusticeNow. I figured that was because they were the same person."

"Why are you asking about JusticeNow? Does this have something to do with where Kelly went?"

"What's Kelly's relationship with this Baily?" Brian asked.

Ian shrugged. "I don't think you can say they have a relationship per se. Their only connection was Candice, and until they ran into each other before Christmas, I don't think Kelly had seen Baily since Candice's funeral, and that was over seven years ago."

"Do you know where Baily lives?" Brian asked.

"I believe she's still living at her parents' estate. Why?"

IF SHE PEED on the sofa's brocade upholstery, would it be a clue to lead investigators to her body? That was just one of the crazy thoughts popping into Kelly's head as she watched a pistol-wielding Baily pace the living room, trying to decide what to do—kill Kelly here or take her somewhere else to do the dastardly deed.

Peeing on the sofa would be fairly easy, considering Kelly had never had to use the bathroom so bad. Yet her discomfort was the least of her problems. The only reason she hadn't started screaming for Maria—who Kelly assumed must be the maid—was that Baily had threatened to kill Maria too. Did Kelly want that on her conscience?

There was no clock in the living room, but Kelly guessed she'd been at the Bradford Estate for at least an hour, maybe longer. She was hoarse from trying to convince Baily not to do this thing—after all, they both loved Candice. What would Candice think?

The second time she asked that question, Kelly remembered the sad truth about her dear friend. Candice was always a little unbalanced, which made her easy prey for Peter Morris. Kelly had always assumed Candice's issues stemmed from abuse at the hands of her mentally ill mother. But watching Baily, Kelly came to realize mental illness ran in the Bradford family.

"Stand up," Baily demanded, the small pistol pointed at Kelly's face.

"What are you going to do?" Kelly slowly stood.

"Your car's parked outside. We're going to move it."

"If you just let me go, I promise I won't say anything. And even if I did, I couldn't prove anything!"

"Shut up and get going!"

"What about Maria? She might see us," Kelly reminded her.

"I'll worry about Maria, just get moving."

FROM THE BACKSEAT of the police car, Ian gave Joe and Brian directions to the Bradford Estate. They only planned to drive by and see if Kelly's car was parked somewhere in the neighborhood. The moment they turned down the street leading to the Bradford Estate, they spied not only Kelly's car, but also Kelly with another woman, walking behind the vehicle. The woman made no effort to conceal the small pistol she had pointed at Kelly's back. It appeared the woman was leading Kelly to the driver's side of the car.

Everything seemed to happen in an instant. Both Kelly and her kidnapper noticed the approaching police car at the same time. They each had the same reaction—run. Kelly ran toward the police car while the gun-wielding woman fled back to her house.

FORTY

"Perhaps things will settle down in Frederickport now that Earthbound Spirits' corruption has been exposed," Marie Nichols said as she filled Danielle and Lily's teacups. The three women sat around Marie's kitchen table.

"Logan Mitcham certainly compiled enough on Morris over the years to put him away for decades—if he was still alive to face the charges," Lily noted.

Marie absently tapped her teacup's rim with a fingertip. "I just wonder what happened to all Earthbound Spirits' money. I find it hard to believe there's nothing left."

Danielle sipped her tea and then said, "From what I understand, loans were taken out on properties they owned, poor investments made, and someone from the organization may have embezzled funds."

"I read in the newspaper about Mr. Mitcham's clients receiving blackmail letters," Marie said.

"Yeah, they found the original file on his computer, so there's no doubt he sent them before he was murdered," Danielle said. "I guess both Arlene and David had a letter waiting for them when they got home, and even Heather received one. Hers was delivered to her house. She didn't see it until she got back in town on Tuesday."

Marie leaned across the table and patted Lily's hand. "How is Ian's sister doing after her horrid ordeal?"

Lily smiled. "Kelly is fine. Which is saying something, considering how Ian tore into her for being so reckless. They were all lucky that woman tripped before she got back into her house, and the police were able to apprehend her without anyone getting hurt. If she'd made it inside and locked the door, it could have turned into a hostage situation, because the housekeeper was inside."

"Horrid, just horrid," Marie muttered.

"Well, one thing Kelly got out of this: Joe Morelli." Lily giggled.

"Joe Morelli?" Marie looked with curiosity from Lily to Danielle.

"Kelly's developed quite the crush on the sergeant. According to Ian, when they rescued her, she fell apart, and instead of running to him for comfort, she threw herself into Joe's arms. Apparently, saving the damsel in distress got Joe looking in her direction. She's spending this weekend with her brother so she and Joe can go out on their first date," Danielle explained.

With a sympathetic smile, Marie reached over and patted Danielle's hand. "I suppose it really is over for you and Joe."

Danielle sipped her tea. "And I couldn't be happier."

"I'm not sure I am," Lily grumbled. "I like Kelly and everything, but why can't Joe go to Portland to take her out?"

"No," Marie said primly, "this is much more proper."

Lily glanced askance at the elderly woman and then looked to Danielle, who grinned mischievously.

"Of course, this means there's still hope for you and my grandson."

Now it was Lily's turn to grin.

FLAMES BLAZED in the nearby bedroom fireplace while Danielle curled up on the small sofa, reading a book.

"We need to talk," Lucas announced when he entered the bedroom.

"I was beginning to think you'd moved on." Closing the book, she set it on her lap and sat up on the sofa, her eyes never leaving the image of her late husband.

"I know it's time for me to move on, but first, we need to talk." Lucas stood before the fire, looking down at Danielle.

"I'm not sure what we really have to talk about."

"When I died, I imagine there were many things you wanted to say to me."

Danielle smiled sadly. "There were, but I've moved on, and so should you."

"But you see, there are things I need to tell you—things you have a right to know."

Danielle studied him for a moment and then nodded. "Okay, go on."

"I've never stopped loving you. I admit I had an affair, but she wasn't my lover. I would never use the word love—in any form—to describe our relationship."

"Then what was it?"

"It was me being a fool, getting caught up in the success, losing all perspective of the dreams we once shared. She initiated the affair, and please don't imagine for a moment I'm attempting to blame her for my indiscretions. I'm not. I was flattered, and at the time, you seemed to disapprove of everything I wanted—the new house, the car, even our portrait."

"I've just never been into all that material stuff," Danielle said.

"I know. And frankly, that's one of the things I always loved about you."

"I don't understand; then why? Why did you do it?"

"I don't know." Lucas began to pace the room. "But when the portrait arrived—and I looked up at us—at you—and I realized in that moment how much I loved you, the last thing I wanted to do was destroy our marriage or hurt you. The night of the accident, I told Kelsey it was over between her and me. I told her I loved my wife, that I always had. I wanted to make our marriage work. I wanted to change—change back into the man my wife used to respect."

"It wasn't that I didn't respect you," Danielle whispered.

Lucas stopped pacing and looked down at Danielle. "I didn't respect me, Danielle."

"What did she say?"

"She was furious. Grabbed hold of the steering wheel, and after that, well, everything got confused after that."

"Kelsey caused the accident?"

Lucas nodded. "I am so sorry. I never meant to hurt you. I'll always love you, Danielle."

A tear slipped down her face, yet she didn't know what to say.

"I know this is a lot to take in right now, and you don't have to say anything back. You've been mad at me for over a year, and I don't expect your forgiveness. Perhaps someday."

"I forgave you long ago, Lucas."

He smiled. "I want you to be happy, Danielle. I want you to find a man who loves you as you deserve to be loved."

Lucas reached out to Danielle and whispered, "Be happy." He disappeared.

THE SCENT of pine filled her nostrils. Danielle opened her eyes. She sat on the front porch of a rustic log cabin surrounded by evergreen trees. Turning her head to the right, she looked into Walt's blue eyes. The two sat together on a porch swing.

Danielle breathed deeply and smiled. "Those trees smell so real."

"You can thank Heather for that," Walt told her.

"Heather?"

"It's that oil she got you to put in that contraption before you went to bed."

"You mean the diffuser?" Danielle took another whiff.

Walt shrugged. "I suppose that's what it's called. As long as she doesn't use one of those voodoo spirit-chasing oils."

"I seriously don't think essential oils can really cast out spirits." Danielle smiled and leaned back, her right foot gently pushing the swing to and fro. She stared out to the forest.

"I guess Lucas left? For good?"

She glanced briefly at Walt. "How did you know?"

"He stopped by the attic on his way to—to wherever he's going —to say goodbye."

"Really? I didn't realize you two had become chummy."

"We hadn't, but we were aware of each other."

"Hmm…"

"He told me he still loves you, that part of him wanted to stay and be with you. But that even if you wanted him to stay, it wouldn't be fair to you."

"Hmm…"

"Danielle?"

"Yes?"

"Did you want him to stay?"

Danielle sighed. "I was thinking about that a while back. How it would be possible for someone like me to stay with my deceased husband—if that were something he and I wanted. And then I remembered, in twenty years I will be fifty—I will look fifty, well, maybe early forties if I take care of myself—but he would continue to look the same age as he was when he died. As the years go by, I would get older while he remained frozen in time."

"You didn't answer my question; did you want him to stay?"

Danielle looked at Walt, her expression solemn. "And then I realized; it's the same with you. You're eternally in your twenties while I'll continue to age."

"That's not necessarily true." In the next instant, Walt looked thirty years older.

Danielle smiled. "You age well, but this is a dream. If you want, you could make yourself look like an elephant."

"No, Danielle, even when you're awake I believe I could appear older if I choose to."

"Maybe, Walt. But it's just an illusion…this is all an illusion."

They sat in silence for several minutes. Finally, Walt said, "Lucas told me about his affair, about how he never stopped loving you. He hopes you'll forgive him someday."

"I already have, months ago. Although, now that I've talked to him and realize he did still love me, in spite of his choices, it's different somehow."

"Do you still love him?"

"I thought I didn't. But now…well, it's like I can be free to remember him with love. It always hurt so much to believe our love, our life together, had all been a lie. But now…well, it's like I lost him, got him back, and then lost him again."

"He told me not to interfere with your happiness."

Danielle turned to Walt with a frown. "He what?"

"He told me he didn't understand why I hadn't moved on, but that if I chose to stay, I needed to make sure I didn't interfere with your happiness."

"What are you saying?"

"I wondered…is my being here interfering with your happiness? Should I move on?"

"Do you want to?"

"What do you want, Danielle?"

"Do you want me to be honest?"

"Always."

"You're one of my best friends. I know when I first moved here, I wanted nothing more than for you to continue your journey. And I suppose in some ways, it's selfish of me to want you to hang around. But when I feel that way, I remember what you always tell me: that wherever you go next, it will still be there when you're ready to move on."

"But you didn't want Lucas to stay, even though you might still love him."

"Oh, come on, Walt, how would that work out? My deceased husband hovering around while I'm going on with my life. I can't even imagine how awkward it might be if I decided...well, you know...to...umm...be with a man. I mean really, with my husband lurking around?" Danielle cringed.

"May I remind you, it'll still be awkward if you choose to do that here."

Danielle grinned. "But, Walt, you're confined to Marlow House, while Lucas wasn't. Trust me; I won't be having a sleepover at Marlow House."

THE GHOST FROM THE SEA

RETURN TO MARLOW HOUSE IN

THE GHOST FROM THE SEA

HAUNTING DANIELLE, BOOK 8

When a shipwreck washes up on a beach across from Marlow House, Frederickport residents wonder what happened to the ship's crew.

Danielle soon discovers the ship brought a stowaway—a spirit with ties to Frederickport that go back to the 1920s—when Walt was still alive.

NON-FICTION BY

BOBBI ANN JOHNSON HOLMES

BOOKS BY ANNA J. MCINTYRE

COULSON FAMILY SAGA

Coulson's Wife

Coulson's Crucible

Coulson's Lessons

Coulson's Secret

Coulson's Reckoning

UNLOCKED  HEARTS

Sundered Hearts

After Sundown

While Snowbound

Sugar Rush

Lightning Source UK Ltd.
Milton Keynes UK
UKHW041146250122
397664UK00003B/694